KU-798-327

TOM CLANCY'S
THE DIVISION
BROKEN DAWN

ALEX IRVINE

TITAN BOOKS

TOM CLANCY'S THE DIVISION: BROKEN DAWN
Print edition ISBN: 9781789091878
E-book edition ISBN: 9781789092134

Published by
Titan Books
A division of Titan Publishing Group Ltd
144 Southwark St
London
SE1 0UP

First edition: March 2019
10 9 8 7 6 5 4 3 2 1

A CIP catalogue record for this title is available from the British Library.

Printed and bound in Great Britain by CPI Group (UK) Ltd.

Did you enjoy this book? We love to hear from our readers.
Please email us at readerfeedback@titanemail.com or write to us at
Reader Feedback at the above address.

www.titanbooks.com

To the Aurelio Diazes of the world, in recognition of the sacrifices they make so the world can be a better place

CHAPTER 1

VIOLET

Violet squished the toe of her boot into the ground at the edge of the flooded zone. Across maybe five hundred feet of water stood the hotel where she and her friends had stayed for a while, right after the Dollar Flu—or the Green Poison, whatever you wanted to call it—had started killing everyone. The authorities had turned it into a refugee camp, under the control of the JTF. Violet didn't know what JTF meant, but they were the people in charge of all the military stuff. Also handing out food and medicine. Everything at the hotel had been pretty stable... once everyone who was going to die had died, at least. Including both of Violet's parents.

She wasn't going to think about that right now. "I miss that place," she said quietly.

Her friends stood in a group around her. "Yeah," Saeed said. "Me, too." The Murtaugh twins, Noah and Wiley, nodded. The other three kids in the group—Shelby, Ivan, and Amelia—just looked. Ivan leaned into Amelia. She was his big sister. Sometimes Violet felt really jealous of the kids in their settlement who still had siblings and parents.

They were supposed to be out gathering herbs and greens, but instead they had decided to take a look at the hotel they couldn't live in anymore. Government agents had brought the kids there right when the plague hit. When the worst of it had passed, Violet and the rest of the kids had helped plant a garden in its courtyard. Now all the seeds were probably drowned. Everything around here was drowned.

Still, coming down here and feeling sorry for themselves as a group had to be better than hunting around for edible greens along the overgrown parts of the National Mall, which was what they were supposed to be doing.

They had to supplement the gardens already growing at the Castle. Maybe they could go to another park or something, to stay away from the Mall. A lot of the old museums and stuff seemed to be full of bad people now. The people up at the Castle would understand.

Violet was still nervous, though. She tended to follow rules more often than not, because she'd seen some bad stuff when the Green Poison swept through Washington, DC. They all had. Seven kids in their group, all between nine and eleven years old, and they'd all lost at least one parent. Not to mention siblings and friends. That was part of what brought them together. It also meant that the other people in their settlement tended to lump them together as the Kids Who Needed Looking After... which was irritating and kind of nice at the same time. Most of the other kids in the settlement tended to avoid them, like being an orphan was contagious.

Until the flood, they had lived with about a hundred other

people in the lower floors of the Mandarin Oriental. The outside of the hotel was boarded up and fortified, and JTF soldiers stopped by often to make sure things were okay. They got water from rain barrels. It was a pretty safe place, compared to some. Or at least it seemed that way, the same way it seemed that things in DC were getting a little better than they had been over the winter. Maybe that was just because it was easier to feel good about things when flowers were blooming and everything was green.

Then in early April, the river came over its banks and they had to get out.

Now they were staying up at the old Smithsonian Castle. It was pretty crowded because a lot of the people from the hotel settlement had gone there. Some of the others were supposed to be up on the other side of the Mall somewhere. A couple of groups had decided to head over toward the east side, hoping that things were more stable near the military base there. She couldn't remember what it was called. "Saeed," she said. "What's the name of that army base over by the river? Not the Potomac River, the other one."

"Joint Base Anacostia–Bolling," Saeed answered. He always knew stuff like that. Just like he knew JTF stood for Joint Task Force, and he could tell you all about how the JTF was put together when military units and first responders died so much that all the survivors were reorganized with a new name. And he could tell you that the Dollar Flu was really smallpox that came from New York. Violet was glad Saeed was around. He was like having the Internet around even though the Internet was gone along with everything else.

Violet wondered if it really was safer over there by the

Anacostia River. The problem was, she knew there were some bad guys between here and there. The whole area around the Capitol Building was a no-go zone for the kids. Everyone at the settlement agreed on that. It had been true since before the floods, and now someone warned them about it almost every morning. Like they hadn't already survived a superplague and all the bad stuff that happened after it. Adults didn't understand that kids could figure out how to survive just as well as adults could.

But they let the kids run in a group, pretty much anywhere they wanted within a certain limit. Today they were pushing that limit. Instead of picking greens along the edges of the Mall, they'd gone the other way. South on Seventh to Hancock Park, where the railroad tracks were above street level at the Metro stop. They followed the tracks until they sloped back down to ground level, and then disappeared at the edge of the flooded zone. Huge empty office buildings loomed around them. To the south, along the regular riverbank, tall skinny condo buildings stuck up out of the water. The river churned along out there, muddy with little whitecaps like bits of frosting. Violet turned up her collar and angled herself so the wind was at her back. Down here by the water it was chilly.

"How long do you think the water's going to stay?" Shelby wondered. She was the youngest of them.

"I think it's still rising," Amelia said. "Last time we came over here, we could get closer to the hotel."

Violet thought so, too. How much higher would it get? She thought the Castle was on higher ground, but not that much higher. Would they have to move again?

At the same time, Wiley and Noah said, "We should probably go." They weren't identical twins, but they looked a lot alike.

They also had a lot of quirks that only identical twins were supposed to have, like getting the same idea at the same time.

"Maybe," Amelia said. "But we really should collect some greens before we go back to the Castle." The adults didn't keep very close track of them most of the time, but they did expect Violet and the other kids to follow instructions.

"Yeah," Violet said. "We can look along the part of the Mall over by the Lincoln Memorial, maybe."

"That's a long walk," Ivan said. Shelby agreed.

They compromised on the Constitution Gardens, halfway between the Washington Monument and the Lincoln Memorial. But first they had to skirt around the flooded area all the way up to Independence Avenue. They crossed the wide, empty street to the Mall and stood there, keeping an eye out for groups of strangers. If December and January had been horrible, February and March pretty good, then April so far was somewhere in the middle. There weren't dead people everywhere and guns firing all the time, like in the winter. But it wasn't as peaceful as it had been for a while in March, when the adults back at the hotel were starting to think that maybe the government was still working and everything would be okay.

Violet wondered who the president was. There were rumors that President Mendez had died, but didn't that mean they had to pick a new one? Maybe they had and nobody knew. There weren't phones or Internet anymore. Violet and the other kids only knew what they overheard adults talking about.

"Violet, you coming?" Saeed was looking back at her. The rest of the group was ahead of him, skimming along the southern edge of the Mall.

She jogged to catch up. The Mall made Violet feel weird.

Everything was a museum. Not just the museums. Everything. The tourist information booths, the National Park Service bathrooms… all of it seemed like it had been made for a different world. Violet was only eleven years old, but she recognized that feeling, like she had lived through something so huge that the world after it was always going to be different from what had come before.

Ivan was looking up and down the Mall. He was always their sentry, keeping an eye out for people who might be a threat. They'd had a counselor tell them lots of kids who had been through a trauma did that. It was called hypervigilance. Sometimes it made Ivan a little hard to be around, but it also came in handy. There were still a lot of bad people in DC. The government was gone, the army was gone, the police were gone. The floods had been hard on everyone. Just when they were getting settled and starting to adjust to the way things were, all of a sudden they had to move again.

Everyone had to look out for themselves. The Division agents couldn't do it all.

When she got to the group, Saeed was looking past her. "I know," she said when his gaze shifted over to her. "You want to go to the Air and Space Museum."

He nodded. "Yeah." Saeed wanted to be an astronaut. Violet remembered going to the Air and Space Museum on a field trip a couple of years before, in fourth grade, but she didn't remember a spaceship. She wasn't big into space. Biology was more her thing. She wanted to be a veterinarian. Or a poet.

But she did remember seeing the Apollo 11 capsule in the huge entry hall, with planes hanging all around it. She wondered if it was still there. The Air and Space Museum was one of their no-go spots. Supposedly some bad people had taken it over.

"What's up, Vi?" Ivan poked her in the arm. "You look sad."

Thinking about museums got her thinking about old things, and how people put them in museums so they would be remembered. Now one of the old things people remembered was the way things used to be before the plague. Field trips, weekend outings with your parents, all the normal everyday things that people used to do.

She wasn't going to cry in front of Ivan.

"Come on," she said. "Let's find some salad."

CHAPTER 2

AURELIO

Division agent Aurelio Diaz picked up the lone civilian coming into the Dark Zone just after noon. He was on a rooftop overlooking Fifty-eighth Street and Fifth Avenue, across from the memorial to William Tecumseh Sherman. He stopped there every day on his normal patrol, if emergent duties didn't take him to other parts of the city. It was low enough to let him get to the street fast if he needed to, but high enough to give him a view of the barricades keeping people out of the Dark Zone.

The woman vaulted the barricades and paused just inside, taking in her surroundings. Diaz's first instinct was to run her face through ISAC's facial-recognition database, using the specialized gear all Division agents wore: advanced contact lenses to capture her image, the SHD smartwatch to sync the images from the contact and turn them into a three-dimensional projection, and the so-called ISAC brick, a communications relay device attached to Diaz's backpack. The brick connected Diaz—and all other Division agents—to ISAC, a proprietary artificial intelligence network.

The problem was, she was moving at an angle away from him so he couldn't get a good capture of her face. Either way, she made him curious. Division agents were supposed to enter and exit through the checkpoints spaced around the zone's perimeter, which ran from the southwest corner of Central Park down Broadway to Twenty- third Street, then around and back up past Grand Central Station all the way to Sixty-fifth Street. In theory nobody else was supposed to go in or out under any circumstances. The zone had been one of the first quarantined spaces in the city when the Green Poison had struck, and the overwhelmed Joint Task Force had walled it off and tried to save the rest of the city.

Now, five months after the outbreak, the Dark Zone was quieter than it had been, but still no place for a lone civilian. Often it was no place for a lone Division agent. Other parts of New York were almost livable, but the Dark Zone was completely lawless. Not just lawless—it seemed to attract the most deranged and dangerous people in the city. They were particularly congregated in the northern end of the DZ, because the Division and JTF work in the city spread south to north. Some of the southern DZ neighborhoods were almost normal again, but up here it was still a war zone. Worse than a war zone, in fact. More like a mass psychotic break, where each individual psycho was heavily armed. Not to mention the omnipresent threat of lingering virus that could start a new wave of lethal infections.

And here was a lone woman jumping a barricade to get in. Diaz watched her head east on Sixtieth. She was calm, purposeful. She knew where she was going—or at least wanted watchers to think she did.

He dropped down to street level and followed her. *Entering the Dark Zone,* ISAC's AI said. Yeah, Diaz thought, I know. The only other people on the street were wandering scavengers.

Earlier that morning, Diaz had figured he would run his patrol and then talk to the JTF command down at the Post Office base of operations about whether they still needed him here. He could have left anytime he wanted to, of course. Division agents were empowered by Presidential Directive 51 to act with more or less unlimited discretion. They had no rules of engagement, and answered to no authority within the military chain of command. They were recruited and trained in secret, and activated only in times of critical emergency, when the American government, and social order, was in danger of collapse. Before the Dollar Flu, Diaz had been a gym teacher in DC, with two kids and a wife who worked at a bank.

All of that had changed on Black Friday, when some nutcase had unleashed a weaponized smallpox on the world, starting right here in New York City. Within weeks it had spread all over the world... and Diaz's wife, Graciela, was dead. Maybe she had touched one of the twenty-dollar bills first infected with the virus—thus the nicknames Green Poison, Dollar Bug, et cetera— or maybe she'd caught it from someone who had. In the end, it didn't matter. She had died along with millions of others.

Now, five months later, order wasn't exactly restored in New York, but spring had brought new hope. Pretty soon, Diaz figured he would be able to leave New York and head back home. His kids were there. Mobilized in DC, he'd come up to New York after the first wave of Division agents were killed or went rogue in the violent chaos after the outbreak. At that time, New York had needed help and things in DC had seemed relatively stable by comparison. He wasn't sure that was the case anymoreçfand either way, he'd been away from Ivan and Amelia for too long. The JTF was supposed to be caring for them, but Diaz wanted to be certain.

Getting back to DC was still his plan, but before he could check in at the JTF safe house down on Forty-fifth and Broadway and exit the Dark Zone, he had to see where this woman was going and why. He couldn't just leave her to wander around on her own.

She stayed on Sixtieth to Madison, then turned south. Fires had raged along this part of Madison, and it was mostly abandoned. Fifth and Park were different. Entrenched bands of raiders and bandits had carved out territories along the entire stretch of those avenues between Fifty-second and Sixtieth or so. The boundaries fluctuated.

Trailing her, Diaz was suddenly sure she was choosing her route to avoid that dangerous stretch of Fifth and Park Avenues. She knew this part of the Dark Zone. That made him real curious. He was also curious about the Benelli Super 90 shotgun slung over her right shoulder, next to a pack that sure looked like Division issue… just like the Super 90 was a standard room-sweeper that some agents preferred. But she didn't have a watch, and there was no brick on her pack. She wasn't an agent. So who was she?

She cut back west on Fifty-fifth, and Diaz's alarm bells went off. At the corner of Fifth and Fifty-fifth, the Fifth Avenue Presbyterian Church was home to a gang of apocalyptic cultists. They would be on her like a school of piranha if she went that far. He stepped up his pace, closing to within a hundred feet of her before she noticed and looked over her shoulder. Pretty good situational awareness, he thought. He saw her clock his Division gear and mentally categorize him as no threat. Interesting. That meant she knew she wasn't doing anything she thought would bring her into conflict with a Division agent.

Even so, she was still walking straight toward the church cult.

Diaz cut up Madison at a run, and then headed west on Fifty-sixth to get ahead of her. He scrambled through the ruins of a restaurant that had burned in the aftermath of the plague. Behind it was a narrow alley that ran between the church and the looming skyscraper just to the north. He hopped the fence and came around to the front of the church.

A fresh body dangled from the gallows in the church courtyard. Diaz filed it away. He, or another Division agent, would have to do something about the cult. But today he had another mission. The heavy wooden doors facing Fifth Avenue opened and a group of the cultists saw him. He stayed facing them, his G36 aimed low, generally in their direction but not targeting any one of them specifically. "Stay cool," he said.

They looked past him and saw the woman. She saw them, too—and she saw Aurelio.

Her response intrigued him even more. She cut across the street to give herself some room, but she didn't panic, didn't run. She was no average civilian, that much Aurelio could tell. She passed down the block, staying on Fifty-fifth toward Sixth Avenue. Aurelio backed toward the street. The cultists came out onto the church steps, their eyes boring into him. He'd seen that look before. They wanted him on their gallows, too. Pulling the trigger on the G36 would solve a lot of problems, he thought... but until they made a hostile move, he couldn't justify it. Per Directive 51, he could have mowed the whole group down and nobody would ever have said anything, but that wasn't what Aurelio Diaz—or the Strategic Homeland Division, commonly shortened to SHD—believed in. He backed into the courtyard gate, opened it, and stepped out onto the sidewalk.

"You stayed cool," he said, and kept walking. None of them followed him. When he got to the corner he saw the woman at the far end of the block, almost to Sixth. She turned north, surprising him. She was definitely taking the long way to wherever she was going, and although it made sense for her to avoid Fifth Avenue, clearly her intel about the area wasn't complete or she wouldn't have gone anywhere near the church.

So where was she going?

Fifty-eighth Street, as it turned out. When she got there, she stood for a long moment looking at a nondescript open storefront on the north side of the street next to a parking garage. A shredded awning flapped over the storefront. The inside looked like it might have been under construction. He couldn't see much.

The woman crossed the street and went inside. Interesting, Diaz thought. There was nothing he knew of in that building. Nothing in the garage would be of interest. Over the old store were a few floors of ordinary windows. He thought he saw light in one of them, but couldn't tell whether it was just reflected through a different window from one of the skyscrapers on the same block.

Diaz decided to stay where he was for a few minutes, see what happened. He'd developed a pretty good sense for when people were up to no good—you didn't survive in this ravaged New York without one—and he wasn't getting that sense from her. Still, she'd walked a good mile or more after entering the Dark Zone within five hundred yards of her target location. That piqued his curiosity.

If she came out soon, he would stay on her trail until he left the Dark Zone. Partly that was just because he thought she might need an escort, but also he was curious. Usually people tried to get out of the Dark Zone, not in. What was she up to?

CHAPTER 3

APRIL

She'd spent the spring looking in the Dark Zone, following clues she'd pieced together over the winter. Over the past weeks she had become familiar with every block of the barrier cutting the zone off from the rest of the city. She knew where there were holes. She knew where underground connections between buildings led in and out. None of those holes and tunnels stayed open long. Either the JTF sealed them or criminal elements took control, making them too dangerous to use. But as quickly as they closed, others appeared. Keeping an area the size of the Dark Zone completely sealed was impossible.

The problem was, the place she needed to go was in the worst part of the DZ, just south of Central Park. The southern areas were a little easier to move around in. Still dangerous, but the main JTF base was closer to the southern edge of the Dark Zone. In the months after the Dollar Bug tore through New York, the JTF—and the Division—had begun to restore a semblance of order from about Thirty-fourth Street south. Not so in the north. Up here, Division agents were rarer and the JTF presence was limited to fortified safe houses scattered along the edges of Central Park and the surrounding neighborhoods. She had learned to assess how dangerous an area was based on how often she saw a Division agent's signature gear: the orange circle on the backpack, the optical and audio gear, and most importantly the autonomy. They moved where they wanted, with no rules of engagement beyond a mandate to do what was necessary to keep civilization from collapsing utterly. The more of them she saw in a particular area, the more dangerous the area tended to be—and areas where they usually moved in teams rather than alone were the most dangerous of all.

The northern sector of the Dark Zone was one of those areas.

So she watched, she played it cool, she took her chances as they came up. She only entered during the day, staying close to groups she trusted and ducking out the minute things got hot. Some days it was impossible to get into the Dark Zone. Division agents or JTF patrols turned her back, or there were firefights... or fires. Entire blocks were burned-out shells, thanks to apocalyptic gangs that popped up like mushrooms after the plague struck. Even when she got in and had a chance to scope out an approach to the building she wanted, sometimes she got into tight scrapes. More often than not, she'd been able to avoid violence, and she owed her life to Division agents three or four times over. A couple of times she'd had to shoot someone. Even though she knew they couldn't have been prevented, those deaths weighed on her. She didn't want to live in a world where lethal violence was as common as hot meals.

But that was the world right now, or at least that was New York. Better than it was, for sure, but still a long way from normal. What would normal even be now, with millions dead, the government collapsed, communications severed, great cities emptied, farms lying fallow... she didn't know. After a while, normal was whatever you woke up to in the morning. People had to adapt. She had adapted.

Partially this was because the plague and its aftermath had taught her she had a resilience she had never suspected. Six months ago, sitting in front of her laptop, she would never have imagined vaulting a crumbling barricade into a quarantined hell. But she had a mission. More like an obsession, burning in her gut as she survived the plague and the murderous chaos that followed. It had sustained her through freezing nights and starving days, keeping her focused, giving her something to live for. Her most important clue was an address:

117 w 58th

Today she had finally made it there, at least in part because she'd managed to draw a Division agent along with her. She'd spotted him on the rooftop back by the corner of Central Park, and chosen her point of entry into the Dark Zone hoping he would either confront or follow her. With him following, she'd been able to focus ahead, and get here faster. Mentally she thanked him, and wondered what his name was.

The front of 117 West Fifty-eighth was open, like it had been under construction or something when the Dollar Bug hit. Inside was a trashed space that at first glance looked like it used to be a bike shop. She stepped inside, trying to keep her breathing level. This was it.

Before she did anything else, she took a moment to listen. Human presence in a building revealed itself in various ways. Not just sounds, the quick intake of breath or the small scrape of someone shifting their weight—no, there was a sense of presence that registered somewhere behind the conscious mind. Empty buildings felt empty. She'd learned at some point to tell the difference.

Ahead of her, at the rear of the shop area, was a stairway leading up, and past it a fire door jammed open. Through that doorway she could see a hallway disappearing into the interior of the building. To the right was another, shorter hallway, with a door wedged open on the far side. She flicked on her flashlight and through the open door she saw a stairway going down.

117 w 58th basement level

She descended slowly, listening hard and hearing nothing except the soft scrape of her feet on the safety strips that lined each stair. When she got to the bottom, she still heard nothing. The basement was a maze of narrow hallways opening into boiler rooms, maintenance closets, electrical panels, the circulatory and nervous systems of the modern high-rise. She looked quickly into each and moved on. Then she came to a larger room and stopped in the doorway.

In the near corner of the room was a large server rack, dark and inert. Bedding and crumpled cardboard boxes were scattered across the floor along with food cartons and loose cigarettes. Those caught her attention. They were valuable, and if they were still here that meant nobody had been in this room in a long time.

And that meant...

She cut off that train of thought, continuing her careful observation of the room even though she could feel her heart hammering against her sternum. In the center of the room was a folding table with a map of Manhattan Island and various bits of scrap paper with notes scribbled on them. On the far wall was a whiteboard with a list of names written on it, each keyed to a set of latitude and longitude coordinates.

One of the names she saw was her own.

This was the right place. Or had been. The man she'd been looking for was not here. From the smell of the room, the staleness of the air, she knew he hadn't been in some time. There was no sign of a struggle, no blood on the floor or bullet holes in the walls. No spent shell casings clinking around her feet.

So he wasn't here, but she guessed he wasn't far away. Why send an invitation if you weren't going to be there to receive it?

April I've gone dark come to 117 w 58th basement level

She'd done that. Now she was looking at one last puzzle. Okay, she thought. First we do the obvious.

She went back upstairs to the open entry, moving slowly, alert to any signs of movement. Inside the entry, she paused again.

The building—at least this part of it—felt empty. She moved forward through the remains of the retail space that had once occupied the ground floor. Behind a broken-down fire door was a carpeted hall stinking of mildew and urine. At the far end, another fire door. She doubled back to the retail space and looked up the stairs. Before she started climbing, she shrugged her shotgun off her shoulder and held it low in front of her. Still no sounds, no sense that someone was watching.

She went up to the second floor and peered out of the stairwell, listening for any hint of human presence.

Nothing. But he had to be here somewhere. She went up another floor.

When she looked out of the third-floor stairwell, she could tell someone was living here. Some of the doors were left open, and the soft hum of electrical equipment came from a doorway halfway down the hall on the left. The power couldn't be coming from the building supply. She'd seen the burned-out electrical panels. So someone had a line on an illegitimate supply. That meant they were connected. To whom, was the question. The absence of guards suggested the connection wasn't to a criminal gang. They tended to flaunt their strength.

So: A Division asset, maybe? Hidden away here in the Dark Zone? That fit what she knew… but it also raised more questions.

She walked to the door and paused. Months of searching had led her to this moment. If she was wrong…

She knew she was not wrong. She stepped into the doorway, the Super 90 braced on one hip.

Before the Dollar Bug, this had been a medical suite. Diagnostic equipment lined one wall, and across from it were two desks near a south-facing window. Bright spring sunshine found its way in through the gaps between the skyscrapers to the south. The wall between the medical equipment and the window was lined with bookshelves. From the rows of titles on epidemiology and cell biology and viral genetics, one book jumped out at her: *New York Collapse*.

She'd lost her copy, the one Bill had given her. She'd used it to stay alive and had kept a diary of the weeks after the plague struck in its margins. Repeated readings of it had revealed hidden clues, and those had led her here, to this man sitting at one of the desks. Maybe sixty years old, his hair a salt-and-pepper wave, reading glasses low on his nose. He was writing in a notebook, pausing to glance at a computer screen on the desk.

She spoke from the doorway. "Roger Koopman?"

He looked up and she saw him register the shotgun before he looked at her face. "I don't have anything of value," he said.

"Maybe I should call you Warren Merchant," she said.

He looked more closely at her and a strange expression came over his face, as if he'd seen someone he'd never expected to see and wasn't sure how he felt about it.

"I'm April Kelleher," she said. "I've been looking for you for a long time."

CHAPTER 4

VIOLET

Late in the afternoon, they were hungry and tired, but they had grocery bags stuffed full of dandelion greens. Around the ponds in Constitution Gardens, they had also found a ton of cattails. None of them had ever thought of eating cattails before, but they weren't too bad. One of the women at the hotel, Luiza, had taught the kids what to look for. She peeled cattail roots and ground them up into a flour. Cattail pancakes were on the menu at the Castle now.

So maybe they hadn't gone where they were supposed to go, but they were coming back with better stuff than Luiza and the others were expecting.

The sky over the river was cloudy. It was going to rain. "Let's get home," Amelia said. "We can't really carry anything more anyway."

Cutting across the Mall past the Reflecting Pool, they passed the Washington Monument, staying to the south side of the Mall. Around the buildings north of Constitution Gardens there were gangs of weirdos. The rumor was, they stole kids sometimes. They also stayed away from the White House. There were always people with guns there. Maybe they were protecting

27

the president, or maybe the president was still somewhere else. They didn't know. Saeed and Ivan always said they could tell the difference between the JTF and the other groups, but to Violet they all just looked like men with guns. Mostly men, anyway.

There were also the Division agents, with orange circles on their gear. They didn't seem to be part of any group. Ivan and Amelia said their dad was a Division agent, but Violet didn't know whether to believe them. All of the kids had lost parents and all of them made up stories about their parents to make themselves feel better. Even Violet did this, and she knew both of her parents were dead. She'd seen them die.

She wasn't going to think about that right now.

When they got to Independence Avenue, going past the Department of Agriculture building, a Division agent ran into view from the south. He saw them going up to the intersection of Twelfth and waved to get their attention. "Get out of here!" he shouted.

They froze, not sure what to do. Get out where? Which way?

"Whoa," Wiley said. "Look at that."

He was pointing to the south, and when Violet looked that way she saw a swirling yellow cloud over Hancock Park.

Yellow powder. They'd heard about it. They didn't know what it was, but they knew it was bad.

"Man," Wiley said. The Division agent was coming toward them. "We were just there. We'd be…"

He didn't have to say dead. They all knew.

"Well, you don't want to go down there now," the agent said. "Where were you headed?"

He took his helmet off and used his sleeve to wipe sweat from his forehead and his beard. Violet remembered her dad's beard. The Division agent was a tall, lean white guy with dark hair and streaks of gray in his beard, just like her dad's.

"We're going to the Castle," Shelby said.

"You mean the Smithsonian Castle?"

"Yeah," Noah said. "We used to live down at the hotel, but it flooded."

The Division agent nodded. "Yeah, that was a good spot. Who knows, maybe you can get back there when the river goes down."

"You think it will?"

"Sooner or later, yeah." The agent put his helmet back on and looked west. "It's going to be dark pretty soon. You ought to get home. This isn't a place to be out after dark. And listen. Whatever you do, don't go anywhere down that way."

"Like forever?" Saeed asked. "Is it radioactive or something? I read that uranium powder is yellow."

"No, that's not it. And I don't know about forever, but let's just say you don't want to go down there anytime soon. I'll try to get the JTF over there to set a safe perimeter, but they've got a lot on their hands." The agent got a faraway look on his face. After a moment Violet realized he was listening to something in his earpiece.

"Gotta go, kids," he said. "Seriously, get home."

"We will," Violet said. She shifted her bag full of cattails and greens to her other hand and flexed her fingers.

"Hey, mister. I mean, Agent," Ivan said.

"What's up, buddy?"

"Do you know my dad?"

"Who's your dad?"

"Aurelio Diaz. He's a Division agent, too."

The agent cracked a smile. "Yeah. I do know him. We went out on a bunch of missions together right when everything was falling apart. He went up to New York in... January, maybe?

February? Things were a lot worse up there than they ever got here. Far as I know he's still there."

"So he's not dead."

"Little man, I make no promises. But the last I saw him he was alive and well, and I haven't heard any different since." The agent looked them over as a group. "You guys stick together."

He jogged northwest, back the way the kids had come.

"See?" Ivan said. "I told you our dad was a Division agent."

"Man, that's cool," Wiley said.

Amelia was watching him go. "He's really alive." She was trying not to cry, but it wasn't working.

Violet tried not to be resentful. "Come on," she said. "We have to get home."

Junie, one of the older women who ran the Castle settlement, saw them coming while they were still out in the garden. The Smithsonian Castle was straight ahead, with two art museums flanking the garden, one on either side. Most of the garden was dug up and replanted with vegetables. Chickens clucked their way around, pecking up bugs and whatever else chickens ate.

"I was starting to wonder if you were coming back," Junie said. "But looks like you got what you were after. Let's get those into the kitchen. Ooh, cattails," she added when she got a closer look at their bags.

"We saw a Division agent!" Ivan said. "He said he knew our dad."

"A Division agent?" Junie looked out over the garden to the south. "Is that something to do with the yellow cloud down there?"

They all looked. The cloud was gone now. Violet wondered if the yellow powder was dangerous even if just a few little particles of it got on you. The wind was blowing straight down the river, so maybe none of the powder had come this way. But thinking of that made her want to take a bath right then, and find some new clothes.

Junie was looking at her. "Violet. What's the matter?"

"The Division agent told us the yellow powder was dangerous. He said we couldn't go down there anymore. Like everything down there is poisoned or something." Violet didn't mean to, but she kept talking. "And we were just there!" she blurted out, and then she was crying.

"Hey, now, hey." Junie folded Violet into her soft old-lady arms. The rest of the kids gathered a little tighter around them. "It's not easy being a kid right now," Junie said. "Hell, it's not easy being anybody. But you guys are doing all right."

She let Violet cry herself out. It didn't take long. Violet didn't like showing other people how she felt. But this day had been too much even for her. Nothing really bad had happened, but seeing the hotel, and then seeing the yellow powder… knowing that, more and more, there were places they couldn't go because they might get hurt. She felt like everything was closing in, like sooner or later they would have nowhere to go.

But she couldn't say all that, so she just got herself under control and wiped her eyes. Junie let her go. "Why don't you get all those greens to the kitchen, like I said," she suggested. "Then you ought to get something to eat. Bet you're hungry after being out all day."

"Yeah," Shelby said. As a group the kids trooped toward the Castle and went inside. Violet noticed they were still gathered around her, like they were protecting her. She didn't want them to feel like they had to do that, but it also made her feel good. They were there for each other.

CHAPTER 5

APRIL

"April Kelleher," Koopman said. He smiled broadly. One of his front teeth was stained brown. "Of course." He stood and reached to shake her hand. "It is a pleasure, and also a surprise, to finally meet you."

"Couldn't be that much of a surprise," she said. "You invited me here."

"That was… what, three months ago? I had given up hope." Koopman sat again. He turned off his computer and closed the notebook he'd been writing in. Then he looked up at April, gesturing to a chair. "Please, sit. I'm sure we have a lot to talk about. Sorry for the location. I know it's difficult to get to. I have my reasons for being here, but I felt bad to inflict this problem on you."

She dragged an office chair over and sat. "It wasn't that bad. All I had to do was watch entrances into the Dark Zone for months, figure out the best approach, dodge some bullets, and presto, I'm here." She paused. "And now I have some questions."

Koopman spread his hands. "Fire away."

"First one is, how did you know to leave that wanted

poster?" She took the poster out of her bag and unfolded it. A bad photocopy of her face over the question: HAVE YOU SEEN THIS WOMAN? Below that, a phone number. She'd almost had a heart attack the first time she saw it, when she realized that meant someone was watching her chase the clues in the *New York Collapse* book. Then when she solved the phone number puzzle she understood that it wasn't just anyone watching her: It was the author himself, Warren Merchant. Whose real name was Roger Koopman.

"I was watching you," he answered promptly. "I had some people out observing certain locations. I knew that people would only visit them if they had discovered some of the bread crumbs I left in the book, and you were the only one they reported seeing. So then I started trying to keep an eye on you, but it wasn't easy. You moved around, and then there was the unfortunate business in the condominium."

Unfortunate business. He meant the time April and two of her friends, Miko and Drew, were kidnapped by convicts escaped from Rikers Island. A Division agent tracking the gang found them and freed them after a firefight, but both Miko and Drew were killed. So was the agent. That wasn't the only bad thing that April had experienced since the Dollar Bug first began to rage through New York… but it was just about the worst. Well, the second worst.

"His name was Doug Sutton," Koopman said. "The agent who rescued you."

"Doug Sutton," she said. "Did he have a family?"

"I don't know." Koopman looked uncomfortable, like he didn't want to think about Division agents being people with families. April waited for him to say something else.

When he didn't, she did. "Tell me about Bill."

Bill. William Gibson Kelleher. Six years her husband, now five months dead. Bill, whom she had loved and started to build a life with and then seen shot in the street. Bill, who had given her the *New York Collapse* book that kept her alive during the early weeks of the Dollar Bug and ultimately led her here. She almost never said his name out loud because the name carried with it all the memories, and every time she said it out loud April was afraid she would start telling stories about him and then not be able to stop. Bill was why she'd done all this, risked her life following clues and plotting ways to penetrate the Dark Zone. The day the quarantine had been declared, she'd gone looking for her husband, and she'd seen him killed in the street outside the biotech company where he worked. That was the worst moment of her life. Since then, finding Koopman and learning the truth about what happened to Bill had become two aspects of the same quest. She wanted answers.

Koopman sighed and his chin dropped, like the conversation was going in a direction he didn't like. "You mean why he was killed?"

Like it would be anything else, she thought. "Yes. What he was doing, why he was killed. Did it have something to do with the virus?"

"Sort of, but not in the way you might expect. Bill was part of a team experimenting with a new vaccine design. I'm not a virologist, so I won't pretend to know the details, but the upshot is that this new design would be able to handle large numbers of mutated versions of a particular virus. This class of design goes by the designation BSAV, or broad-spectrum antiviral." Koopman flipped open his notebook and showed April notes and drawings.

She could tell they were diagrams of molecular compounds, but not much beyond that. "Before I moved into management, I was a lab scientist myself, working on water quality issues. So I keep track of things as a sort of interested party. Your husband's company, SBGx, had significantly advanced BSAV research, and what you see here is a simplified sketch of the work other scientists have done, using SBGx's work to prototype a design for a BSAV that would combat Amherst's virus."

"Amherst," April repeated. "He created the virus? One person?"

"Hard to believe, but yes. A skilled virologist with the right tools can design both miracles and catastrophes. Amherst was very skilled. Fortunately there are surviving scientists who are just as gifted. It's a good thing, too, because Amherst's virus could mutate enough to begin spreading again. He designed it to do exactly that, so no single treatment would eliminate it permanently."

Another plague, April thought. The first one had brought everything to the brink of collapse. A second—and a third, and more?—would just about surely finish the job.

"You see how important the work is," Koopman said after a pause.

"So Bill was working on this BSAV. You think that's why he was killed?"

"I don't know for sure," Koopman said. "Maybe Amherst and Tchernenko were cleaning up loose ends; maybe they were trying to delay the production of a vaccine. It was a chaotic time."

"Were there other people killed like Bill?" April had been rehearsing these questions in her mind for months, since she'd first figured out there was more to the book than just survival advice. The whole time she'd imagined the person behind the pseudonym and considered what she would ask when she eventually found him.

"You have to understand," Koopman said. "I was on the run, too. I wrote the book because I knew Amherst was up to something. He designed the virus alone, but you can't do something like that without drawing at least a little interest from other apocalyptic types. They all frequent the same websites, that kind of thing. And megalomaniacs can't help boasting, at least a little. That's how I started to get suspicious. No one knew exactly what he was doing, but quite a few people knew he was doing something, and approved of it. They would have killed me the minute I said anything out loud. I was hoping someone would follow the bread crumbs in the book, so at least in the end someone would learn the truth about what happened." He smiled at her. "Then when I learned you were hunting through the puzzles, I gave you a little assist."

"The wanted poster."

He nodded. "I thought you might want to know you were on the right track. But after I saw what happened to Bill, and some others, I couldn't risk coming out into the open to find you. I had to wait for you to find me. And I'm glad you did."

Glad wasn't the emotion April was feeling. She kept her mouth shut so she wouldn't say anything to anger Koopman, or alienate him. At least not until she had learned everything she'd come here to learn.

"Now since you're here," Koopman went on, "I've got some news for you. The broad-spectrum antiviral Bill was helping to prototype? It exists."

"It…" How was that possible? "Where? Why isn't anyone making it?"

"It's still just a few doses. There are precious few places left where one could manufacture a vaccine. But Dr. Jessica Kandel, working in the JTF lab here in New York, prototyped a vaccine for the existing strain of *Variola chimera*—the Green Poison. She managed to get her design to a surviving lab in Ann Arbor, Michigan. They, in turn, have used it—and your husband's work on broad-spectrum antivirals—to design a vaccine that will combat mutant strains of the Green Poison. And this vaccine works on every observed mutation of the disease… or, at least, so I am told." Koopman spread his arms, indicating the space around them, and by extension his isolation inside the Dark Zone. "The JTF doesn't tell me much, and I certainly am in no position to keep tabs on what people are doing in Michigan. But rumors travel as fast as anything else, and I hear through various channels that the vaccine exists, at least in a few samples."

"In Ann Arbor."

Koopman nodded and shut his notebook again. "The lab in Ann Arbor had some time to prepare before the virus began to spread there, so some of their lab staff had already quarantined themselves so they could continue the work."

The idea of this vaccine was irresistible to April. Could it be true? What were they doing with it? Were things in Ann Arbor that much better than they were in New York? If they were, why was the JTF keeping people quarantined in New York? April started to realize just how distant the rest of the country had become to her. She didn't know what was happening in Hoboken, let alone Ann Arbor, or Denver or San Francisco. She didn't know who was president, or if there was a president. Or if there was a Congress… or, in the end, if there was still a United States.

"And these people in Ann Arbor," she said. "They knew Bill? Would they know what happened to him?"

Koopman shrugged. "Maybe. They had a working agreement with SBGx. I wouldn't be surprised if they knew him, and possibly even survived attacks themselves. But having said all that, I don't even know if the rumors are true. They could all be wishful thinking. There might not be any broad-spectrum antiviral at all."

The words were out of her mouth before April meant to speak them. "I'm going to Ann Arbor."

Koopman did her the courtesy of not laughing. Instead he gave her a long, contemplative look, and then he said, "You'll forgive me saying so, April—can I call you April?"

"I don't care. Sure."

"Okay, then. That's insane. You can't just go to Ann Arbor. It's, what, six hundred miles away? Do you have any idea what has happened in all those states?"

"No. Do you?"

Now Koopman did let out an exasperated chuckle. "I hardly know what's happening on Fourteenth Street."

"Right," April said. "So things might not be as bad out there. Maybe that's why they've kept the quarantin on."

"I don't have any indication that that's the case," Koopman said.

"But you also just said that the JTF doesn't really share much information with you. So you don't know." April stood up and adjusted her backpack. "I've followed this question through some of the worst I can imagine a human being would do. Now it's spring, the virus isn't spreading anymore, and I'm going to follow it right to the end."

She wasn't usually the type to make snap decisions, but this felt right. Now she knew where the truth of Bill's work and death was. Ann Arbor, Michigan. All she knew about it was that the University of Michigan was there.

Six hundred miles, she thought. But most of it will be empty. Probably none of it will be as dangerous as the ten blocks of the Dark Zone I crossed to get here.

"You know," Koopman said, "when I wrote that book, I didn't think anyone would ever follow the clues all the way to the end."

"Here's how I feel about that book," April said. "Probably I'm alive because of it. You know Bill gave it to me as an anniversary present? He meant it as a joke, but it kept me alive. So thanks, I guess. But then if you'd never written it—if you'd just told someone instead—I never would have needed the goddamn book in the first place. Even if they killed you, a lot of other people would still be alive."

Koopman considered this for a long time. "From one angle, you could call it cowardice. I understand that. But there's something else you have to understand, if I have not already explained it clearly enough. Thanks to associates in various intelligence communities, I suspected there was an active plot to release a bioengineered virus. But I did not know anything beyond that—no hints of who was doing it or when it might happen. All I knew was that the plot existed, and that elements within the government also suspected it—and were supportive of it, if you can believe that. To raise the alarm in public would have caused a panic without materially changing Amherst's plan. He might have moved, gone underground to a different lab. Also there was a strong possibility that... well, you know what happened to Bill. He wasn't the only one. As I said, there are rogue elements in the government and military who saw a possible catastrophe as a means to power, and I could easily have ended up dead. So I took another approach, hoping someone would be interested enough to run down the truth. Then the virus was released, and a number of people in a position to have suspected Amherst's project began dying, so I... well, I went dark, as I told you. As dark as I could get, in the Dark Zone. The only people who would know my location were certain Division personnel... and whoever followed the bread crumbs I left in the book. Which you managed to do."

"Five months too late," she said. "And how many millions dead?"

Koopman was quiet for a long time. In the end all he said was, "Well. I don't think I could have changed that. But I tried to do something."

Conflicted, April watched him. The dimming light from outside seemed to lengthen the shadows under his eyes and along his jaw. She understood what he was saying, but that was in her mind. In her gut she blamed him: for Bill dying, for her dogged hunt through the dying city for clues that would lead to "Warren Merchant," for her belief that in meeting him she would somehow learn the great secret behind the Dollar Bug.

But her feelings didn't matter. April had gotten what she needed from Koopman. Some answers, and some more questions, and a path forward. April got up and paused, feeling like there was something else she should say. She and Koopman had a strangely intimate connection by way of the book. But he knew that as well as she did.

In the end what she said was, "Do you know how I can get out of Manhattan?"

"I can reach out to someone," he said, after a pause so long

she'd become certain he would say no. "But not until morning."
Outside it was dusk. "Look," Koopman added, "as determined
and resourceful as you are, you still don't want to be out in this
area after dark. Stay the night here. In the morning, if you still
want to go, I'll put you in touch with someone who can help."

CHAPTER 6

AURELIO

Aurelio watched the open storefront on Fifty-eighth until night fell. The woman didn't come out. Twice he saw people on the street pause in front of the storefront, as if considering whether or not to go in. If they had, he would have followed, but both times they went about their business. A block north, near the barricades separating the Dark Zone from the southern end of Central Park, he heard a brief burst of gunfire. A minute later, another single report, this time a shotgun.

He called in to the nearest JTF safe house, over on Madison. "Diaz here. Shots fired along the Fifty-ninth Street DZ barricade. Any JTF involvement?"

"Negative." Diaz recognized the voice of Ed Tran, the intel officer working out of that safe house. "No JTF presence in that area."

"Acknowledged, Ed. Diaz out." He looked back at the storefront, and then at the building's upper floors. There was a dim glow on the third floor, as if one of the rooms in the rear of the building had a light on.

Something about the situation was bugging him, but he couldn't figure out quite what. He pinged the safe house again. "Ed, can you run an address for me? One-one-seven West Five-eight."

The JTF kept meticulous records about the locations of their various assets, be they scientific, technical, or logistical. It was unusual, to say the least, for a JTF asset to be housed in the Dark Zone, but that was one thing that could explain why whoever lived there didn't have visible security. There could be a guard detail inside, or other active security measures installed.

"Recorded as the location of Koopman, Roger," Ed came back. "Status unclear. I don't know who he is or why we're tracking him."

"Can you find out?"

"Sure."

"Thanks, Ed, I'll call you back." Diaz shifted his weight and considered his options. He heard another shot from near the barricade. Sometimes random assholes got drunk on home-distilled booze, or high on industrial solvents, and just shot into the air... but more often than not, gunshots meant trouble.

Whoever she was, the woman inside that building wasn't going to head out into the Dark Zone by herself at night. Diaz knew that much about her from watching her move through the area in daylight. She knew it was dangerous and she knew how to handle herself. She would stay holed up, or shacked up, with Roger Koopman until morning.

And if she didn't, Diaz thought as the shotgun boomed again, she was on her own. He couldn't sit here watching the door when there was an active firefight nearby.

He slid out of his cover and headed around the corner onto Sixth, moving quick with his G36 held low. More shots came from just around the corner to the west on Fifty-ninth.

When he got to the corner he looked left. The HUD embedded in his contacts picked up a single running figure, heading west. Male, not visibly armed. Aurelio sighted on him out of reflex, then let him go. No way to know whether he'd been involved, or why.

There were bodies in the street just inside the Dark Zone wall. One slumped against the Jersey barriers that formed the base of the wall, with corrugated sheet metal and plywood above it, topped with razor wire. Other parts of the DZ's perimeter were made from shipping containers butted up against each other, or other construction materials. It all depended on what the JTF had available when they were walling the DZ off in December.

Two other bodies lay close to each other in the middle of the street. A third was twenty feet or so away from them, straddling the curb in front of a burned-out hotel. Aurelio thought he saw motion there. He moved forward, thinking he didn't have the field medical equipment he would need to treat a bad gunshot wound. Even so, he had to see if there was something he could do. And if the wounded person survived, she—Aurelio was close enough to see it was a woman—might be able to tell him what had happened. Random street violence wasn't really the Division's main concern, but a new organized gang or militia was a whole different story.

When he was within twenty feet or so of the woman, he heard a faint scuff behind him on the sidewalk. He just had time to duck his head and start leaning to the left when something hit him hard, high on the right side of his back. His backpack took some of the force, but Aurelio still went to his knees. He rolled to his right, instinctively assuming the attacker was right-handed, and therefore a roll to the right would be away from the next blow. He was right. A metallic clang sounded on the sidewalk where he'd been a moment before. Aurelio looked up. Towering over him was a mountain of bald and bearded hate, one of the Dark Zone's resident sociopaths. He held a crowbar and was already rearing up for another swing.

Still sitting, Aurelio brought up the G36. He squeezed off a short burst, letting the recoil walk the fire pattern up from the target's legs to his upper torso. The crowbar clanged on the sidewalk a second time, falling from the target's hand. He folded up and dropped where he stood.

Aurelio stood and turned a full circle. The HUD embedded in his contacts displayed no other people on the street. He glanced back at the man he'd just shot, making sure he was going to stay down. There wasn't much doubt. Two ragged exit wounds in his back told the story, and even if he could have survived those, Aurelio's first shot had punched through his left leg just above the knee.

This wasn't the same man who had been running away in the other direction. Too big, and there was no way the guy could have run around the whole block and come up behind Aurelio so soon. So there was at least one other witness to what had happened, but Aurelio put that aside for now. He stepped up to the woman and squatted at her side.

She was dead. The left side of her torso, under a leather jacket and flannel shirt, was shredded by a load of buckshot. Near her, in the gutter, lay a small black automatic.

He turned to examine the other bodies. None of them wore any kind of uniform. The two lying in the street were facing each other. One of them had the shotgun, the other a Glock that looked like police issue. At a glance it looked like they'd killed each other. The third man, crumpled at the base of the Dark Zone perimeter wall, had clearly met his end courtesy of the same crowbar that had nearly caught Aurelio in the back of the head. Two deep valleys showed in his skull, one along the left side just above the ear and the other right along the crown. Either would probably have been fatal.

So what he had was an apparent encounter between two hostile groups of Dark Zone residents. It happened all the time. If he'd gotten there two minutes earlier, he might have made a difference—but on the other hand, he might also have gotten killed, and for all he knew both groups were drug runners or human traffickers.

Sometimes the Dark Zone made Aurelio a little depressed. Out in the rest of the city, he could see signs that the work and sacrifice of the Division was making a difference. In here, not so much.

He headed back down Fifty-ninth and out through a checkpoint just north of the memorial, along the eastern edge of Central Park. "Housing on your brick thing is cracked," one of the JTF guards noted as he passed.

"Thanks," Aurelio said. "I'll check it out."

Thirty minutes later he was at a JTF safe house in the building that had once housed the 92nd Street YMHA. He checked in with the JTF duty officer, just as a professional courtesy, and got something to eat. Then he cleaned the G36 and looked at the ISAC brick. The housing was indeed cracked, thanks to the crowbar, but it wasn't going to fall out.

Diaz let out a long breath. It was sixteen hours since he'd left the JTF safe house down in Murray Hill. He wondered about the woman who had gone to visit Roger Koopman. He wondered about the man he'd seen running away from the gunfight. He wondered how Ivan and Amelia were doing. Pretty soon he was going back to DC.

That was his last coherent thought before he pulled off his boots, stretched out on a cot, and fell asleep.

CHAPTER 7

VIOLET

Dinner in the Castle was catch-as-catch-can, with small groups of people clustered at small tables or sitting on the floor around their plates. The main gathering area was on the second floor, in a huge hall lined with windows. Violet and the rest of the kids were down at one end, a little bit away from the main groups of adults but still close enough to hear some of their conversation. They had learned that this was a good way to learn things the adults didn't want them to know.

Tonight's dinner was military surplus MREs, with extra salad of dandelion greens. They were bitter and none of the kids liked them, but they ate everything on their plates anyway. They'd learned about hunger in the weeks after the Dollar Bug hit. Some of them might have been picky eaters before, but none of them were now.

Junie was at a table near one of the gallery's big windows, deep in conversation with three other adults. One of them was Mike Walker, who had led a group from the Mandarin Hotel to the Castle after the flood. That was almost three weeks ago, Violet realized. She was already starting to think of the Castle as home.

"We have to be careful," Mike was saying. "There was already pressure from over toward the Capitol, and now they've taken over the Air and Space Museum. Won't be long before they come here."

"Maybe, maybe not," Junie said. "We don't have anything they want."

"They're not just bandits, Junie. They don't want to steal anything from us. They're lunatics who want power. So they're going to go looking for people they can have power over." Mike talked like a teacher, always explaining everything in small stages. It bugged Violet, and she thought it probably bugged Junie, too.

"I know who they are, Mike. And I think if we keep our heads down, just go about our business, we can trust the JTF to keep things under control." Junie cut a glance over at the kids. Violet looked away quickly, but not before Junie had seen her watching. "Anyway, this is a conversation for another time."

Mike looked over at the kids, too. "If you say so. Seems to me they should know."

Junie set down her fork a little harder than she had to. "They know a lot more than is good for them already.

We're the adults. We should protect them when we can."

"Junie, there are mass graves two hundred yards outside the window. Protect them from what?" Mike leaned in closer to Junie as he spoke, but he was still looking sideways at the kids.

"We should go somewhere else," Amelia whispered. Wiley and Saeed started to gather up their plates. Then the others did, too. Violet waited as long as she could, but Mike didn't say anything else and Junie was staring at him. Violet could tell she was mad.

Even though the conversation made her uneasy—like it always made kids upset to see their parents fighting, only none of them had any parents—Violet didn't want to go yet. She wanted to know more about what was going on around them. After all, they were the ones who were going to be dragged off to some new place if it wasn't safe here anymore. She knew there were different groups in the city, and they fought with each other. Some of them just seemed to be random crazy people who wanted to ruin everything, but there were others who wore uniforms, or at least dressed kind of the same. They had a goal. Power, Mike had said. That got Violet wondering about the president again. Who was in charge?

Was anyone in charge?

Shelby was pulling on her arm. "Come on, Vi," she said. "Let's go upstairs."

All of the kids stayed in one big room upon the third floor, all the way at the east end. There were windows looking out in three directions: north over the Mall, east toward the Capitol, and south toward L'Enfant Plaza. There weren't enough couches for all of them, but they had sleeping bags and pillows, along with rugs dragged in to cover the stone floor. It wasn't too bad. For a while, Violet had gone to sleep every night thinking about her old room in the house on School Street in Alexandria, but she didn't do that as much anymore. Tonight, though, she couldn't get it off her mind. Was anyone living in the house now? Was there another kid sleeping in her bed, playing with the stuffed animals she still kept even though she never really played with them anymore?

Probably not. Probably the house was empty, with broken windows and its rooms all messed up from people looting it. In the first couple of days after things started to get bad, Violet's parents had reported to a quarantine site. Her mother was already sick then, and her father caught the Green Poison soon after. Both of them were dead two weeks after Black Friday. The people running the quarantine site had kept her there for another two weeks, putting her with other kids. Other orphans. She made a point of using that word because it was true and she had to face the truth. Her parents were dead.

Saeed was in that first group of kids, too. Some of the others were claimed by relatives, but Violet and Saeed got cycled out of the quarantine and into the Mandarin Hotel camp. That was where they met the other kids. They'd been together since.

They finished their food without saying much. All of them were thinking about what Mike and Junie had said, but none of them were ready to talk about it yet.

Noah took their dishes back down to the kitchen and they all brushed their teeth. The adults were very strict about this. There weren't many dentists around, and apparently people could die from infections in their teeth. Violet had never known this.

It was well dark by the time they all got done with their bathroom stuff. Their room had a couple of candles. The rule was, they had to put them out before they bedded down or the adults would take them away, and Amelia was in charge of that. So she waited until all the other kids were wrapped up in blankets or sleeping bags and then she blew out the candles and stretched out on her couch.

Then it was only a matter of time. Violet didn't mind talking about things, but she didn't want to be the one to start. So she was glad when Ivan said, "If we move, our dad won't be able to find us."

"Sure, he will," Amelia said. "Don't worry."

"I don't think we'll have to move," Saeed said. He always believed the best. "Or if we do, we'll be able to go back to the hotel once the flood's gone."

"The hotel's going to be ruined," Wiley said. "Everything will be under, like, a foot of mud, and there'll be mold everywhere." He had relatives from New Orleans who had told him stories about flooding from Hurricane Katrina.

"Then we'll go somewhere else," Saeed said.

"Yeah," Shelby said. "But where?" Her parents were diplomats or something from China. Sometimes she talked about her uncle in Beijing who was going to come get her, but they all knew that wasn't happening. There wasn't any fuel to fly airplanes, except once in a while they saw a military jet or helicopter. China might as well be the moon.

"Do you think it's getting more dangerous, Vi?" That was Shelby again. She'd started treating Violet kind of like a big sister, which was okay with Violet most of the time, but right now Violet didn't know what to tell her.

"I don't know," she said, thinking of the yellow powder and the way the gunshots out over the Mall seemed closer now than they had a couple of weeks ago. There were more JTF soldiers around, too, which was good because they helped protect everyone—but also bad because it meant the JTF thought they needed more protection. "But if we do," Violet added, "we'll be okay. We'll stick together and we'll be okay."

After that, none of them had much to say. Pretty soon Violet heard them sleeping, breath regular and deep. She stayed up for a while, thinking about all the things she didn't want to be thinking about. There were fires burning near the Capitol, and she wondered if those fires would spread in their direction. Where would they go?

She didn't know. None of them knew. Violet watched those flickering fires and wondered if things would ever be normal again.

CHAPTER 8

AURELIO

Aurelio was up early, cleaned up and full of eggs by seven o'clock. He still had the woman and Roger Koopman on his mind. Before heading out, he took in a morning briefing—as usual, things were more or less under control south of Thirty-fourth Street, then progressively more chaotic up to the north end of the Dark Zone and surrounding areas. Scouts were reporting that the northern end of Manhattan Island was fairly secure, largely because it was mostly depopulated. Since JTF resources were concentrated down around the main bases at Hudson Yards and the Post Office, most of the people who survived the plague had headed in that direction.

Having run more than a few missions up into Washington Heights and Harlem, Aurelio thought the last part of that assessment was a bit rosy. But he only had his own experience to go on, and it was possible the JTF scouts, and other Division agents, had better overall intel than he did. So he kept his opinions to himself, and after the briefing he went to find Ed Tran again.

Ed, as usual, was in the operations node up on the second

floor, surrounded by communications equipment and computer screens. Heavy power cables ran from his workspace down a hall toward the back of the building, where presumably a generator was grumbling away on a fire escape or rooftop. He looked up when he saw Aurelio coming. "Still looking for intel on whatsisname?"

"Koopman. Yeah." Aurelio waited while Ed searched through the JTF's various databases.

"His name pops up here and there," Ed said after a while. "Mostly as a coauthor or editor on scientific papers that Kandel and her group are using to do antiviral research. I don't see anything about him being directly involved with... oh. Wait a sec." Ed tapped and swiped some more. "There is a note in operational logs for that address. Something about installing passive security, keeping twenty-four-hour surveillance... huh." He leaned back. "I don't know what it's all about. Above my pay grade. But somebody somewhere wanted to make sure this guy was safe even though he was hiding out in the Dark Zone. Anything else I can tell you?"

"Yeah. He's a scientist. Is he working on something with Kandel and her people?"

"Doesn't look like it. Not directly. But I can't access the logs themselves. I do see that he visited a certain Dr. Liu down at the Post Office lab, and he's one of Kandel's researchers." Ed kept scanning, then gave up. "That's all I got, man. Sorry."

"Thanks, Ed." Aurelio checked in on the mission board to see where the day's hot spots were. The JTF satellite base on the Manhattan side of the Queensboro Bridge was seeing increased hostile action from a group trying to get off the island. The Midtown Tunnel, right down the street, had flooded over the winter. Rumor was that the JTF had done it when they had too many exit points to guard. Same with all the subway tunnels under the Hudson and East rivers, along with the Brooklyn–Battery Tunnel. The Holland Tunnel was still open to keep a surface supply route available. Made sense, since that tunnel's Manhattan entrance was only a couple of blocks from the JTF's main Hudson Yards base.

That situation looked under control, so Aurelio kept scanning. Part of his mind kept running over the question of what a random woman had wanted from Roger Koopman that would lead her to brave the Dark Zone by herself. If Koopman was a known JTF asset, that put a different spin on her visit. By the time he got back to the DZ, she would in all likelihood be long gone, but Aurelio was tempted to go anyway and ask Koopman what it was all about. On the other hand, the city of New York was offering him plenty of other high-priority uses of his time. Roger Koopman wasn't killing anyone. Eventually Aurelio decided to let it go. He couldn't serve both his curiosity and his mission to save lives. People did all kinds of weird things. He guessed they always had, and now after the virus there was just less to hold them back.

"If you're looking for something to do," Ed called across the room, "I've got a document package that needs to get to the Lighthouse today."

"Is it important?" Aurelio didn't want to spend his day being a courier while other agents were in the line of fire, unless the documents in question were of the life-saving variety. But if the docs were headed to the main JTF base of operations in the Post Office—known as the Lighthouse—they were probably crucial to something.

"Yeah. It's intel recovered from a mission yesterday. Some of our guys intercepted a paramilitary group trying to get onto the island from under the Triborough Bridge. The higher-ups want to see it pronto, and the agent who brought it in can't make the trip." Ed held up the packet, a thick sealed plastic envelope.

Aurelio reached to take it. "Why not?" he asked.

"Died last night," Ed said. That was when Aurelio noticed the traces of dried blood on the envelope, like someone had made a half-hearted effort to wipe it clean.

"Who?"

"Laila Khan. You know her?"

Aurelio shook his head. "Nope." He'd known plenty of other agents who hadn't made it this far, though. On operations with a fire team, ISAC tracked each member's vital signs and pinged out notifications when a comrade was dying, so the team medic could render aid. Or, if it was too late for that, ISAC also had its way of telling team members one of them was dead. *Fatal trauma detected,* was how the AI voice usually put it.

Aurelio stashed the envelope in his pack and notified ISAC that he was on-mission headed to the Lighthouse. His contacts' HUD was overlaid with a high-level map of the optimal route, across Central Park and straight down Eighth Avenue. The base was in the old post office, right across the street from Madison Square Garden, where Aurelio had run one of his first New York missions. There'd been a field hospital there, and when it was overrun by rioters, the JTF called in help to get their medical personnel out. Aurelio had only been in New York for a couple of days then, but he'd helped establish a secure passage for the evacuated personnel to get to the Lighthouse. He wondered if Jessica Kandel was one of the doctors he'd helped get out. By the end of the op, he'd been too exhausted to get any of their names or remember what any of them looked like. He probably wouldn't recognize Jessica Kandel if he ran into her on the street.

Now that he was thinking about her, Aurelio had half a mind to stop into the medical wing and see what Dr. Kandel would tell him about Roger Koopman. First he'd have to get the documents where they needed to go.

He filled his water bottles, checked his loads, and headed out into the bright spring morning on Ninety-second Street. The JTF presence in the area drew food trucks and other traders, so there was a little bazaar most days around the Cooper Hewitt Museum and the edge of the reservoir. Aurelio strolled through, enjoying the smells of cooking. He caught the odor of fresh bread and stopped at the stall. "Man, smells good." He dug in his pockets for something a baker might want in return for a loaf of bread. It had been months since anyone in Manhattan had used money.

"Ah," the baker said, looking up and seeing Aurelio's gear. "A Knight of the Orange Circle." He picked a loaf and held it out, grinning through his flour-dusted black beard. "This one's on me. But don't tell all your friends, all right?"

"Thanks," Aurelio said, smiling back. He didn't like taking gifts, but he also realized that it was a strange kind of obligation. When you spent most of your days interacting with people trying to kill you, it was easy to forget that the world was also full of kindness and generosity. People who knew what Division agents did were grateful, and Aurelio had come to understand that it was important to accept their gratitude without abusing it.

"Tell you what," he said, tearing a piece of the bread off and smelling it. "Next time I pass through, I'll bring you something. What do you need?"

"Need? Oh, you know. Reliable electricity, ice cream, baseball on TV. But I'll tell you one thing I really miss. I used to walk across the Brooklyn Bridge every week. But since all this, I haven't been south of Union Square. If you happen to run across anything that says Brooklyn Bridge on it, like a street sign, anything, I'll hang it right here." The baker tapped the awning he had set up over his stall. "And you get free bread forever."

"Sounds like a good deal," Aurelio said. "I'll see what I can do." He tried to remember the last time he'd been down around city hall, or anywhere near the Brooklyn Bridge. February, maybe.

He held up the chunk of bread as a farewell salute and started chewing on it as he walked around the south end of the reservoir and picked up the Eighty-sixth Street Transverse over to Central Park West. Most of Central Park was a patchwork of mass graves, but here and there people had started gardens. Aurelio even passed by a pen full of goats along the bridle path. Where had anyone gotten goats? New York was full of mysteries.

There was another market in front of the Natural History Museum, and then things got desolate as he got closer to the northwest corner of the Dark Zone at Columbus Circle. He flexed his fingers on the grip of the G36, keeping himself loose and alert. ISAC didn't detect any hostiles, but ISAC couldn't see everything. It relied on facial recognition and uniform detection in conjunction with the JTF's current database of known locations of hostile gangs, cult groups, et cetera. Overall, ISAC did a good job of making an agent aware of the general characteristics of a given area, but in the end nothing could substitute for observation and situational awareness. Eyes and ears.

He ran into JTF patrols just south of Columbus Circle, before the perimeter wall of the Dark Zone bent away, following

Broadway while Aurelio stayed on Eighth. Burned buses and hollow-eyed vagrants surrounded the Port Authority. They all took one look at him and gave him a wide berth.

When he got to the windswept plaza outside Madison Square Garden, another big market was in full swing. This was the safest place in the city, with the JTF base of operations right there. All of the buildings in the surrounding blocks were occupied by people who clustered in this area to feel secure. Of all the parts of New York, this was the place that felt closest to normalcy. Even so, almost everyone got inside after dark, and Aurelio knew many of the vendors and wandering pedestrians were armed. The veneer of civilization was very thin, even here.

Seeing his Division gear, the guards at the Post Office waved him in and he went looking for the duty officer, who, according to the guard, was one Lieutenant Hendricks. He found her in the security wing. She was a serious- looking black woman in her early fifties, with short salt-and-pepper dreadlocks and little patience for people who took her away from her current task involving an operational map and some kind of checklist.

"What can I do for you, Agent?" she said briskly, looking him over and then returning her attention to the map.

"I came down from the 92nd Street Y," he said, showing her the envelope. "Supposed to deliver this to an intel officer."

Aurelio watched her register the smears of blood. "Somebody got that the hard way," she said.

"The hardest," Aurelio agreed.

After a pause, Hendricks held out a hand. "You need to convey in person, or can I deliver it?"

Ed hadn't said anything about the handoff, so Aurelio gave her the envelope.

"I'll see that it gets there ASAP," she said.

Aurelio watched her walk away to an inner office. One of these days, he thought, there's going to be a memorial to all the Division agents who died holding the United States of America together after the Green Poison.

He hoped he wouldn't be on it.

CHAPTER 9

APRIL

April slept until late morning, the first time that had happened since the quarantine. She didn't remember having any dreams, and woke up feeling the kind of stiffness that came from lying in one position for hours. Reaching the end of an obsession was like that, maybe. She didn't know. She'd never had an obsession before.

And she didn't have one now, not really. She did still have a purpose, though. She was going to go to Ann Arbor and find out the truth about the BSAV, and the truth about Bill if anyone there knew it. Either way, she considered, the trip would be a kind of honor to his memory. She would be closing the circle on his presence in her life by seeing for herself the final product of his life's work. The decision felt good.

She was in a room that used to be some kind of small office, across the hall from the room where Koopman slept and worked. She stood, stretched, felt joints crack. God, she'd slept hard.

All of her gear was exactly where she'd left it. Just to be sure, she popped the magazine off her Super 90 and checked its load. All good. She didn't like carrying guns, but the world was what it was. Also, she had an emotional attachment to this gun. She'd picked it up from the floor next to the body of the Division agent who had died saving her. Doug Sutton. Who had he been before the virus? Did he have surviving family, a lover, anyone other than April to mark his sacrifice? She would probably never know.

This was a hell of a train of thought to have first thing in the morning, and April tried to reset it as she walked out into the hall and saw Koopman through the open doorway just opposite.

"Good morning," Koopman said. "Hope you slept well. Bathroom's down at the end of the hall."

Thank God for gravity, April thought as she flushed the toilet. New York's water supply was gravity fed, so most of the smaller buildings in the city still had water. She couldn't imagine how people in other parts of the country got their water… but she would be finding out pretty soon, now, wouldn't she?

When she came back into Koopman's office, he was setting out a pot of coffee and two mugs. "My God," April said. "Where did you get coffee?"

"I have a connection here and there with the JTF, and some other people in the city who know how to get things done. Once in a while those connections pay off with small luxuries."

April smelled it, feeling the wash of memories that came with the simple act of letting that coffee aroma drift with the steam around her face. It used to be mundane and precious at the same time, she thought. Something I did every day, but looked forward to every day. Now it's like a miracle because God knows when it'll happen again.

She took a sip and almost started crying, because it was good and also because it seemed to her like a sign of everything that was lost because of Amherst and his doomsday madness. But instead of crying, she took another sip and said, "Thank you. This is... well, it's an unexpected treat."

"I'm happy to do what I can," Koopman said. "You've been through a lot."

"Not as bad as some," she said, thinking of Doug Sutton. Also Miko and Drew, all the other people she'd seen die in the past months. And Bill.

"So," she said. "You said you might know someone who can get me across the Hudson."

Koopman set down his mug and cleared his throat. "You know this is a terrible idea."

"I know I'm going to do it one way or another whether you think it's a terrible idea or not." April kept her tone level. She needed Koopman for this one last thing, so she had to walk a fine line between standing her ground and irritating him. She sipped the coffee, again lost in the simple sensory delight of it.

"Well," Koopman said after a while. "What I can do is get a message to the Riverside Templars."

It turned out that when Koopman said he would get a message to the Riverside Templars, he meant he would write a letter for April to carry. "They're suspicious, but good people," Koopman said.

"If they shoot me before they see the letter, it won't really matter how good they are," she pointed out.

"I promise you they won't." Koopman finished the letter and folded the sheet neatly in thirds. He handed it to April. "I know I said this was a terrible idea, and I still believe that. But I also believe that you're as likely as anyone to pull it off. This note ought to get you started on your way." After a pause he added, "I'll also make sure the JTF checkpoint around the corner knows to let you out."

She'd finished her coffee and it was time to go. Anything she needed, April always had with her. She kept a room downtown, in the back of an old souvenir store on Twenty-eighth Street, but there was no reason to go back there now. She got her pack and settled it on her shoulders. Then before she left she had one last thing to get off her chest.

"Merch," she said. That was the nickname she'd coined in her head when she was having long internal conversations with the writer of *New York Collapse*, trying to understand the puzzles in the book and through them the author's motivations. He'd called himself Warren Merchant, and that pseudonym was one of the final clues. Koopman was the Dutch word for merchant. She'd braved the stacks at the New York Public Library to find that out.

Koopman was back at his desk, writing something down in a notebook and referring to his computer terminal. He looked up. "Merch?"

"For Merchant. I had to give you a nickname while I was working through the book." She paused, trying to figure out exactly what she wanted to say. "Listen, I want you to know that I'm grateful. Your book kept me alive, and when I started to see there was more to it than the survival advice, that kept me going. I don't know whether Bill would still be alive if you'd called CNN instead of writing the book. I guess I'll never know. But I do know I wouldn't be here. So thank you."

He stood and inclined his head, almost bowing. There was something courtly about his bearing. "I should be thanking you," he said. "Everything you did to get here validates what I was trying to do in the book. I wish you good luck, April Kelleher. I hope you find what you're looking for."

Koopman directed her to the JTF checkpoint nearest his hideout, where Sixth Avenue dead-ended into Fifty-ninth Street. Moving fast and keeping the Super 90 visible, April got there with no trouble. The checkpoint was a fortified sandbag emplacement on top of a cargo container, covering a gated gap in the Dark Zone barrier. JTF sentries called out when she was still in the middle of the street. "Do not approach! You will be fired on!"

She slung the Super 90 and kept her hands out in front of her. "My name is April Kelleher," she said. "I was told to come to this checkpoint."

"By whom?"

"Roger Koopman. Just a few minutes ago."

"Approach slowly."

She did, looking up at the two sentries. One of them said, "She fits the description."

The other sentry looked down behind the barrier and said, "Open the gate."

As the gate racked open, April walked over and slid through the minute the gap was wide enough for her to pass. Two more JTF soldiers were at the base of the wall on that side. They kept guns on her as she came through, then shut the gate behind her. April turned west along the southern border of Central Park, thinking of the other times she'd gone into and out of the Dark Zone. If she was lucky, she'd never have to do it again.

She caught breakfast at the market in front of the Natural

History Museum and then kept going north, staying at the edge of the park all the way up to 110th and then cutting over to Riverside Drive for the rest of the long walk up to the far northern tip of Manhattan Island. The closer you stayed to the river, the more often you ran into JTF patrols. April wanted to be visible to them in case she ran into trouble.

But she didn't, and an hour later she passed the 190th Street subway station and followed a winding road into Fort Tryon Park. This was a beautiful part of Manhattan, and one she'd only seen once before. High forested bluffs fell away on her left toward the Hudson River. Beyond the river she could see the Palisades of New Jersey, spotted with condo towers. The Henry Hudson Parkway, below her at the edge of the river, was empty and silent. She passed the old fort itself, and a few minutes after that she became aware that someone was following her.

When she turned around, she saw that in fact there were three of them. They were fifty yards or so behind her, trailing her along the park road. She stopped and took in their appearance. Three men. Two white, one black. Full beards, matching handmade tunics bearing what she recognized as some kind of medieval cross. All three carried rifles.

"You not from around here?" the black guy asked.

"No," she said.

"Didn't think so, or you would have known not to come. This is a sacred place. Visitors are not permitted. If you want to join, that's another story. You have to talk to the Master." He nodded past her, toward—she assumed— the tower of the Cloisters, which was where she was going anyway.

"I don't want to join," she said. "Thank you. But I do need to speak to the Master."

"I am Brother Michael. I decide who sees the Master. What is your errand?"

She started to shrug her backpack off, but thought better of it. From Koopman's brief description of the Riverside Templars, surprising them didn't seem like a good idea. Instead she said, "I have a letter for him."

His eyebrows rose. "A letter? From whom?"

"It's for the Master," April said. "Please take me to him."

He held her gaze for another moment, then said, "Very well."

One of the white guys took her shotgun while the other gave her a respectful pat-down. Then they fell into step next to her while Brother Michael led the way toward the Cloisters.

The one other time she'd been up here was right after she'd moved to New York, fresh out of college and determined to take in all the sights as fast as she could. It had been quiet then by New York standards, with the traffic noise from the Hudson Parkway muffled by trees and most other people picnicking or walking dogs or walking the grounds in tour groups. Now both the traffic and people were gone, and the only sounds were their footsteps on the road against a backdrop of birdsong and leaves ruffling in the wind.

The Cloisters was a museum complex built a hundred years before from pieces of various medieval monasteries. She remembered that much from taking the tour. Now it was reborn as an actual monastery, from the looks of it, but the Riverside Templars weren't the contemplative type of monks who spent their days transcribing manuscripts and singing vespers. She saw them at work on the grounds outside the museum. They were building fortifications, conducting combat drills, sending out patrols. She saw a few women, but mostly men. No wonder it was quiet, April thought. Any criminal gang or band of thieves would only make the mistake of testing the Templars once.

Brother Michael guided her through an entrance, nodding at the guards on either side. April remembered there being a café in the building somewhere, but she didn't see it as they passed deeper into the building and came out again into a courtyard. The gardens were manicured and the stone walkways swept.

The Master stood by himself near the center of the courtyard, looking down at the still water in a large basin. He was tall, thin, with head shaved but beard thick and white against the dark brown of his skin. "Brother Michael," he said as they approached. "Who is this?"

"She says she has a letter for you, Master," Brother Michael said.

The Master still had not made eye contact with any of them. "Then let her produce it."

April set her backpack on the stones and took the letter out. Brother Michael plucked it from her fingers and walked to the Master, who opened it and read it. "Thank you, Brother Michael," he said. "I will speak to her."

He looked up at them for the first time and saw one of the other Templars holding two guns. "One of those is hers, Brother Javier?"

"Yes."

"You may return it to her."

Brother Javier held the Super 90 out by the strap and April took it. She slung it over her shoulder, very careful not to give anyone the impression she might be pointing it at the Master along the way.

"You will excuse us, Brothers," the Master said.

The three Templars nodded and went back inside.

The Master was looking at the letter again. "Roger Koopman," he said. "How do you know him, Miss Kelleher?"

"April is fine," she said. "What do I call you?" She didn't have a lot of patience for ceremonial titles in any circumstance, and the whole warrior-monk performance was already wearing on her. Maybe they needed it to keep themselves together, but she didn't feel like participating.

"My given name is Andrew Bartholomew Rhodes," the Master said. "Colonel, United States Marines, retired. Also Doctor. I acquired a PhD in medieval European history during my service."

That started to clarify things a little, April thought. A retired marine officer with an interest in medieval history, faced with the collapse of civilization. Why wouldn't he do what some medieval Europeans had done, and create a monastic order to preserve what otherwise might be lost?

"So do I call you Dr. Rhodes or Colonel Rhodes?" she asked.

He cracked a smile. "Andrew will be fine for now," he said. "But you have not answered my question." He didn't repeat it.

"Roger Koopman knew some important things about how my husband, Bill, was killed," she said. "I found him so I could learn what he knew. Now I need to find some other people, and to do that I need to get across the river."

"So his letter explained," the Master said. "Now perhaps I should explain why he suggested you approach us for aid. We, the Riverside Templars, have taken up the cause of protecting the innocent while the United States of America is in the process of deciding whether or not it still exists. The influence of the Joint Task Force rarely extends this far north, and without us, the entire area north of the George Washington Bridge would be a lawless waste."

That fit what April had already assumed. "You must be doing a good job," she said. "It's quiet up here."

He nodded. "We keep it that way. We also understand that some of the actions of the JTF impose undue hardships on those innocents we are charged to protect. People need food and medicine, yes; but they also need news of their loved ones beyond this island. And, every so often, they need to—as you said—get across the river."

Warrior-monks who were also smugglers, April thought. This was a strange new world the Dollar Bug had made. "I see," she said.

"I expect you do," the Master said. "Koopman speaks highly of you in this letter, and he is not by disposition a man who speaks highly of many people."

He folded the letter and tucked it away inside his tunic. Then he glanced up at the sky. Heavy rain clouds hung over New Jersey, and the first drops of rain were already spattering the stone walkways and dimpling the surface of the water in the basin. "It is five hours yet until sunset," he said. "We will get you across the river, but not until dark. In the meantime, permit me to extend the hospitality of the Riverside Templars. You are welcome here. Rest, refresh yourself. Bathe if you wish." He looked past April, and she turned to see that Brother Michael had reappeared.

"Conduct our guest to a room, Brother Michael," the Master said. "See that she has what she needs." To April he added, "Someone will call for you at approximately ten o'clock. It is important you be ready."

"Thank you," she said, and she followed Brother Michael back inside.

CHAPTER 10

AURELIO

When the rain moved in late that afternoon, Aurelio was on a mission clearing a group of smugglers out of a condo building in the Meatpacking District. He was sweaty from running stairs, dusty from the clouds of drywall particles kicked up in the fight, and limping a little because a ricochet had clipped him on the right ankle. It was already sapped of most of its force, so it hadn't even penetrated his boot, but it still felt like someone had cracked him with a baseball bat.

He was better off than the smugglers, though.

Privately Aurelio didn't have a problem with some of the black-market commerce happening all over Manhattan. People had to get things, and there were dozens of vendors bringing in food, pharmaceuticals, and various mundane items. As far as Aurelio was concerned, they weren't hurting anybody. But there were also groups bringing in guns and hard drugs. Some of them also offered coyote services, claiming they could smuggle people out. This particular group specialized in wringing everything they could out of desperate people who wanted to get to Jersey or points west. Then those people ended up in the river. Word never spread because none of the people who wanted out ever planned on coming back anyway, but JTF patrols farther south started finding bodies with their throats cut. They investigated and traced the grapevine right back to its roots in a condo tower at the far western end of Fourteenth Street.

The first JTF strike team had run into trouble and called for fire support. Aurelio, who had just delivered the document package into the capable hands of Lieutenant Hendricks, headed down the High Line to see what he could do. Just south of Fourteenth, the High Line path ran underneath the building, creating a small elevated plaza. He'd shot his way in, cleared the stairwell leading down to the floors occupied by the smugglers, and kicked through the fire door just in time to save the JTF team from getting caught in what would have been a lethal crossfire. They were fully engaged with a group at the far end of the hall, and just as Aurelio came out of the stairwell, four of the smugglers burst out of a door near him. Since they were looking the other way, toward the embattled JTF team, Aurelio had put them down *tout de suite*. He ducked into the doorway they'd come out of, to pop a fresh magazine into the G36, and that was when he noticed that the smugglers had punched holes through the walls between condos.

He ran the length of the hall, coming out in the last corner unit. The hole there was in a bathroom wall. He came through, stepping into a master bedroom with three terrified civilians huddled against the wall behind the bed. Aurelio motioned for them to stay put. ISAC told him the hostiles were in and around the unit's front door, on the other side of a big open living room.

When he stepped sideways out into the living room, he saw six smugglers, all focused on the JTF team that was hopscotching down doorways toward them. Aurelio stepped back into the bedroom, pulled the pin from a grenade, and hooked it around the bedroom doorway across the living room.

He heard the thunk of it landing on the wood floor. Then one of the smugglers shouted, "What the fuck!"

Then it went off.

With the sound still ringing in his ears, Aurelio sidestepped into the living room again. Through the smoke he saw four of the smugglers down and still. ISAC tracked two more. The first of those had ducked out into the hall to avoid the grenade, but that put him right in the sights of the JTF team, who didn't miss.

The last smuggler popped up from inside a laundry closet on the far side of the unit's front door. He got off a haphazard burst from what looked like a TEC-9, and Aurelio's right leg went out from under him.

As he was hitting the floor, though, Aurelio was firing, a long burst that splintered the closet door frame and sent the smuggler staggering back. He hit the far side of the doorway and sank down, dead by the time his ass made contact with the floor.

Aurelio got to his feet. "Hostiles down!" he called out into the hall. He tested his leg. It hurt, and the outside of his foot was numb, but he could stand.

Two of the smugglers were still moving, but judging from the amount of blood on the floor and the walls, they wouldn't be for much longer. Aurelio decided he would leave it up to the JTF whether they got medical attention or not.

"Identify yourself!" one of the JTF officers called. ISAC, combing deployment status notifications, told Diaz his name was Franklin.

"Division agent Aurelio Diaz," he called back. "You're Sergeant Franklin?"

"How the hell do you know that? Stay where you are. We're coming in."

Typical, Aurelio thought. Call for help, then get suspicious when you show up and give it. "There are three civilians in the master bedroom," he said when Franklin entered, his M4 pointed in Aurelio's general direction. Aurelio tried not to take offense. People got jumpy after a firefight.

He pointed behind him. "Back that way."

Franklin lowered the M4 and looked down at the bodies of the smugglers. One of them was still breathing, but barely. He looked back at Aurelio. "You know if this is all of them?"

"There were guards at the High Line entrance, and they had the stairwell guarded, too," Aurelio said. "All clear now. Another four of them at the far end of the hall. I took care of them. Then these."

He let that hang in the air. That's right, he didn't add. I just smoked a dozen hostiles while you were trying to get three doors down the hall. Maybe you could show a little respect.

"Understood," Franklin said. He called back into the hall. "Civilians inside! Let's get a medic in here!" When he looked back at Aurelio, he added, "We'll take it from here. Appreciate the help."

"*De nada*," Aurelio said. He waited until the JTF medic was past him into the bedroom, ignoring the last dying smuggler. Then he limped back out, back up the stairs, and out into the rain. On the way he passed two dead JTF soldiers.

Now, already soaked, he stood for a while on an overgrown stretch of the High Line elevated park that ran from Gansevoort Street up to the Javits Center. The JTF tried to keep the High Line open and relatively safe, because it gave quick access to the entire stretch of Manhattan's west side from Hudson Yards all the way down to Greenwich Village, with superior sight lines down the east–west streets along the way. The problem with the High Line was that it was lined with high-rises, so JTF teams were routinely under sniper fire whenever they operated. The rain and wind made that less of a problem, so Aurelio felt reasonably safe as he leaned on a railing and looked down the empty canyon of Fourteenth Street. Beyond Eighth Avenue, it disappeared into the rain.

He flexed his ankle. Feeling had come back to his foot and he didn't think anything was broken, but the next time he took off his boot he was going to have a hell of a time getting it back on. The ankle was going to swell.

Problem for another time. He was thinking about the three civilians in the smugglers' condo. One of them had been a girl maybe twelve or thirteen. Now that he thought about it, they were probably a family group. Unlikely all three had survived the Green Poison as a nuclear family, but the adults had gotten together in the aftermath. Now they were trying to get out, and if Aurelio hadn't shown up—with some credit to the JTF, too, sure—all three of them would have been facedown in the Hudson sometime later that night.

His daughter, Amelia, would turn twelve in about a month. June 3.

Something clicked when he had that thought, and Aurelio decided he would be there for her birthday. Ivan would be ten in August. Aurelio planned to be in DC for that, too.

It was time for him to go home. There would always be work for a Division agent in New York, but there was plenty of work in DC, too. He'd overheard chatter in the Post Office that the government was still in flux. Aurelio knew President Waller was dead. Reports were, he'd succumbed to the virus sometime in January. His VP, Mendez, was supposed to be in DC trying to hold everything together, but the rumor mill suggested he was having a hard time. Too many competing interests, too many people seeing the aftermath of the Green Poison as their chance to claim power.

One more reason for Aurelio to get back to DC. Winter was over, people were beginning to adjust, adapt, rebuild... it was time to make sure that the nation's capital was safe and stable. That was the Division imperative. But he could also keep a closer eye on Ivan and Amelia.

He shoved off the railing and started walking north. When he got to Thirtieth Street, the High Line curved west and Aurelio dropped down to the street. Two long blocks east, he hung a left on Eighth Avenue and was back inside the Post Office at about seven o'clock.

The first thing he did was hang up his gear to dry in the former sorting area, now a makeshift barracks. Then he toweled himself off and went looking for Lieutenant Hendricks over in the security wing.

She was just getting off duty, but he begged five minutes of her time and she sat down with him at her desk. "Just as a courtesy," he said, "I thought I'd let you know I'm going to head back to DC. From what I hear, the situation on the ground there is deteriorating, and things here seem pretty stable. At least by comparison."

"Well," she said, "maybe by comparison. You and I both know I can't tell you what to do, Agent Diaz. But I can tell you I would appreciate it if you stayed another three days. JTF is planning a large-scale operation to reclaim the area around city hall and the approach to the Brooklyn Bridge. We're going to need every asset we can muster, and that includes you and your fellow Division agents."

Aurelio could understand the symbolic importance of reestablishing city hall. The scale was different, but to the people of New York, having a reliable local government would mean as much as a stable White House and Congress.

Three days, he thought. He'd been in New York four months. "Okay," he said. "Unless—"

"I know," she interrupted. "Unless you decide there's something else more important. I've read Directive 51, too, Agent Diaz."

He stood. "Thanks for your time, Lieutenant. This op rolls out in three days, or you think it'll be over in three days?"

"The current plan is to roll out in…" She glanced at her watch. "Fifty-nine hours and thirty minutes."

"Got it," Aurelio said. "One more thing. You have access to records from DC?"

"Not all of them. What are you looking for?"

"Amelia and Ivan Diaz," he said. "They were housed at the Mandarin Oriental Hotel when the JTF turned it into a refugee camp. I'd like to know if they're still there."

"Your kids?"

Aurelio nodded.

"Okay." Lieutenant Hendricks swiped and tapped through a sequence of screens on her tablet. Then she paused, finger hovering, as she studied the result of her search. "That entire part of the city is currently flooded," she said. "The Potomac's been over its banks for three weeks. Operational notes from the logistics people in DC suggest that most of the Mandarin population moved to another settlement, in the Smithsonian Castle. Others headed north, to a couple of other settlements."

She looked up at him. "I'm afraid I don't have any specifics on which of them went to which location."

Aurelio had to fight a reflex to stand up, get his gear, and head for DC right that minute. He took a deep breath, got it under control, and asked, "How detailed are casualty reports on settlement populations?"

"I'm sorry, Agent Diaz," Hendricks said. "I don't have anything like that. Except the JTF deployment logs do not show extensive contact with hostiles at the Mandarin, or for that matter at the Smithsonian Castle. I hope..." She set the tablet down and sighed, closing her eyes for a long moment. "I'm sorry. That's all I have to offer you."

Reading between the lines, Aurelio realized the odds were still pretty good that Amelia and Ivan were all right. He knew they'd survived the initial outbreak, and there was no record of a mass-casualty attack on either place they'd been since then.

That would have to be good enough for now.

Three more days, he thought. Then maybe three more to get to DC, depending on how much of the distance he would have to cover on foot.

Then he'd be back in DC, to defend the republic against all enemies foreign and domestic. And while doing that, he would find his kids.

It was twenty minutes to eight. Time to get something to eat, get some rack time, be ready for whatever would happen tomorrow. Aurelio got back to his cot. His coat was still dripping in the corner. He sat on the cot, hungry and sore and wanting nothing more in the world than to look his kids in the eye and tell them he was back.

Then he shook it off. Three days. He had a job to do.

CHAPTER 11

VIOLET

It rained all day, a steady downpour that started before dawn and kept up until late in the evening. To Violet it seemed like there had been nothing but rain since the last snowstorm in February. She and the rest of the kids were stuck inside all day, doing chores until Junie ran out of ideas to keep them busy. Then they spent the afternoon in their room, inventing new card games and trying not to talk about what was on all of their minds.

In the middle of the night, just before the rain started, a huge explosion had woken them all up. Rushing to the windows, they'd seen flashes and fire near some of the museum buildings across the Mall from the Castle. Violet knew one of them was another Smithsonian museum, maybe for art? Or maybe the Natural History Museum? She wasn't sure which building was which. But all around it were fires and explosions. It went on for more than two hours, until the rain moved in. Then whoever was fighting seemed to decide that neither of them were going to win so they might as well get dry, and the Mall was quiet again.

On the Castle grounds outside their window, they saw armed

adults watching to see if the battle was going to start up again. That meant they were worried it was coming their way. "What do we do?" Shelby asked.

They had an escape plan. Junie had told them that if there was ever trouble right in the Castle, they were supposed to all run out the nearest exit and then get together in the art museum just on the western edge of the gardens. Then she had walked them through the Castle, showing them all the stairways and doors. All of them knew the plan, but it didn't answer all their questions. What if the closest exit was where the bad people were coming in? Then they would have to go to another one. But what if they couldn't get across the gardens?

Junie had sighed at that point and said, "I know, I know. There's no way to predict everything. What's important is that you have the idea: Get out fast, worry about getting together again after you're safe."

This was on their minds while they watched the flashes across the Mall, only maybe two soccer fields away. "Is that close enough? Do we run?" Saeed clutched a little stuffed animal, a zebra he'd gotten at the zoo. He wasn't afraid to like stuffed animals even though he was going to be eleven in the summer. That was one of the things Violet liked about him.

"I don't think so," she said.

"Me neither," Amelia agreed. She still had her retainer in, so it was kind of hard to understand her. "I think if we see people here starting to... you know, shoot back, then that's when we run."

"Yeah," Noah and Wiley said.

Violet also thought that made sense.

Someone turned their doorknob. Clustered by the north-facing window, they all turned around. Junie was there, peeking around the door. "Hmm," she said. "I was hoping you'd all slept through this, but I guess that was never going to happen."

She came in and shut the door behind her. "Okay. Back in bed, everyone."

"What's going on out there?" Wiley asked.

"Shooting," she said. "Other than that, I don't know. Don't know if it's JTF or bandits or that militia that's been out over by the Capitol. Or any of the other bands of lunatics. A lot of people in this town are crazy. Probably the same everywhere else. And sometimes they get crazy at each other." As she spoke, she was going from kid to kid, settling them in sleeping bag or couch, tucking them in and smoothing their hair before she moved on. "That's how it is, and there's no point pretending it's not. But whatever it was, it's over now, and it didn't come this way."

She was tucking Amelia in as she said that. "But what if it does?" Amelia asked.

"You remember the escape plan?" Junie asked. Amelia nodded. "All of you?" Junie added, looking at each of them in turn. They all nodded. "Then you know what to do. I don't think any of those crazy people care about us."

Saeed piped up. "That's not what Mike said at dinner."

Junie sighed. "I could kill that man." Quickly she added, "Not really. You know what exaggeration is, right? I'm exaggerating."

"We know," Saeed said.

"There's a lot of arguments sometimes about what we should do. You know why? Because none of us ever had to do it before. So we all have to learn." Junie settled herself on a long couch at Shelby's feet. "Mike and I don't always agree on how to do things. That's natural. But we both want the best for everyone in the Castle. Especially you kids. You didn't make this world, but you're going to be the ones stuck with it."

"Thanks, grown-ups," Wiley cracked.

Violet felt the same way.

Junie was quiet for a bit after that. Violet listened to the rain, and wondered what else was happening out there in the dark where she couldn't see or hear it.

Then Junie started talking again. "You're doing good, you know. You're sticking together. You'll be all right. I hear President Mendez is getting things under control. Pretty soon there might be a Congress again. Then we can get back to moaning and groaning about how dumb they are."

She sat with them a while longer, yawning once in a while. Then she pushed herself up off the couch. "You going to be okay in here?"

They all said they would. Or rather, Violet and Amelia and Saeed did. The others were already asleep.

"Okay. It's late. Early, really. I'm going to get some sleep. You should, too."

She left them, and they lay wrapped in their blankets and sleeping bags, listening to the rain and wondering when the shooting would start again.

Because they'd been up so late, they slept in, waking up to rain and more rain. The whole day seemed out of joint, like it was already close to bedtime even though they'd just gotten up. Junie's chores took their minds off everything for a while, and then so did the card games. Saeed and Amelia were good at inventing them. Violet was better at seeing a new game and suggesting little ways to improve it. Noah and Shelby were mostly good at complaining that nobody wanted to play the games they wanted to play. Wiley and Ivan just went along, staying quiet and not really participating in anything. Violet could tell they were still really scared about what had happened the night before.

At the end of the day the rain barrels they used to collect water from the Castle's downspouts were overflowing. Junie sent the kids out with gallon jugs to gather whatever they could. "Last chore," she said. "If it's going to keep raining, the barrels will fill right back up. We can get a lot of water saved."

Outside, a grumbling group of adults were already tapping the rain barrels into big buckets and jugs. The kids got in line, wet and miserable, waiting their turn to fill up their jugs. Violet was glad it wasn't a thunderstorm. Usually she liked them, but right now she thought thunder might sound too much like a bomb or a gunshot. She hated whoever was shooting for turning something awesome and beautiful like thunder into something that scared her. Then she felt bad about hating. Her parents always said she shouldn't hate. Maybe she was just angry, then. Anger was okay as long as you didn't let it bottle up inside. This was the problem, though. If you talked about what was making you angry, adults tended to misunderstand it and start telling you how you should feel. So the kids only talked about bad feelings with each other… at least when they could keep their feelings under control. Violet was still a little embarrassed about crying in front of everyone after they saw the yellow powder.

What was that, anyway? Nobody seemed to know, but everyone agreed that since the Division agent had warned them not to go down there anymore, it must be something serious.

It was her turn to fill her jugs. She carried them back into the Castle and down to the far end of what had once been the main art gallery on the first floor. There were still some paintings hanging on the walls. One of the other adults in the Castle, an old white-haired guy named Raúl with a big mustache, was arranging the jugs in blocks and rows. He took hers. "Pretty heavy for a little girl like you," he said. There was a twinkle in his eye. She knew he didn't mean anything bad by it.

Still, Violet didn't like it when people talked down to her, and she wasn't too morose or worried to roll her eyes. "I can carry them just fine," she said and went to get two more. She heard Raúl chuckling to himself as she went. That was fine, she thought. Let him. He didn't know how tough a little girl could be.

CHAPTER 12

APRIL

At ten o'clock sharp there was a knock on the door of April's room. She was ready. She'd bathed, changed her clothes, eaten, repacked her gear, and even caught up on her journal. She had long since run out of room in the margins of the *New York Collapse* book, which she'd used as a diary in the weeks after the quarantine. It had happened without her meaning to do it at first, but she was alone and terrified and putting words on paper calmed her. Now she kept doing it as a way of organizing her thoughts and helping to keep her oriented. In many ways she was no longer the same person who had scribbled those first lines in the book, back in December. She was more capable, more sure of herself. She'd looked the worst of humanity in the face a couple of times and also seen people at their best. Maybe she'd even been able to help a few people here and there.

She mused on this in the journal for a while, as the sun dropped behind the Palisades across the river. Then she made her final preparations, and when she opened the door to see Brother Michael in the hall she was ready to go.

He led her through Inwood Hill Park in the rain, not using

a light until they got to the steep slope that took them down to a tidal flat at the edge of Spuyten Duyvil Creek. Then he shut the light off again and they waited for their eyes to readjust. "There's a JTF checkpoint at the maintenance yard over there," he said, pointing. April saw it, a floodlit cluster of trucks behind sandbags under the Manhattan side of the Henry Hudson Bridge. The creek itself was only maybe five hundred feet across at this point.

"Please tell me we're not planning to swim," she said. She was a good swimmer, but maybe not with her pack and the Super 90. Also, one of the things she'd read in *New York Collapse* was that swimming across any of the rivers that surrounded Manhattan Island was nearly impossible due to their treacherous currents and undertows.

"Oh no," he said. "I'm just pointing it out because we have to get around it along the shore before we arrive where we're really going. The rain is good, it masks a lot of noise, but this is a time to be very careful."

April nodded. "Okay. Lead the way."

Brother Michael tramped through the undergrowth, finding a footpath that ran parallel to the creek. As they got closer to the checkpoint, other sounds resolved out of the background patter of the rain. A generator, a truck engine. The crackle of static on radios. Brother Michael kept going, not even looking up at the checkpoint. April followed. The hair on the back of her neck was prickling and she had to fight an urge to run.

When they were under the bridge and briefly out of the rain, Brother Michael stopped. "Okay," he said, his voice barely above a whisper. "We keep going here, out to a railroad bridge. The JTF runs river patrols, so we have to wait until a patrol passes.

Then we go across. There are motion sensors on the tracks, so we can't just walk over. We have to jungle-gym the whole way on the outside."

April took a moment to digest this. She'd seen that railroad bridge before. It had a center section that swung open to let boat traffic pass. Once she remembered driving over the Henry Hudson Bridge and looking over at it when it was open, with a passenger ferry chugging through toward the Hudson. "You've done this before?" she asked.

Brother Michael grinned. "Yeah. It's kind of a rush. Might be a little slippery in the rain, though."

"You don't say." April took off her hat and retied her hair into a ponytail. "All right. Let's do it."

They came out from under the Hudson Bridge and kept working their way along the edge of the creek until they came to a cleared space near the southern end of the bridge. The shore here was huge granite blocks dumped around the bridge foundation to hold it in place. The bridge itself was made of steel girders.

"We can get under here, get out of the rain a little," Brother Michael said, crouching to squat on one of the tilted blocks.

April joined him. The rain got through, but not as much, and by this point she was so wet it had stopped making any difference. "How often do JTF patrols come by?"

He was looking under the bridge to get a view of the Hudson. "Varies," he said. "Over the winter they had a garrison here, but it packed up in March. I guess they figured since the virus wasn't spreading as much they ought to focus on more dangerous places. But like I said, they left motion sensors. And the patrols, well…" He shrugged. "Put it this way. If we see one go by, we'll have time to get across before another one shows up."

It was nearly an hour before a patrol boat appeared from the south, sweeping a spotlight across the riverbank and the bridge pilings. The boat steered in toward the bridge, close enough that even in the rain April could make out the figures of its crew. One of them was looking through binoculars. If they've got thermal imaging, we're in trouble, she thought.

At the same moment Brother Michael said, "Duck down behind the rocks."

They scrambled down toward the water together, hiding themselves from view. "They don't usually come in that close," Brother Michael said. "Must be figuring someone might be using the rain as cover."

The boat idled on the far side of the bridge for a minute or so. Then they heard its engines rev. April peered up over the blocks and saw its lights arcing back out into the river. It headed back south, and soon it was lost in the rain.

"Okay," Brother Michael said. "Now we go."

April watched him climb up the stone blocks and then get a grip on the outside of the bridge structure. He scooted a couple of steps ahead and looked back at her. "See?"

She nodded and climbed up after him. The steel was rough in most places, either rusted or covered in corroding paint applied in multiple layers over rust. It wasn't as slippery as she'd feared after Brother Michael's warning.

"You ever do any climbing?" he asked as they started to work their way out over the water.

"No."

"Three points of contact," he said. "Move one hand, one foot at a time. Keep that in mind, you'll be fine."

April fell into the rhythm of it pretty quickly. The bridge superstructure had trusses in a vertical zigzag pattern extending from the span up to arches. They were spaced closely enough that she could always keep a hand on one while reaching for the next… barely. She learned to lean her weight in over the bridge deck when she was making the reach between trusses, so if she missed she would fall on trestles instead of water. About halfway across they came to the platform that supported the swinging part of the bridge. "Rest here for a minute," Brother Michael said. She was glad to. The rain drummed on the platform, a harsher sound than the white-noise patter it made on the surface of the creek. That thought got April looking back toward the JTF checkpoint at the Henry Hudson Bridge. She could barely tell it was there. Just a few smeared lights.

"We're doing fine," Brother Michael said. "In this rain they probably wouldn't see us from the checkpoint even if they were looking."

"What would they do if they did see us?" April asked.

"It's a little far to start shooting, unless they've got a sniper there. Who knows?" Brother Michael shrugged. "It's never happened."

He sounded pretty confident. Much more confident than April felt. "How many times have you done this?"

"This is the fourth," he said. "Better keep going."

Her forearms and calves were trembling by the time they got to the far side and dropped down into the brush on the Bronx side. She shook them out and flexed her cramping fingers. Then it occurred to her that for the first time in nearly five months, she was off Manhattan Island. She looked down at her feet. The Bronx. She'd escaped the quarantine.

"Feels pretty good, right?" Brother Michael said.

April nodded. "Yeah. It does. I'd kind of forgotten what it was like to be able to go where you want."

"And where is that?"

"Michigan."

"Michigan? Man, that's a long trip. Hope you have some friends along the way."

It hadn't even occurred to April to think of this. She'd been assuming that everyone she knew, in New York or anywhere else, was dead. After all, those were the odds. But now that Brother Michael had put the idea into her head, she started running through possibilities. She didn't have any siblings, and her parents had retired to Montana. She hadn't heard from them since the quarantine came down. A couple of her college friends were living, or had lived, in places along the way—one in Pittsburgh and another somewhere near Toledo. Maybe she would be able to stop at one or both places and try to find them, depending on circumstances. If Toledo or Pittsburgh were as bad as New York, she would want to give both places a wide berth. Probably the best thing to do would be to stay in the country as much as possible, as long as she could find water and food.

"I'll figure it out," she said.

"All right, then," Brother Michael said. "Here's what you do next. Get up the hill here and then stay on the tracks for about two miles. You'll run into the Riverdale Yacht Club. Ask for Blake and give him this."

She could barely see his extended hand in the rainy dark, but she held out her own hand. He put something in her palm and closed her fingers over it. She could tell it was some kind of figurine. Turning it over in her fingers, she tried to discern details. Human, maybe?

"It's a jade Buddha," Brother Michael said. "Song dynasty."

"I can't—" She didn't have anything worth trading. "I don't have anything to offer you in return."

"It's a gift from the Master and the Riverside Templars." Brother Michael climbed back up onto the outside of the bridge. He raised a hand in farewell, and April thought: three points of contact. "Consider it our blessing," Brother Michael said. "It's a long road to Michigan, April Kelleher. You better get going."

CHAPTER 13

VIOLET

The rain finally let up before the next morning, and they could all get out of the Castle, so of course that was how Wiley got shot.

They were all running from a group of robbers: the seven kids, plus Junie and four other adults. Twelve of them. They'd gone out along the edge of the Mall, following Jefferson west until they hit the edge of the flooded zone just past the Washington Monument. The Reflecting Pool was invisible under the muddy floodwaters, and the river lapped at the bottom steps of the Lincoln Memorial. They squished across the sodden ground to Constitution Gardens again. The harvest had been good enough last time that Junie wanted to see the place for herself. "Maybe if things get a little more stable we can set up a farm there," she said. "Be nice if we could do it a little closer, but..." She trailed off. Violet knew what she meant, though. Nobody was going to be planting anything on the parts of the Mall right by the Castle. It was all a mass grave.

The south side of the garden pond was marshy after all the rain, so they went around to the north, along Constitution

Avenue. Everything was overgrown here. From the north side of the pond a little footbridge went out to an island, and it was like a little piece of jungle there. A rabbit bounded away from them into the underbrush. Junie was in heaven, spotting edible greens everywhere she looked. Not just cattails and dandelions, but all kinds of other plants Violet had never known you could eat: garlic mustard, yellow sorrel... and violets, which gave Violet a funny sense of pride. Junie set the kids to gathering them, and she was picking some herself, talking about all the sources of nutrition nobody ever paid attention to, growing right in everyone's backyards.

It felt good to be out in a big group, with adults. Violet liked having time with just other kids, but she also knew that they were safer with adults around. It also helped that they were close to the JTF's main base in the White House. Violet imagined the president—there had to be a president, didn't there?—working hard to get America back on its feet. The JTF had soldiers and some vehicles all around the White House grounds, from the Ellipse right up to Lafayette Square. Being so close to it made her feel more secure.

"Wonder if there are any fish in this pond," Mike said.

One of the other adults stood next to him, hands on hips. "Don't know," he said. "But there'll be frogs."

Violet didn't know if she could eat a frog.

She was considering the question, wondering just how hungry she would have to be to eat a frog, when people appeared from the little building just across Constitution Avenue from the middle of the garden pond. They were ragged, wearing mismatched clothes and looking different from each other. Not one of the organized groups of bad guys. Just a band of scavengers and robbers, was Violet's first thought. She'd seen groups like them before. DC was full of them. They were scary, but not any more than yellow particles drifting over L'Enfant Plaza, or the ever-present midnight crackle of gunshots echoing over the Mall. Not when she was part of a big group, with five adults.

Then one of them raised a gun and started shooting.

Violet knew what to do. She got low and looked around at everyone else. Were they running? If they were, she should run, too. Mike had drilled this into the kids back at the hotel, and she knew it applied here, too. The rest of the kids hit the ground, too, as Mike and the other adults got their guns up and started shooting back.

Her first thought was to get out of there, to run and not stop until she was back in her room in the Castle. But Wiley cried out and fell, right at the edge of the pond, and Violet ran to him instead. She dropped onto her belly and crawled right up next to him. Wiley was panting and crying from the pain, and there was blood on his shirt. They huddled together in the cattails. "You're okay," Violet said automatically, not knowing whether or not it was true.

"It hurts," Wiley moaned through gritted teeth. "They shot me, Vi. I'm going to die."

"No, you're not," she said. He rolled over, clutching at the wound. She could see that he really had been shot, and part of her wanted to run all the way to Alexandria and hide forever in her old room with her old posters and stuffed animals, sleeping until someone came to tell her that everything was going to be all right.

But it wasn't. There were more gunshots.

Around her, everyone was getting down into the weeds

around the pond, trying to hide. She saw Mike shooting back, but the robbers kept coming.

Violet slid along the muddy bank into the water, pulling Wiley with her. The other kids were running to the other side of the little island—except Noah. He crashed down next to Violet, grabbing Wiley's hand. Wiley was groaning with the pain and kicking his legs.

Bullets slashed through the cattails over their heads. Violet couldn't see Mike anymore. She couldn't tell where any of the adults were.

She crawled out of the water to get a better view. There was Mike, on his hands and knees by their end of the footbridge. He was trying to get up, but couldn't put any weight on one leg. The robbers were in the trees between Constitution Avenue and the north side of the pond. She could see them moving. Four of them together started out from the trees, headed for Mike. Where were the other adults? Violet tried not to panic, but she didn't know what to do. Noah and Wiley were pretty well hidden, but it was too cold to stay in the water, and Wiley needed a doctor.

Junie crawled up next to her. "Don't move," she said.

"But Mike…"

"There's nothing we can do." Her face was grim. "Maybe in a minute we can get Wiley out of here."

Behind the first four robbers, six more came out of the trees. "Wrong part of town to pick flowers," said the robber in the lead. He started over the footbridge, the rest of the robbers behind him.

Violet wondered if she was going to die. She was shaking. Junie put a hand on her back. "Ssshhh, now. If things get bad, just don't look."

Mike heard the robbers coming and started crawling away, toward the little monument in the middle of the island. Nobody was shooting now, but somehow that made everything worse.

Beyond the robbers, she saw another motion in the trees. More of them, she thought. Maybe she could swim across the pond and get away. Where were the other kids? Her mind was jumping from idea to idea, but her body was stuck in place. Junie stayed with her. Violet saw she had a gun, a square black pistol. But it wasn't going to be much help against ten robbers. Or more, if that was who was coming through the trees.

It wasn't.

A tall white guy wearing a backpack and carrying a rifle stepped into view. He raised the rifle and sighted down it. Violet saw a glowing orange circle on his left wrist and she felt a tiny glimmer of hope. A Division agent. Only one, but in her mind they were like superheroes. And this one was left-handed like her. None of the robbers had noticed him yet. They all had their eyes on Mike, and their minds on what they were going to do to him.

He fired, shifted his aim, fired again. Shifted once more, fired again. All in two seconds. Then he stepped behind the tree again. By the time Violet had looked from him to the robbers on the footbridge, one of them was hitting the water and two others were facedown on the bridge itself.

The rest of them spun around and pointed their weapons in every direction, screaming at each other to find out who was shooting at them. The leader pointed back toward the little stand of trees.

The Division agent stepped out again. One shot, then he ducked back into cover. Another robber fell down and didn't get up.

"He can't get us all with a fucking deer rifle," the leader shouted. "Go after him!"

The robbers charged. Junie jumped up from the cattails and ran to Mike, dragging him behind some bushes where at least there would be some cover. Violet looked back at Noah. "How is he?"

Noah was crying, cradling his brother's head in his lap. "He's hurt, Vi. He's still bleeding." Wiley was quiet and pale.

"Get him out of the water. Here, I'll help." Violet scooted over to them and together they got Wiley up on dry ground again. He was soaked to the waist from being in the pond, and above that his right side was wet with blood.

A rattle of gunshots sounded from the trees. Violet spun around and saw the robbers firing into the trees. She couldn't see the Division agent. No, wait, there he was… but no. This was an Asian woman, another agent, calmly stepping out to flank them. She had a different kind of rifle, one of the ones with the curved magazines. When she fired, it was a long burst that raked the group of robbers. They started to scatter, at least the ones that still could. Then the first Division agent reappeared at the other end of the trees and calmly shot another one of them.

That left only two of the original ten. They ran for their lives through the trees back toward Constitution Avenue. The Division agents didn't go after them. They converged on the footbridge and crossed together. "You can come out now," the man called.

Junie stood up from behind the bushes and said, "We need help! Two of us are shot. At least two. I don't know where everyone is."

The woman agent tapped her watch face. "Base, Fujikawa here. Civilians in need of a medic, this location, stat." She paused, listening. "Threat neutralized. Situation stable for the moment. Pearson and I will stay until you're on-site."

She looked back to Junie. "Help is on the way."

The other agent was carrying Wiley up from the edge of the pond. He knelt and set Wiley down gently on a sidewalk. Noah was right there. "Help him," he pleaded.

"Hang in there, buddy," the agent—Pearson—said. "JTF'll be here any minute."

Fujikawa dropped her go-bag and found her first-aid kit. She applied a field dressing to one of Mike's wounds. He'd been shot twice, once in the arm and once in the leg. The leg wound looked worse. "You're going to be okay," she said. "Might be a while before you can start jogging again, though."

"Ha-ha," he said weakly.

Less than ten minutes later, the JTF response team arrived. Four medics and a dozen armed escorts. Watching them approach from the footbridge, Fujikawa held out a fist to Pearson. He tapped it. "Catch you later," she said. They walked in separate directions, he going north and she headed west. Pearson nodded at the JTF team as he passed them, pointing at the island to indicate where they should go.

Violet followed Fujikawa's figure as long as she could, until the agent was lost in the trees growing around the Vietnam Memorial. Agent Fujikawa is never scared, she thought. Agent Fujikawa can handle any situation. I want to be like her.

While the medics treated Wiley and Mike, Junie rounded up the rest of the kids. The other three adults came out of the bushes looking both sheepish and grateful. Violet memorized their faces and told herself not to trust them in the future. Only Mike and Junie had stood up and tried to protect the kids.

She stayed close to Wiley, holding Noah's hand just so he wouldn't be scared. The other kids clustered like they always did, the smaller ones in the middle. Shelby and Ivan were talking to each other, but Violet couldn't hear what they said.

The medic looking at Wiley stood up. "Okay, buddy. We're going to get you a stretcher." Off the patrol leader's look, he said, "Through and through, mostly got fat and muscle, but it nicked a rib and grooved a little deep on the way through. Should get it cleaned and closed up so we don't have to worry about peritonitis."

"Does that mean surgery?" Mike asked. He was sitting up, his arm in a sling and his leg bandaged from knee to hip.

The medic shrugged. "Technically, yeah. But we won't have to put him under. Couple of shots, couple of stitches, course of antibiotics. He'll be good as new."

Wiley was sobbing. Noah and Violet held his hands while the medics got him onto the stretcher. "Can I go with him?" Noah asked. "He's my brother."

"Can't take unaccompanied juveniles," the medic said.

"I'll come, too," Junie said. "The rest of you, get home with all this salad we collected."

Mike stood up with the help of another JTF medic. He tested his weight. "Son of a bitch, that hurts. You sure it's okay for me to walk on it?"

"Won't hurt anything, if that's what you mean, sir," the medic said. "The bullet pretty much carved a piece of muscle off the outside of your thigh. Keep it clean and you should be good as new in a couple of weeks."

"Good news," Mike said. "So all I have to worry about is a broken arm."

"It's not displaced." The medic skimmed one palm off the other. "Bullet glanced off it. I got it cleaned out. Same as your leg, keep it clean and it'll heal just fine."

"I don't have anything to keep it clean," Mike said. They were pretty much out of all medicines at the Castle.

"I'll send some meds along with you." The medic dug in his pack. He shook a few pills out of a bottle and held them out to Mike. "This is about all we can spare. Once a day, with food."

The patrol leader looked the group over. "How about we come with you on your way home? We'll call in another team to get the kids and your den mother back to base."

"Thanks," Mike said. "Maybe you can ask them to bring a crutch."

An hour later they were all back at the Castle. Safe and sound, Violet thought.

For now.

CHAPTER 14

APRIL

It was morning by the time April finally made contact with Blake. She'd made it to the Riverdale Yacht Club just after midnight, and found it dark and quiet, with a padlocked gate closing off the driveway that led down to the clubhouse.

This was not what Brother Michael had said would happen. Had something gone wrong up here? If so, April was still off Manhattan Island, but she would have to figure out another way to get across the river. The most obvious solution would be to walk across the Tappan Zee Bridge, but that was miles north.

The other possibility was that Blake didn't know she was coming. That seemed likely enough, since telecommunications were only a fond memory, at least in this part of the country. Only the JTF and some other government organizations still had phone and data networks.

Well, she wasn't going to stand on the railroad tracks all night. She swung up and over the fence surrounding the yacht club property. The clubhouse was dark, and all of the cars in the parking lot looked like they had been there since November, with drifts of sand and grit around their tires. April didn't see any boats anywhere. She didn't hear any voices nearby, but the rain could account for that.

She was sick of the rain.

Across the parking lot, attached to the main clubhouse building, was a white tent. She ducked under it, working her way through plastic chairs tumbled over by winter storms. The tent was torn in several places, but near the clubhouse door was a sheltered spot. She dropped her pack and sat. Hell of a thirty-six hours, she thought. I found Merch, learned more about what happened to Bill, and got smuggled out of New York.

Oh, and found out that there might be a vaccine for the Dollar Bug.

Could that be true? Was someone even now making it? Maybe in another year, everyone in the United States—and wherever else the virus had spread—would be looking back at Amherst's virus. Putting it in the past where it belonged.

She had to know. Mostly because if Bill's work had helped the process along, that would make it a little easier to deal with him being dead.

She hadn't meant to fall asleep, but the next thing she knew someone was kicking her feet. "Hey. Wake up."

A man was standing over her, pointing a gun at her heart. He had one foot on the barrel of her shotgun. Beyond him, she saw sun gleaming on the river. Slowly she raised both of her hands. "Are you Blake?" she asked.

He blinked. Then she saw understanding dawn. "Did Andrew tell you to come here?"

Andrew… oh. She put it together. The Master.

"Yeah," she said. "He said to give you…" She paused. "I'm going to reach into my coat pocket."

"Slow," he said.

She found the small Buddha and held it up. The milky jade caught the sunlight reflected from the river, making it look like the Buddha himself was glowing. "He said to give you this," April repeated.

"For what?"

"To get across the river."

Blake considered her for a long moment. Then he considered the Buddha. Then he holstered his gun and lifted it from her palm. "Nice piece," he commented. His demeanor had completely changed from the suspicious scowl he'd worn when kicking her awake. "So why is Andrew doing you a favor?"

"Because someone else asked him to."

"And who is that someone else?"

"You know Roger Koopman?"

"Nope. But I wanted to see if you would tell me. Okay. Where do you want to go?"

"Eventually, Michigan," April said. "But today I'll settle for New Jersey."

"Michigan? Jesus. I won't ask why, but that sounds nuts to me."

"You're not the only one," April said with a faint smile. She stood and stretched. "So… I don't see any boats."

"I don't keep my boat here. JTF assumes any boat on this part of the river is smuggling something." Blake looked the figurine over one more time, rubbing his thumb across the Buddha's belly. He put it in his pocket. "Here's how this is going to work. You go inside, get yourself something to eat if you want. I'll be back in an hour with the boat. Then there are two places in Jersey I can drop you. I mean, two boat landings. If you'd rather, I can just swing in close to the riverbank somewhere and you can hack your way through the woods."

"Should I do that?"

"Is the JTF after you? Usually that's why people are trying to get out of New York."

"No," she said. "I don't think the JTF even knows who I am."

"Then you might as well use one of the marinas. Right that way"—he pointed southwest across the river— "that's the Englewood Boat Basin." He swung his arm ninety degrees to the right, now pointing northwest. "Up there about three miles is the Alpine Boat Basin. Englewood's probably quicker, but shit, if you're going six hundred miles I guess you don't have to sweat an extra couple hours of walking."

"Which place has fewer people?"

"Probably up by Alpine. It's right in the Palisades Park, and then once you get inland it's all golf courses and suburbia for miles. Englewood's closer to I-80, but lots more people."

April considered, but not for long. "Alpine."

"Done." Blake opened the clubhouse door. "Like I said, come on in. Make yourself at home. I'll be back in an hour."

Before Blake went to get the boat, he showed April the clubhouse kitchen. In the fridge, sealed but of course not cold, there was dried fruit, canned tuna, cheese. All kinds of stuff. She realized she was very hungry.

"Take whatever you want," Blake said.

She looked over at him, figuring he must be joking. "Really?" In New York, this much food was enough to make you a target. He was just giving it away?

Blake saw what she was thinking. "You're not quarantined anymore... what was your name?"

"April."

"You're not quarantined anymore, April. Things are tough out here, but after a while it's going to seem like paradise compared to where you've been."

She ate until she was full, and then she added some cheese and a couple of cans of tuna to her pack. Then she took a bag of raisins, too. No reason to refuse someone's generosity when generosity overall was in such short supply.

Blake was back right on time, easing a twenty-four-foot Parker fishing boat up to the retaining wall at the river's edge. She saw him through the big windows facing the river and gathered up her gear to go meet him. He held out a hand to help her aboard, but she was already stepping down onto the boat's gunwale without it. The boat had two swivel chairs in its open cockpit, with the steering wheel on the right side. April dropped her pack behind the left-hand chair and laid the Super 90 on the deck next to it. Blake was already dropping the boat into gear. "You get everything you need?" he asked, raising his voice over the sound of the boat's motor and the rush of the wind.

"I did, thanks," April called back. She wondered where he was getting fuel for the boat, then decided she didn't need to know. Ex-military guys probably had all kinds of contacts in the JTF. Or maybe beyond New York it was still possible to actually go out and buy gas. Now she did want to know. "I haven't traveled in anything with a motor for months," she said. "Can you get gas out here?"

"Well, you can't just pull up to a pump and get it," Blake said.

"But it's possible to find, if you know where to look."

That was about what she'd figured. Now she was wondering what other differences there were. Even being a couple of miles from Manhattan had galvanized her curiosity about the rest of the country. Also, now that she'd found Koopman, all the parts of her brain that had been devoted to that obsession were freed up to think about other things.

"So it's more normal out here?" she asked.

Blake laughed. "For certain values of normal," he said. "I don't know much about what's going on in the rest of the world. Or what's happening in Washington. I heard President Waller died, but I don't know if that means Mendez is president now, or somebody else. That kind of news doesn't get around. Truth is, things are still pretty shitty. But like I said, compared to Manhattan, you're going to think you're in Shangri-la."

She thought about that for a few minutes, as Blake powered the boat north against the current. April remembered reading in Koopman's book that it was four miles an hour. That was a brisk walk. Faster than her average speed would be between here and Ann Arbor. "Is that for everyone, or just people with connections in the military?"

"I'll be honest with you, April. I have no idea. I do have those connections here and there, and I use them. Once in a while I can help someone out. It's kind of funny," he added as he slowed the boat and steered across the river. She could see the Alpine Boat Basin ahead, with the green bluffs of the Palisades rising behind it. "Andrew and I deployed together a couple of times, back in the late nineties. Never figured we'd still be in contact now."

"That's weirder than him leading an order of warrior-monks?"

Blake laughed. "If you'd known Andrew when I knew

Andrew, that part wouldn't surprise you at all."

He steered around a tree trunk drifting with the current, slowing as they approached the western bank. "Hey, listen," he said. "If you're seriously going to Michigan, there's probably a faster way than walking from here. At least at the beginning."

"What would that be?"

"This is going to sound funny, but the Erie Canal."

"Seriously? Isn't that way upstate?"

"You can pick it up in Albany and it goes all the way to Buffalo."

April thought about this. Buffalo was a long way north of the direct route.

"I know it seems out of your way, but you'll get to Buffalo in a week. How far can you get on foot in a week?" "I don't know," April said. They were approaching the marina. "Probably not that far. Are you sure?"

"One of the things about fuel shortages is people start going back to nineteenth-century modes of transportation," Blake said, sounding for a moment like a college lecturer. "There's all kinds of cargo traffic on the canal now. As long as you have something to trade, you can catch a ride on one of the barges."

"That's... huh." April had a few things in her pack she could trade. In a pinch, she could offer herself as a guard, literally riding shotgun. "You sure you want to take me all the way up to Albany?"

"Ah, why not? It'll get me out of the house. Plus, I like seeing what's going on in other places. You can never trust what you hear through the grapevine, you know?" Blake slowed the boat near a sign that said NO WAKE at the outer edge of the boat basin. "What do you think?"

Around them, abandoned boats floated in their berths. Several of them were partially sunk. The boathouse looked like nobody had been in it for months.

April surveyed the area. Long narrow parking lot to her left, with a park road switchbacking up the bluff behind it. Open grassy area to her right, with more docks and more sunken boats. Not a human, or sign of human presence, to be seen. "Are there many people in Albany?"

"Some, yeah. It's a mess like everywhere else, but a lot of people have started coming there to trade because it's on the river and the canal." Blake held the boat steady against the current. "So...?"

"All right," April said. "Albany it is."

Eleven hours later, Blake was holding the boat steady again, this time at a landing in Waterford, New York. A largely abandoned, once-touristy downtown street ran parallel to the landing, lit by torches set into the streetlights. A few people walked along the street. Straight ahead, up a short side channel of the Mohawk River, April saw a canal lock gate, also lit by torches. A crew was manually cranking the gate open, revealing a barge in the lock. The barge was piled with crates, and three horses stamped and tossed their heads on its deck.

So it was real, April thought. The Erie Canal.

Blake pointed. "You go right up to the other side of the lock there, and you'll find a... well, I don't know what you call him. Customs officer or something. He's the guy who keeps track of what comes and goes. Tell him you want to go to Buffalo and he'll put you in touch with someone."

"Tonight?" It was almost ten o'clock.

Blake shrugged. "Maybe. Barges go as long as there's water. Might be easier to pick up a ride in the morning, but you might get lucky tonight."

April picked up her pack and gun and stepped up onto the stones of the landing, feeling the boat rock behind her. When she turned around, Blake was dropping the boat into gear and backing slowly away. "What are you going to do with that Buddha, anyway?" she asked. "Trade it for something?"

"No. God, no. I'm a collector. That's how Andrew gets me to do dumb things like smuggle people across the river." Blake touched the brim of his cap. "Take it easy, April. But not too easy. You might not be in New York anymore, but it's still pretty rough out there."

"Thanks," she said. "I will."

Blake finished backing the boat around and chugged back out onto the Hudson with a final wave. She waved in return, wondering what his story was. Art collector, smuggler, cheerful cynic... she would never know the rest of it. Still, it comforted her to know that there were people like Blake out there, not just clinging to the bare edge of survival. The Dollar Bug hadn't killed kindness.

When she couldn't see his boat anymore, April stood there for a while, looking around at the little town of Waterford. No skyscrapers. No burned-out ruins. No roaming gangs, no JTF. Just people walking around on a cool spring evening. Some of them looked at her, some of them didn't. It took April a minute to figure out what was different about them. Then it hit her: None of them acted like they could be attacked at any moment, which was how everyone in Manhattan acted.

She was free. Now she could find out the rest of Bill's story.

And if the BSAV was real, she would find that out, too.

CHAPTER 15

IKE

Six forty in the morning, sun shining low over Long Island and a pleasant chill in the air, Division agent Ike Ronson got the call.

"Sentinel, this is Mantis. Acknowledge."

"This is Sentinel." Ike checked his watch to make sure his response wasn't being picked up by ISAC. All communications with Mantis were on an encrypted frequency and should appear as noise on ISAC's spectrum scanning. Everything looked good. "Go ahead, Mantis."

"We have intercepted comms indicating a civilian in possession of valuable intel has left Manhattan. Your orders are as follows: Pursue the individual. Engage and assist as needed. Ascertain her destination and observe."

"Who is she?"

"Name Kelleher, April. White female, early thirties, hair red-brown, eyes blue, height approximately five- seven, medium build. May be in possession of Division backpack. Armed."

"She has Division gear, but she's a civilian?" More often than not, that meant the civilian in question had killed a Division agent.

"Affirmative."

"Engage and assist," Ike echoed. The standard, unspoken protocol when an agent encountered a civilian wearing a dead agent's gear was to put them down, no questions asked. But Ike was already way outside protocol. He would have to adjust. "Where is she now?"

"Last known location was the Cloisters. Analysis is, she's across the river and headed west. Probable destination Ann Arbor, Michigan."

Ike had trouble believing a lone civilian had just up and decided to walk from New York to Michigan. "Confirm, Mantis. You said Michigan?"

"Correct."

"Roger that." Ike envisioned the route in his head. Pretty much a straight shot out I-80, across Pennsylvania and Ohio until you hit Toledo. Then up U.S. 23 and there you were.

"Report every forty-eight hours," Mantis instructed. "Frequency-switching schedule is as before."

"Understood."

"You are to depart immediately. Mantis out."

In the silence that followed, Ike leaned against the wall and considered his options.

He was posted up at the corner of Duane and Hudson, running a parallel mission to the JTF's big push down at city hall. His task was to keep the local bad guys off the JTF's six so they could stage in Foley Square before moving down Centre Street to City Hall Plaza. From his position, he could see all the way down Duane to the southern edge of Foley Square. Between him and the JTF force, which was running final checks before moving out at seven, the street was empty. He was listening in to their chatter over the mission frequency. Everything seemed normal.

It was normal where Ike stood, too, which was to say that the ordinary band of murderous thieves was stirring in the lower floors of the apartment building on the northeast corner, right across from where he was leaning against the wall of the Duane Park Building. They called themselves the Duane Park Family— DPF for short— and exacted tribute from any ordinary citizens they ran across. As a result of their brutality, there weren't very many ordinary citizens anywhere near this area anymore.

JTF intel officers suspected the DPF was allied somehow with the larger and even more murderous gang currently living in city hall. That likely meant that once they heard the shooting start, they would head that way. Ike was supposed to send up a flare if that happened, and slow them down as much as he could.

The problem was, he now had a new mission. Mantis had called him into action, and he couldn't say no.

He also didn't want to leave the JTF force, and his fellow Division agents, open to an ambush while they were engaged with city hall. Conflicted loyalties were a bitch.

It was five minutes before seven.

Ike glanced over his shoulder at the building behind him. The ground floor was empty—looted small businesses—and above it maybe twenty stories of apartments. He'd never seen anyone go in or out.

A plan started to come together. Ike slid around the corner to the building's main lobby door. Diagonally across the intersection, he saw some of the Family clock his presence. Perfect.

It was three minutes before seven.

Ike raised his M4 and hosed down the DPF members milling around outside the building across the intersection. Then he dropped his magazine and ducked inside the apartment lobby, snapping a new magazine into place as he sprinted past a reception desk and ducked behind it.

The plan was simple. Play cat-and-mouse with the DPF for a few minutes, get them completely focused on him, then ghost on them and call in an engagement report. That would pull them away from the action over at city hall, and also give Ike a head start on his mission for Mantis. Everybody wins, except the DPF.

The Family members still walking after his initial barrage charged across the street after him, with more coming out of the building behind them. Ike waited until they were converging at the doorway, and then he popped up and emptied another magazine. When the hammer clicked on an empty chamber, he turned and ran down a side hallway. He wasn't worried about running into a dead end. Thanks to updated fire codes, newer buildings like this almost never had them.

Fifty feet down the hall, he had a choice of left, back toward the Hudson Street side of the building, or right, which would take him to loading docks and a fire exit. He chose right, making the turn just as bullets from the pursuing Family punched into the far wall.

The right-hand hall ran straight down to a fire exit door. But between Ike and that door were three others, all open.

And all with civilians peering out, eyes wide and terrified.

Shit, Ike thought. There wasn't supposed to be anyone in this building.

Guns appeared in the civilians' hands. They saw Ike's Division gear and aimed past him as he got to the far end of the three doors, with the fire exit at his back. The civilians were firing down the hall, keeping the Family members back for the moment, but it wouldn't last.

Ike had a decision to make. He was far outgunned, and needed elsewhere, but he didn't want a bunch of dead civilians on his conscience.

He backed into the fire door, shoving it open. "Get out! Everyone!" he shouted. "Now!"

The civilians started to spill out of the open doors. One of them opened into a laundry room, Ike saw, another a row of connected offices. At least a dozen people came out, half of them kids. Still in the doorways, the few of them who were armed kept watch down the hall.

Ike glanced over his shoulder. The fire door opened into a small elevator atrium. On the far side was a glass door with a parking garage visible through it. "Go," Ike urged the last of the civilians, nodding at the glass door.

The first of them put her hand on the door's push bar... and the door glass blew out in a shower of glass as bullets from outside tore her apart.

The DPF had guessed where they were going, and gotten there before they did.

Screaming, the armed civilians charged into the atrium, firing through the door at the DPF out in the garage. Now they were in the way. Ike had no field of fire on the Family. Besides which, there were probably more of them still in the apartment lobby hall, waiting to make their move.

He looked back through the fire door and saw he was right. They were coming. Time to take drastic action. Bullets rang off the steel fire door as Ike ducked behind it. He pulled grenades from his belt and rolled them down the hall, one, two, three, then braced himself behind the door.

The three explosions were like three sharp kicks in his

shoulder. He pivoted around the door and ran down the hall, passing bodies and fallen ceiling tiles. His boots crunched on broken glass as he passed the hallway juncture and dove out through a broken window on Hudson. He ran south as far as Chambers, then hooked a right.

It was eight minutes after seven. He could hear the crackle and stutter of the battle over at city hall.

Ike tapped his watch face. "This is Agent Ronson," he panted as he ran. "Need fire support and medical, Duane and Hudson. Multiple hostiles, civilian casualties. Repeat, need fire support and medical, civilian casualties."

He kept running until he was out in Battery Park City, then slowed to a walk. JTF comms chattered in his ear. *Fully engaged, no resources available.* Then ISAC pinged him a notification that a fellow Division agent was en route to Hudson and Duane.

Good luck, brother, Ike thought. Or sister.

He headed down the esplanade to the Battery Park City ferry terminal. It had been abandoned over the winter, but the JTF had reclaimed it a month back and now used it as a launch for river patrols.

He hailed the crew of a boat that was just coming in. "Need to get to Jersey," he said, jumping aboard. "Like, now."

Thanks to the orange circle on his watch and the matching one on his pack, they didn't ask any questions. Ike was grateful for that.

CHAPTER 16

AURELIO

Aurelio caught the call from Ike Ronson five minutes after he'd engaged a group of hostiles who were firing from the entrance to the Chambers Street subway station at the corner of City Hall Park. Mostly he was keeping them pinned down so the main body of the JTF force could get into place around city hall without taking fire from the rear. When he got Ronson's distress call, Aurelio had a decision to make. The JTF force was mostly in place, but he was pretty sure some of the gang's perimeter guards were still down in the station, around the stairwell where Aurelio couldn't get at them... unless he went down and rooted them out.

The call to protect civilians was what decided him. Ronson had called from Duane Park, not even a half mile away. Aurelio held his position until the last of the main JTF force had passed Chambers Street. Then he peeled off and headed around the back of city hall along Chambers, jogging up Broadway to Duane Street and keeping up the pace all the way to Duane Park. Behind him, the sounds of the battle faded into a confusion of echoes. ISAC showed him the location of the firefight where

Ronson had called in: toward the back of an apartment building on the south side of the small park.

Aurelio went in, noting bodies all around the entrance. He didn't know Ike Ronson well, but he knew Ronson could fight. All Division agents could. Putting the scene together as he went, Aurelio saw that the firefight had spread down a connecting hall that ran to the back wall of the building. There he found more bodies, and signs of explosions. Three open doors on the right-hand wall ahead of him were blackened and speckled with shrapnel. At the far end of the hall was a steel fire door, dimpled with bullet impacts.

He got to the end of the hall, glancing in each of the open rooms in turn. They were full of bedding, extra clothes, the flotsam of desperate people. The air was thick with the smell of cordite.

The fire door was almost closed, showing a two-inch gap. Aurelio could see blood on the floor in the doorway. He leaned on the door and felt it bump up against something soft and heavy. His contact-lens HUD didn't show any other Division agents in the area. Where was Ronson? ISAC hadn't pinged out a notification of an agent fatality.

Aurelio set his feet and leaned harder against the door. It slid open, slowly. A thick smear of blood spread along the arc it made as he cleared the doorway and stepped into a small elevator lobby with a shattered glass door hanging open on the far wall.

That was where he found the civilians Ronson had mentioned. Fourteen of them. Five men, three women.

Six children.

All dead.

Automatically Aurelio checked the time. Seven thirty-one. Ike Ronson had called in twenty-three minutes ago.

He took in the scene, trying to suppress the part of him that rebelled against seeing murdered children and keep cool long enough to understand what had happened here. Three of the adults had been armed. They were near the shattered door, cut down trying to defend the rest. The concrete floor of the parking garage beyond the door was littered with shell casings. The rest of the civilians were grouped together in the corner away from the glass door. Aurelio had pushed two of them aside when he wedged his way in.

There was no sign of Ike Ronson. Whoever had killed all these people had come in from the garage, that much was clear. But Ronson had done his fighting out in the hall. The grenade explosions and the multiple bodies ISAC tagged with the identification *DPF* told that story.

The DPF had pursued Ronson into the building. He had fought back. Somewhere along the way he had gotten all the civilians into the elevator lobby. Then they had died defending themselves.

"ISAC," Aurelio said. "Pinpoint location of Agent Ronson's distress call."

A small hologram spawned from Aurelio's watch face. It showed the area bounded by Hudson, Chambers, Greenwich, and Duane. A red dot blinked on Chambers just west of Hudson… a good five hundred feet from where Aurelio stood.

It took him a long time to be certain of what he was seeing, but Aurelio Diaz was a man who believed in evidence. And the evidence stated that Ike Ronson was nowhere near the fight when he'd called in.

That meant these fourteen civilians had died because he ran out on them.

Aurelio felt pure fury, like heat running through his face and hands. This would have been cowardice if a civilian had done it, but understandable cowardice. For a Division agent to do it was absolute treachery.

He looked down at the bodies around him. The kids could have been his kids. The adults could have been the people in the DC settlement taking care of Amelia and Ivan. They were dead because of Ike Ronson.

As of that moment, Ike Ronson was a rogue agent.

"ISAC," Aurelio said. "Locate Agent Ike Ronson."

There was a brief pause. Then another hologram from Aurelio's watch face showed a bright red dot in the middle of the Hudson River, moving steadily toward the Jersey side.

That son of a bitch, Aurelio thought. He's running.

In that moment, Aurelio decided he was going to follow.

In the next moment, ISAC's AI voice sounded in his ear. "Warning. Identified hostiles entering the building."

Aurelio's HUD spread to include the entire first floor. A group of hostiles had come in the building's front door. ISAC labeled them DPF. They must have seen him come in. Did they think he was the same agent who had run out on the civilians before?

Didn't matter. Aurelio counted nine bogeys on the HUD, clustered together in the building lobby. If they were after him, they would come straight to the back of the building and down the hall toward the fire door. He reoriented the HUD to include part of the parking structure as well. Nothing out there. At least not yet.

As a practical consideration, the elevator lobby was a bad place to make a stand. The bodies made footing uncertain, and as long as Aurelio had to worry about more of the DPF showing up from the garage, he was potentially fighting on two fronts.

He ducked through the fire door and sidestepped into the

closest open door. Kneeling in the doorway, he waited as the group of bogeys came down the hall.

He got visual on the first and put him down, three shots to center mass. A second and third target were already emerging into view as he took the first down. They brought their guns up, but Aurelio was already locked in, and they dropped right next to the first. He ejected his magazine and reloaded. Six left.

Wild gunfire sprayed down the hall. None of them knew exactly where Aurelio was, so they were just trying to pin him down. Meanwhile others would be trying to get to a better firing position, or looping around to come at him through the parking structure. Even a violent rabble had usually watched enough TV to absorb some basic tactics.

Squatting low, he hooked the G36 around the door frame and fired a burst to chase them out of the hall. Someone started screaming down the hall, but Aurelio didn't look. He sprinted up one doorway and ducked in. It was another thirty feet or so to the juncture where the back hall met the way to the front door. Aurelio figured he probably had another minute or so before they could get around the block and into the parking structure.

When he heard the DPF's return fire, he could tell they were still focused on the third door. Good. They hadn't seen him. Now they thought they knew where he was, but didn't, and he could use that against them. A grenade would come in handy here, but he was out. He'd used them all on the Chambers Street subway entrance back over by city hall.

He did have smoke, though. He popped a smoke grenade and rolled it down the hall. Cries of alarm went up as the gang members saw it. They didn't know the difference between smoke and frag grenades.

That gave him time to go the other way, back out the fire door. He shut it behind him and tiptoed among the bodies, out through the shattered glass door into the parking structure.

The street entrance was ahead and to his right, a narrow driveway with a pedestrian door next to it. Aurelio cut diagonally across the space, giving him a good angle on part of the street outside. He pressed against a concrete pillar and watched, glancing back when he heard bullets smacking into the fire door. The DPF inside were still firing blindly. Sooner or later they would come out, but Aurelio's plan was to be somewhere else by then.

There they were. Three of them, jogging into the garage driveway. They slowed and approached the elevator lobby door. "Fucker's never going to see us coming," one of them gloated.

"He will if you don't shut up," another said.

Aurelio shifted around the pillar. They were forty feet away, holding still while they decided how to go into the lobby. A long burst from the G36, belt-high, dropped all three before they had a chance to turn around.

Now it was time to go. Let the others come out and see what had happened...

No. Then they were going to think he was the same agent who had run out on those kids. Aurelio couldn't live with that. He didn't want them spreading the word that a Division agent had betrayed his pledge. Later Aurelio would settle things with Ike Ronson personally, but right now he had the reputation of the Strategic Homeland Division and all of its agents weighing on him. He waited.

A couple of minutes later, the fire door opened. A man peered through. Aurelio waited. The man pushed the door farther open, scanning the garage from the glass doorway. Holding the door, he waited for his pal to come through. Counting in his head, Aurelio thought that made nine. Six killed, one wounded, two at the door. He called up the combat HUD again and saw that ISAC wasn't showing any more hostiles in the area.

All right, then. Aurelio switched to single shot. He sighted on the man holding the door open and squeezed off a shot. Blood spattered the door frame and the target went down. The second man ducked, glancing in Aurelio's direction. That's right, Aurelio thought. See me. You go through this city killing children, I'm the last thing you're ever going to see.

He pulled the trigger again.

CHAPTER 17

VIOLET

Two days after the attack at the pond, a JTF patrol showed up at the Castle to bring Wylie home. Noah and Junie were with him. It had been a strange time around the Castle without Junie. Mike limped around and did the best he could to keep things organized, but he didn't have much energy so the kids were pretty much on their own.

Violet ran to greet her, and then stepped back as Noah and Wylie came in. Wylie looked pale, but he was walking on his own. "You okay?" Violet asked him. It sounded kind of dumb and obvious when she said it, but it was the only thing she could think of.

He nodded and sat down in a big chair off to one side of the big entry room on the first floor. "Yeah, I'm feeling better. Wasn't so good the first day."

"They had to clean the wound out a couple of times," Noah reported as the rest of the kids gathered around. Junie watched from a short distance away, where the JTF escort was waiting.

"Violet," Junie said. "Can you go find Mike? Tell him to meet us in the library."

"Okay." Violet ran upstairs and located Mike resting in one of the Castle's towers. They had cool windows that looked out in every direction. She told Mike that Junie was back and he said he would be right there.

When she came back down and reported that, Noah and Wylie were gone. Shelby and Ivan, too. "Helping Wylie get settled upstairs," Junie explained. "The rest of you can go, too."

Amelia, Saeed, and Violet looked at each other. They knew they were being dismissed, but they wanted to hear whatever Junie was trying to get them not to hear. So they wandered away through one of the Castle's downstairs galleries, but they stayed close enough to be able to see where Junie and the JTF patrol went once Mike got downstairs.

The meeting spot turned out to be the old librarian's office, which was later some other kind of office. It had a conference table and a bunch of chairs and useless computer stuff. The kids couldn't get too close to it, but they could get to the main stairwell, which was right outside the door. About a week before, they'd figured out that the stairwell conducted sounds from the ground floor. They crept up to the second-floor landing and listened.

"I'm here to give you some difficult news," someone was saying. Since they didn't recognize the voice, it had to be the lead JTF officer. "The militia that's been exerting pressure on the eastern side of the city, specifically the area around the Capitol and the northeastern parts of the Mall... they're getting stronger. They've moved into Smithsonian museums on both sides of the Mall—the Air and Space Museum, along with the two just across from the Castle here."

"Who are they?" That was Junie.

"Well, this isn't easy to admit, but the core of the group is a JTF unit that went rogue. They may be allied with other armed militia elements that were already present in the city, but we're not sure. Gathering intel isn't easy. Also, we're stretched particularly thin because there are two other groups growing and getting more organized in the west and north of the city. Our base of operations in the White House and surrounding grounds is secure, but… I'm not sure how to put this, so I'm just going to say it. We—"

"You're not going to be able to help us anymore," Mike cut in.

"I wouldn't say that exactly," the officer said. "But it is true that we won't be able to respond as quickly to threats. You might want to consider relocating."

"To where?" Junie snapped. "There's floods and poison south of us, and crazy people with guns everywhere else."

"There are settlements at Ford's Theatre and—"

"There's no room for us there," Junie interrupted. "Where's the rest of the JTF? Where's the rest of the military? This is Washington, DC! Where are the people who are supposed to hold everything together?"

"Easy, Junie," Mike said.

"Easy, hell. We're talking about dying here. Where are the people who are supposed to keep us safe?"

"They're coming," the officer said. "Believe me. There's a lot going on outside DC right now, and the government's going to get back on its feet. I don't know all the details, but I do know that. Believe me."

"Why should I?" Junie had a head of steam now, and she wasn't stopping.

"Because I've got no reason to lie to you. And if I was going to lie to you, I would for damn sure come up with a better lie than the embarrassing truth I just laid out." The officer was trying to control his temper, the kids could tell that. His voice was tight with tension.

There was a pause. Then, "Okay," Junie said. "Fair enough. So while we're waiting for all this to happen, what do we do?"

"Stick very close to settlements. Try to contact us and arrange supply transfers instead of scavenging. Whatever you do, avoid the eastern end of the Mall. In general, don't travel outside approved zones."

"Where are approved zones?" Junie asked.

"Well," the JTF officer said. "Those boundaries are fluid."

"That's very helpful," Junie said. "Thank you."

"Look, just stay as close to home as possible," the officer said.

"The other night, we watched a firefight from our home," Junie said. "We heard the shots. We saw the flashes. Two hundred yards from our house. How close do we need to stay to be safe?"

"What do you want from me?" the JTF officer asked. "We're doing everything we can."

"Okay," Mike said. "We get it."

"But we don't like it," Junie added.

"Yeah." Mike paused. "Can you tell us what happened down in L'Enfant Plaza, at least?" Mike asked. "With the yellow smoke, or powder, or whatever it was?"

The JTF officer shook his head. "I can't really say anything about that."

"The children said a Division agent told them it was dangerous," Junie said.

Violet could almost hear the JTF officer rolling his eyes. He came across like one of those adults who didn't put much stock in what children said. "Listen," he said with a frustrated sigh. "That much is true. Don't go down there. But there are a lot of reasons not to go a lot of places in this city right now. So don't get too worked up about whatever it is a bunch of kids think they saw."

"So it is dangerous."

"Sure. Yes."

"Is it dangerous to us in the Castle?"

"I... don't think so," the JTF officer said. "Honestly, that's the truth. If I were you I wouldn't get anywhere near it, but it's not going to move, if that's what you're worried about. Especially not after all that rain. A lot of it's probably washed down into the river by now."

"Bad news for the fish," another voice muttered in the stairwell below them. Violet peeked down and saw the JTF soldiers were all hanging out there. She looked back at Saeed and Amelia, pointed down, and put a finger over her lips. They nodded.

"Floodwaters have risen again over the past few days," the JTF officer went on from inside the conference room. "Whatever happened down there, it's underwater now. You really don't want to go anywhere near it."

"So basically we're cut off," Junie said. "Like I said. Floods and poison to the south and west, armed lunatics everywhere else, and you don't know if you can help."

"Remember: We're to the north. We will keep patrols up in the area south of the White House all the way to the flood zone, and west to this location. We do the same for the other settlements where large numbers of survivors are grouped."

Chairs scraped in the conference room and they heard the clump of boot heels as the officer rejoined the rest of the JTF patrol. "Listen," he said, "I'm glad we could help out over at the pond. And we'll be there whenever we can in the future. But DC is going to be a difficult place to live for the foreseeable future. I would consider it a dereliction of my duty not to tell you that."

Mike's crutch made a squeak on the stone floor as he came out of the room. "So I guess we should schedule a supply transfer now?"

"Since we were coming anyway, I brought quite a bit of stuff," the officer said. "We'll help you get it loaded in."

They ate well that night, celebrating the new supplies a little. But the overall mood was pretty downcast. Word of the JTF officer's warning had spread through the Castle even before dinnertime, and it was all anyone was thinking about—even if they kept trying to talk about other things. "So basically he means we're screwed," Saeed said.

"No," Amelia said. "That's not what he meant. He was just telling us we have to be careful."

Ivan looked up at her and said, "We knew that. Right?"

"Yeah. Right." Amelia rested her hand on her little brother's shoulder.

"Hey, I have a question," Saeed said, like he'd just noticed they were there. "Your dad. How did you know he was a Division agent? Did he, like, announce it before he stood up and walked off?"

He was looking at Ivan when he said it, but Ivan looked up at Amelia. "I don't know," Amelia said. "We weren't there. Our mom just told us he was gone. Then... then a week later she was, too."

That wasn't quite the answer Saeed—or the rest of them—

had been expecting. Violet decided to change the subject. They were all jumpy because of what they'd heard the JTF officer say. "Hey, Wiley," she said. "Can we see the bullet hole?"

She was surprised when he grinned and said, "Yeah, check it out." He pulled up his shirt and carefully peeled back the dressing. The bullet wound on the right side of his rib cage was a purple pucker, stitched up and surrounded with little black specks. They must have been dried blood, Violet thought.

"Whoa," Saeed said. "It looks like one of those craters on the moon, you know? With the lines coming out of it where debris and stuff sprayed all over?"

Ohhhh, yeah, a couple of them said. It did look like that. Saeed even reached out like he was going to poke it, but Noah stopped him. "Hey, don't."

Saeed pulled his hand back. "Okay. Sorry. But it really does remind me of that. You guys know what I mean?"

They did. "What about the back?" Amelia asked. "Is that the same?"

"I don't know," Wiley said. "I haven't seen it." He was enjoying the attention. "It didn't really hurt that much, you know."

None of them reminded him how he'd been crying and sobbing at the time he'd been shot. After all, they probably would have been doing the same thing.

Looking at the wound, they got quiet after their initial burst of interest had passed. Wiley set the dressing back in place and Noah helped him make sure it was taped up again. They were quiet for a while after that. It could have been any of them. And it could have been much worse.

"What do we do?" Shelby asked. "If we're cut off, I mean. What do we do?"

"We're not cut off," Violet said.

"Yeah," Saeed agreed. "We just have to be careful."

"We were already being careful," Shelby pointed out. "And look what happened."

"Well," Wiley said. "Be more careful, I guess."

They all laughed, but they were scared, too. The adults weren't telling them anything, and they knew that was a bad sign.

CHAPTER 18

AURELIO

By the time Aurelio had lost twenty minutes taking out the remnants of the DPF, the main op at city hall was already in its mop-up stage. JTF brass had predicted the gang would crack as soon as the JTF penetrated their perimeter security. This was usually the case with gangs. They pretended to keep paramilitary hierarchies and discipline, but when push came to shove they fell apart.

He tried to raise Lieutenant Hendricks back at the Post Office, but she was wrapped up in operational duties. Next Aurelio checked Ronson's status on ISAC. If he was going to file a report on Ronson for dereliction, he wanted to have all his ducks in a row. Declaring an agent rogue was a serious step. Aurelio had never made such an accusation before, but he didn't know how else to interpret what Ronson had done.

ISAC showed Ronson as currently deployed on a mission. That was it. No notes about him bailing out on an operation and getting a bunch of civilians killed.

Thinking about that nearly made Aurelio boil over with

anger again. What he really wanted to do was get on a boat and hunt Ronson down.

Instead he went back to the Post Office and waited until Lieutenant Hendricks had finished her after-action reports and consults. Stationed by her desk, he could see her through a window into a briefing room. At one point she looked up and saw him, but that didn't seem to make her hurry. It was a good hour after he'd gotten to the Post Office before she emerged from the briefing room and returned to her desk.

"Agent Diaz," she said. "What brings you here?"

"Nothing good," Aurelio said. "I pulled off the city hall op this morning to answer an SOS from Ike Ronson. When I got to the location, I found a bunch of dead civilians and no Ronson. I pinged his location and he was on a boat headed across the river."

Hendricks took all this in for a moment. "Are you saying what I think you're saying?"

"I'm saying Ronson called in for fire support and then hightailed it out of a combat zone. As a result of that, a lot of people died."

Hendricks brought the ISAC interface up on her desk workstation. "According to ISAC, the op was completed and he is conducting a follow-up that took him across the river."

"I saw that, too," Aurelio said. "But if you want to come down to Duane Park with me, I'll show you something different."

"This is a very serious accusation, Agent Diaz."

Aurelio nodded. "Yes, it is. I do not make it lightly. Ike Ronson issued a false alert and abandoned his duty. He endangered my life and caused the deaths of at least a dozen people he was supposed to protect. Any way you slice it, that makes him a rogue agent."

"I'll enter that status in ISAC," Hendricks said. "When he sees his watch go red, either he'll head to the closest SHD base and get things sorted out, or…"

Or he'll keep running toward whatever he's running toward, Aurelio thought.

He knew which outcome he thought was more likely.

"Why hasn't ISAC tagged him already?" Aurelio asked. Typically the system could tell by an agent's movements and actions whether that agent had gone rogue. It should have tagged Ronson the minute he ran out on the op down by Duane Park.

Hendricks was studying the display. "I don't know," she said. "I can't make a formal judgment from here about whether he did anything wrong. For one thing, that's above my pay grade even for regular JTF personnel. For another, as you well know, we don't decide whether Division agents are rogue or not."

"I get that," Aurelio said. "But when I saw ISAC hadn't tagged him, I figured I should say something."

"And now you have. I've added your report to his operational profile." Hendricks stood. "ISAC still isn't tagging him as a rogue. Maybe there's something about this situation you don't know."

Aurelio considered this. "Could be," he said. "But I'm going to find out."

"Thought you were going back to DC."

This was the crux of the problem. Aurelio wanted to go back to DC. He could do better work there, and he could maybe keep an eye on Ivan and Amelia.

But if he headed for DC now, he would be letting Ike Ronson walk out on a bunch of dead kids who had every bit as much to live for as Ivan and Amelia did. That cut against everything he'd sworn to do when he became a Division agent.

Ike Ronson had chosen another loyalty. Aurelio wasn't going to do that.

"Ronson didn't skip out on that op just to go get a sandwich," Aurelio said. "He had a reason. He's answering to someone else now. The most important thing I can do is find out who."

"Makes sense to me," Hendricks said. "If he's gone rogue, I hope you find him and nail him to the wall, Agent Diaz."

"I will." He waited a moment as Hendricks nodded and swiped open a new screen on her workstation, but Aurelio wasn't quite done yet. "But I need a hand with something."

She looked back up at him. "What would that be?"

"His comms. Someone must have been talking to him." ISAC had nearly universal surveillance over digital and voice comms for both Division agents and JTF personnel. That was a crucial part of the Division's rapid- response capability. Aurelio reasoned that a capture of Ike Ronson's comms from that morning might help narrow down his location and direction.

"You want me to sweep up his comms?"

"It would be a big help. If we can find out who he was talking to, that might shed some light on where he's going. And why."

He could tell Hendricks didn't like the idea. Aurelio was asking her to eavesdrop on a Division agent based solely on his field analysis of a combat operation that from her perspective might have been just a disastrous failure. Part of the latitude granted by Directive 51 meant Division agents weren't answerable to the JTF, so essentially Aurelio was asking Hendricks to exercise oversight of an agent outside her command structure.

"I'm not asking you to judge," he said. "All I need is information so I can make the right decision."

"Okay," Hendricks said, after a long pause. "I can do that. But it won't be until later in the day."

"Fair enough." Aurelio stood. "Thanks, Lieutenant."

"You're welcome. I hope you're wrong about Ronson, but if you're right, go get the SOB."

"That's the plan."

Aurelio walked away, out of the Post Office and west on Thirty-fourth Street toward Hudson Yards. Ike Ronson had a three-hour head start, and ISAC said he was still in New Jersey. Aurelio knew that much. So the logical next step was to get on a boat and figure things out once he was across the river, too.

It was late afternoon by the time he could catch a ride over to Jersey on a JTF patrol boat. He hopped off the boat at a marina in Weehawken, now a JTF staging area that spread over the adjacent park and the approach roads to the Lincoln Tunnel. ISAC said Ike Ronson was on Interstate 80, already most of the way to Pennsylvania. Still no change in his status, either. As far as ISAC was concerned, Ike Ronson was a Division agent in good standing.

He was also seventy miles ahead of Aurelio. Given the nationwide shortages of fuel, that probably meant he'd caught a ride with a JTF convoy. But given Ike's betrayal, he might have met up with someone else.

There were too many variables in that line of thought, so Aurelio refocused on what he could do right then. He headed over to the staging area and found a command shed at the edge of the concrete expanse of the tunnel's approach lanes. The smell of diesel fuel was thick in the air. Standing in the open doorway of the command shed was a harried-looking JTF officer. He saw Aurelio and nodded.

"How you doing," Aurelio said. "Listen, any way I can catch a ride on one of these trucks?"

"A ride to where?"

That was the problem, Aurelio thought. Where was Ike Ronson going? He pinged Ronson's location on ISAC, and it showed Ronson stationary just outside Stroudsburg, Pennsylvania. "Stroudsburg?" he suggested.

The officer consulted his schedule. "Nobody going that way tonight. But I can get you to Harrisburg."

Harrisburg, Aurelio thought. That was way past Stroudsburg, and he didn't know whether Ronson was staying in Stroudsburg or just getting some rack time before hitting the road again. Still, Harrisburg was closer than he was now. "I'll take it," he said. The officer pointed out a truck idling on the other side of the tunnel approach. Aurelio walked across and found the driver in the trailer securing a pallet jack to the wall.

"You headed to Harrisburg?"

The driver snapped a bungee cord into place and climbed down from the trailer, pulling the door shut as he dropped to the asphalt. "Soon as I take a leak and get a sandwich," he said. "Why, you want a ride?"

"Matter of fact, I do," Aurelio said.

"Cool." The driver started walking toward a low building near the command shed. Over his shoulder he called, "You want a sandwich, too?"

"Sure," Aurelio said. The driver shot a thumbs-up back in Aurelio's direction. Aurelio went around the passenger side of the truck and climbed into the cab.

CHAPTER 19

APRIL

By her fourth day on the canal, April was finally beginning to relax.

She was on a barge about the size of two semitrailers lashed together, fifty feet long and maybe twenty wide. The deck was divided into three parts: crew quarters, animal pen, and cargo. The crew quarters, toward the bow, was a lean-to nailed together out of two-by-fours, plywood, and tarps. The animal pen, occupied by a dozen sheep and lambs, was at the stern. In between was a huge jumble of sacks, crates, and piles of items that couldn't be put in a sack or a crate: furniture, pieces of wrought iron, a car engine, a small pyramid of tires. Lying along the starboard railing was a mast and carefully folded sail.

They'd spent the first three days winding their way from the Hudson up the Mohawk River and then to Utica and Rome. Usually the barge moved twenty-four hours a day, pulled by horses or mules walking along the edge of the canal. Once there had been a towpath there, but now the animals did their work mostly on paved bike trails. They had to stop fairly often when they arrived at locks. Each time, a local crew would drain water out of the lock until it was at the downstream level, open the gate, then let water back in until the water level matched the upstream gate. All that work had to be done manually, so each lock transfer took about an hour. Luckily none of the gates had jammed yet. The boat's pilot said that usually happened at least once every trip. Her name was Sonia Whitmore, ex-navy, recreational sailor, now crewing a cargo barge with her spouse, Julia, and their two boys.

April had been amazed to see an intact family of four. The odds on such a thing in Manhattan were tiny. "Yeah, we all made it," Sonia said. The boys, twelve-year-old twins named Tim and Jake, were coiling rope in the bow and watching the horses on the towpath. "Just lucky."

According to Sonia and Julia, the Dollar Bug had gone through Albany and the surrounding area, but without the ferocity seen in bigger, more densely populated cities. She didn't have any specific idea what percentage of people had died. "A lot, though. It's a lot quieter, even if you account for no electricity, so no TV, no car stereos, that kind of thing."

As soon as it became clear that neither electricity nor gasoline was coming back anytime soon, people along the Erie Canal started seeing it as a substitute for road traffic. The interstate highways had killed commercial canal traffic in the 1950s; now the worm had turned again. "So we went down the river until we found some barges we could use, hauled them back up here, and got to work," Sonia said.

"I heard you can get to Buffalo in a week. Is that true?" April still wasn't sure how she was going to get the rest of the way, but she tried to be methodical about planning. That character trait had gone a long way toward keeping her alive these past few months.

"If there's no jammed locks and no trouble along the way,

yeah," Sonia said.

"How often is there trouble?"

"Well, I've only done this run… let's see." Sonia thought for a moment. "This is the fourth time. We had to wait until the weather was good enough to make the trip. And we've only had trouble once. But"—and here she nodded at April's shotgun leaning against the railing near the lean-to—"that was enough to make us take precautions."

At the first lock, where Blake had dropped her off, April had asked around about a ride and the first question she got in return was about the gun. You know how to use that? When she said yes, one of the lock crew called over to Julia, who called over to Sonia, and two hours later April was moving at a steady pace west on the Erie Canal. They kept a watch around the clock, one armed person fore and aft. The fore job was better because you couldn't smell the sheep pen.

That was where April was on the morning of the fourth day, as they cleared the last lock before a long stretch of open water, crossing Oneida Lake. There was no way to use horses here because there were too many houses close to the lakeshore, so they had to sail. April helped get the mast and sail up, then got out of the way. She didn't know anything about sailing. It being spring in upstate New York, there was plenty of wind, but it was mostly out of the west, so Julia and the boys were hard at work tacking back and forth in a zigzag across the lake. "It's a twenty-mile stretch to the other canal mouth, but we'll sail more like fifty by the time we get there," Sonia commented, watching Julia and the boys working the sail. "Plus, this thing wallows like a pig. It's going to take a while."

"I'm in no hurry," April said. It wasn't true, but it was the right thing to say. She was still trying to wrap her mind around the idea that in the twenty-first century, she was sailing on a cargo barge as part of a transit of the Erie Canal. How fragile all of the trappings of modern civilization had turned out to be. Take away electricity and you stepped back more than a century... unless you were part of the government, or the JTF. In a few places along the canal April had seen electric lights. Sonia explained that people were finding ways to tap windmills and other power sources here and there, but it was all local.

Everything was local. That was the big difference between now and the world before the virus.

And in this new reality where circumstances could change drastically in the course of a few hours' walk, April was going on a six-hundred-mile trip, chasing the ghost of a vaccine, and beyond it the ghost of the truth about why Bill had died. She didn't have to do it. She could go to work on one of these boats, or make a new life for herself in one of the small towns and cities dotting the canal route. Not everything was like New York City. Sure, even here on Oneida Lake there were people with guns on the deck, watching from the bow and stern for any threats that might come out of the woods, but the sentries didn't really believe there would be trouble. You could tell the difference in the way they watched, their weapons casually leaning against a deck chair or a railing. In New York those same sentries would have been ready to fire any second. April realized how much she'd gotten used to that way of life, thinking that at any moment someone might try to kill you for whatever you might have in your pockets.

Not what you did have; what you might have. For the past five months she'd been living in a place where lives could be snuffed out for the potential gain of a can of bouillon cubes or a pocket multitool.

Now… there were burned-out houses along the lakeshore, but whole ones, too. Someone fishing from a dock waved to the barge, and April waved back.

She could get used to this.

But she wouldn't. She had a task to complete, and she would complete it. After that…

Let the future take care of itself, April told herself. Handle what's in front of you.

"Once we get back in the canal," Sonia called over the wind, "we'll need to be a little more careful. There's a… I don't know what you'd call them. Gang, cult, something. They try to stop us sometimes, and they always demand ridiculous trades to let us use their horses."

"I'll be ready," April said.

"Sorry," Sonia said. "I saw you looking all peaceful there and figured I'd better ruin your mood ahead of time instead of surprising you later."

April laughed. "Thanks, that's very considerate."

The wind shifted, and the barge swung around. They were halfway across the lake. "I've never been sailing before," April said.

"This barely qualifies," Sonia answered. She stepped over to the cargo and shoved a crate back into place. April joined her, making sure the cargo wasn't moving around too much as the barge rocked through its turns. "One of these days," Sonia went on, "when this is all over, you should go sailing for real. Who knows, you do your thing in Michigan and come back this way, maybe look us up."

What a possibility, April thought. To be done with this and move on. "That would be great," she said.

Sonia caught her wistful tone and got a little more serious. "What are you doing out there, anyway? I mean, planning to do."

How much to tell, April wondered. "Well, this is going to sound a little crazy, but my husband was killed right after Black Friday and I think someone in Michigan knows why."

"Oh," Sonia said. "I'm sorry."

April nodded. "I wish sometimes he had died of the virus. Then I could just grieve and get it over with and move on. But this... I can't let it go."

Sonia was quiet for a while. Julia and the boys hadn't heard any of the conversation. They were still fully engaged with wrestling the sail to keep it at the right angle to the headwind. Then Sonia said, "Well, with the world falling apart around us, I guess it's good to have an obsession to get you out of bed in the morning."

April couldn't help but smile. "I've thought that, too, sometimes. But it'll be good to know and... I hate this word, but closure. It'll be good to have some closure."

Now Sonia was looking over at her family. "Yeah. I don't know what I'd do if I lost any of them."

"You all got through the virus," April said. "That was the hard part."

Unless it comes back, she thought. But she wasn't going to say that out loud.

Late that afternoon, they reached the town of Baldwinsville, where they had to pass through a lock to avoid rapids on the Seneca River. They had taken the mast down after coming off the lake and stowed it again along the starboard railing, almost exactly as long as the barge hull. "This is the place I was telling you about," Sonia said as they waited for the lock to drain. Julia was onshore, paying the kid who had led their horse team from the western end of Lake Oneida.

The lock gate ground open and the boy led the horses forward. As soon as they were in the lock, he cast off the towrope and got his team out of there fast. April could tell he didn't want to be anywhere near Baldwinsville for any longer than he had to.

A group of bearded men, all armed, emerged from an old hotel on the other side of the canal from the towpath. One of them, older and grayer than the rest, took the lead. "You'll need horses."

"That's right, Deacon," Sonia said. "We're happy to make a fair trade for their use."

"We'll see about that."

April didn't pay much attention to the haggling that ensued. She was watching Deacon's men from the bow of the boat, the shotgun in her hands but pointed low at the water. They had the look common to isolated fanatics everywhere, suspicious and hungry, like they were hoping something would go wrong so they could kill in the name of whatever they believed.

She was so focused on them, she didn't realize right away that Deacon was pointing in her direction and had just said something to her. "I'm sorry, what?"

"I said where'd you come from?"

"Albany," April answered.

"Before that. I've seen those backpacks before. You're one of the government agents."

"No. It's just a backpack." April held up first one arm and then the other, after switching her grip on the shotgun. "See? No watch. If you've seen them, you know about the watches."

"Well," the elder said. "We seen a lot of government around here lately. Convoys, helicopters. Traffic on the thruway. They pass us by and don't give us trouble, but if you're one of them, you carry the word. They don't bother us, we won't bother them. We're free people."

"Got it," April said.

"Do we have a deal, Deacon?" Sonia was holding a plastic tote in both hands. April couldn't tell what was in it, but from the set of Sonia's feet she could tell it was heavy.

Deacon looked at her like he was thinking of something he wasn't quite ready to say. Then he nodded at one of his men, who broke away from the group and jogged across the bridge just downstream. A few minutes later, he appeared on the other side of the canal, leading a mule team. A boy walked with him.

When the towlines were attached, Deacon's man tousled the boy's hair and walked back toward the bridge. "You'll make sure he has a place to sleep," Deacon said.

"Just like last time," Sonia said. "We will."

Deacon nodded. Then he pointed in the direction of Tim and Jake, who had just finished making fast the towlines. "You ought to leave those boys here," he said. "We'd bring them up right."

April could see Sonia biting back anger. She glanced over at Julia and saw the same emotions playing out on her face. This was a delicate moment. April shifted her weight, bringing the shotgun up just a little off her hip.

"No, thank you, Deacon," Sonia said. "I need them to help around the boat."

He held her gaze for a long time, distaste and scorn clear on his face. "Offer stands. You'd better go."

The upstream lock ground open and the barge moved slowly through, back into the main channel of the Seneca River. April kept watch on the group until they were around the first bend in the river. Then she let out a long breath. "The virus sent us all back in time," Julia said in the dusk. "Some of us farther than others."

CHAPTER 20

VIOLET

After the attack over at the pond, the adults at the Castle laid down some new rules. All excursions to search for supplies had to be in large armed groups. They were going to talk to the JTF daily to get briefings about what the armed gangs in the area were up to. They were going to petition the JTF to get them some guns, or maybe even a permanent garrison.

Also, the kids couldn't go farther than a block from the Castle grounds in any direction without an adult.

They protested, but looking at Wiley, they knew it was probably a good idea. DC had seemed pretty safe for a month or so, but now it was getting more dangerous again. They had to adapt.

So they took to spending their days on the grounds, doing chores when they had to but otherwise playing games. Junie was talking about starting some kind of school, but everyone in the Castle was too busy to get that started.

Three days after Wiley returned, the weather changed. It was sunny and humid, the kind of day that made Violet wish there was a swimming pool on the Castle grounds instead of just a couple of small pools full of stagnant water and bugs. Saeed had found some chalk somewhere and they were playing foursquare with a soccer ball Ivan had brought from the first camp at the Mandarin Hotel. Wiley watched from a chair they'd dragged out from the library.

"Keep that ball out of the garden," one of the grown-ups said as he passed by. They promised they would.

"You think they'll know if we go somewhere without a grown-up?" Ivan asked when it was just the seven of them outside. All of the adults were out on supply runs or doing things inside. "I mean, they can't watch us all the time."

"Maybe not," Violet said. She was already feeling trapped. But at the same time, it was good to know someone was looking out for them. Mike and Junie cared enough to make sure they were safe. There were probably a lot of kids out there who didn't have someone to care about them.

After a while she got sick of playing foursquare. It was too hot to stay outside all day. She went inside thinking maybe she could find a book that wasn't some kind of old history or reference. The inside of the Castle, especially by the thick stone walls, was much cooler, and Violet took her time looking around the ground floor where the library was. Most of the books were gone—someone had said people burned them over the winter to keep warm— but there were still a few here and there. Mostly it was boring stuff about the history of Washington, DC, and the Smithsonian, but she ran across a couple of cool picture books about expeditions to places all over the world.

Paging through them, Violet wondered if she would ever see any of those places. She'd never been out of the United States, except to Toronto once when her dad brought all of them along to a convention. She remembered the view from the top of the CN Tower. It had been a clear day, and she could see the city of Niagara Falls. That was where they had crossed into Canada, and on the way back from Toronto they stopped to see the falls.

Now the world was a mess and she would probably never go that far again. Seeing the pictures of fabulous faraway places depressed her. She would never get to the Taj Mahal or the pyramids or the Great Wall of China.

She couldn't even go around the block by herself.

Violet closed the book and sat in the cool dimness of the library. She heard people walking in the atrium between the library and the Castle's main doors. They were talking about the supply run they'd just been on. "Tell you what, we're going to have to start going farther. There's nothing left around here," one of them said. Violet recognized the voice and could picture the man's face—red hair, sunburned even in April, missing one of his bottom front teeth—but she didn't know his name. "If we could get across to Alexandria, though…"

"Be easier if we could go up toward Maryland, wouldn't it?" The second voice was another man Violet could picture. He was Indian, or maybe Pakistani, with a thick mustache. And he was really tall. She remembered his name. Dileep. He'd worked for the government, but she couldn't remember what he did.

"No, man, the whole area around that… well, you know what happened at that quarantine site over past the Lincoln Memorial?"

"Yeah, that was bad."

"Real bad. And it's worse now. I don't think the JTF even goes over that way unless they're in vehicles. But we could probably get across the bridge and see what we can find in Virginia."

"I'd go," Dileep said.

"Yeah, we'll talk to Junie and Mike about it. One way or another we have to figure something out. We got, what, a hundred mouths to feed?"

"Something like that."

"Yeah. Can't do it with dandelion greens and whatever we can grow in the courtyard. Anyway, I'm gonna go find Junie. Later, Dileep."

"All right, Darryl. Let me know how that conversation goes."

Violet heard clomping boots on the stairs. Then she heard the front door open and close. Dileep must have gone outside.

So the adults were starting to worry about food. That wasn't good. They had a pretty big garden, and the JTF had made sure they had seeds, but the other man—Darryl—was right. The garden wasn't going to feed a hundred people.

The door opened again and Violet heard all of her friends come in, complaining about being hot and thirsty. She got up and made it out into the atrium before they went upstairs because they were waiting for Wiley. Even though his wound wasn't very bad, it still hurt when he moved fast.

She'd meant to tell them about the conversation between Darryl and Dileep, but instead she said, "Guys. What's the farthest you've ever been from home?" Pointing at her own chest, she added, "Toronto."

Ivan and Amelia had visited their mother's relatives in Zacatecas, Mexico, once.

Wiley and Noah had been to Florida and Chicago. "I'm not sure which one is farther," Noah said. "I think Chicago."

* * *

Shelby said San Francisco, where her parents had lived before their work brought them to DC.

"I was born in the Sudan," Saeed said. "So technically this is the farthest I've ever been from home."

"Jeez, you win," Wiley said. "Violet, why were you thinking about that?"

"Because I was wondering if we were ever going to be able to go places again," Violet said. "I mean, I don't want to bring everyone down, but I got thinking about... there's this tower in Toronto, it's, like, the tallest building in the world. Or it was until a couple of years ago. You can go up in it and look out, and it feels like you can see forever. So I was thinking that one time I was, like, a thousand feet in the air, and maybe I won't ever be again. And I was in another country, and maybe I won't ever be again. And..." Her eyes were starting to prickle and she took a deep breath. "Anyway. That's why I was thinking about it."

"I bet we will," Ivan said.

Shelby nodded and added, "Yeah. Everything's going to get better."

Just like that, Violet snapped back into big-sister mode. She'd never been a big sister before the virus, but she had to play one for the little kids. "I bet you're right," she said. "Everything's going to get better."

"It's not going to get better for me if I don't get a drink of water," Saeed said. "I'm going to dry up and blow away."

They went upstairs to the kitchen. It was too early for lunch, but the cooks gave them some snacks and a gallon jug of water. They went out on a balcony on the shaded side of the building, looking north over the Mall. The air was hazy enough to make the outlines of the White House a little fuzzy. To the right was the Capitol, with barricades all around it. There was a stretch of the Mall between them and the Capitol where a lot of people had been buried right after the virus happened. It was in front of the Air and Space Museum.

Saeed was looking in that direction, too. "That's where I'd really like to go," he said.

"The museum? It's, like, full of bad guys with guns now, isn't it?"

"No," Saeed said. "Space. I don't want to be a thousand feet in the air. I want to be a thousand miles in the air. A million. And I'm gonna do it. There's been plagues before. Everything always gets better in the end."

Maybe, Violet thought. But she was also hearing Darryl's voice in her head. None of them were going to get anywhere if they didn't have enough to eat.

CHAPTER 21

AURELIO

The sun was going down when the empty semi pulled into a truck stop just off Interstate 83 in Harrisburg. "We're here," the driver said. His name was Abdi. During the ninety-minute drive, swerving to avoid abandoned cars the JTF hadn't had the time or manpower to clear, Aurelio had gotten his life story. Born in Somalia, spent most of his childhood in a refugee camp, came to the States just in time for the virus to tear apart any vision he might have had of the American Dream. "But hey," Abdi said. "I'm breathing, man. And I have a job."

It was more than a lot of people could say. Aurelio shook Abdi's hand. "Thanks for the ride," he said and climbed down out of the cab. Abdi got out, too, heading around the front of the truck to check in at the JTF logistics office to see what he would be hauling next.

Interstate 83 ribboned away to the north and south. Aurelio ached with the realization that he could get on it, head south, and be through Baltimore and into DC in four or five hours. He could find Ivan and Amelia, feel their embrace, the strength of tiny arms wrapped around his shoulders.

But instead he was headed the other way, west and north, because that was his duty.

They would be okay, he told himself. They were with a group, and someone was looking after them. They would be okay. "Abdi," he said. "Is all the JTF command in that one office?"

"Far as I know," Abdi said.

Aurelio walked over to the office and introduced himself. He mostly needed a place to stay for the night before he kept up his pursuit of Ike Ronson. The duty officer pointed him to a makeshift barracks in a repurposed motel just north on the access road. Aurelio got there and the guard on duty issued him a room. The first thing he did was turn on the faucet in the bathroom. Nothing. That figured. Most places didn't have running water. New York was an exception. For all the bad things about deploying there—ongoing violent chaos, scarcity due to the blockades, recurrent threat of the virus returning to a close-packed population—at least it had running water.

So Aurelio was looking at a bucket shower in the morning, but at least there was a bed. He sat on it, bouncing a little. Months of sleeping wherever he could find a flat spot had conditioned him to love any place that had a bed. This would be a good night's sleep if he could somehow stop himself from thinking of his children.

That thought returned him to the elevator lobby south of Duane Park. All those dead people. Dead kids. Aurelio had seen plenty of dead people in the months since the plague had struck, but none of the people in that lobby had to die.

In his mind, the evidence was clear: bodies all bunched together, with no sign that Ronson had mounted any kind of defense from the elevator lobby, or even covered them while they got out through the parking structure. Ike Ronson had killed those civilians by running out in their moment of need. Whatever else Aurelio was doing, he would make sure Ronson answered for that.

His comms pinged. Diaz answered and heard Lieutenant Hendricks's voice. "Agent Diaz. I found something that might be of interest to you."

"All right," he said. "Let's hear it."

"I'm sending it to you now. A little background: This was an encrypted transmission. ISAC didn't initially pick it up, but I looked at Ronson's comms records and found a conversation from oh six forty this morning that didn't match any of the recorded audio we have from him. So I went back to that time and heard static on his channel. I clipped the static and ran it through some decryption utilities. Most of it was still garbled, but I sent you the parts of it that are intelligible."

"Care to give me a sense of what's in there?"

"I'll put it this way: I was skeptical of you this morning, Agent Diaz. I am less so now."

"Thank you, Lieutenant." Hendricks ended the transmission and Aurelio saw a blinking icon on his watch face, indicating the audio file. He tapped it and listened.

Sentinel, this is Mantis... intercepted comms... left Manhattan... engage and assist...

That wasn't Ike Ronson's voice. So Ronson must be Sentinel, and the other person was Mantis.

Then Aurelio heard Ronson: *You said Michigan?* More squeals and garbled noises followed until the other voice, Mantis, returned.

Frequency switching... Mantis out.

The audio clip ended.

Aurelio played it again, but couldn't hear anything new. He wondered if Hendricks was going to keep working on it. Counterintelligence was a big part of what she did, so Aurelio figured she would. In the meantime, he had learned a couple of things.

One, Ike Ronson was loyal to someone other than the Division.

Two, his contact with that other organization called herself Mantis.

Three—this one was speculative, but Aurelio felt pretty solid about it—Mantis had sent Ronson out to find someone who had left Manhattan.

Four—also speculative—someone was going to Michigan. Was that Ronson, or the person Ronson was supposed to engage and assist?

Questions: Who was Mantis? Who was Ronson looking for, and why? Where were they going?

Only one way to find out, Aurelio thought. He knew Ike Ronson was headed west, so that was the way he would go. Even if he had to walk all the way to Michigan.

He stretched out on the bed and realized he was hungry. Back at the truck stop was a JTF commissary, mostly to feed the drivers. Aurelio went out and made a pass through it, gathering up sandwiches and coffee and candy bars. He took all of it back to his room and sat, thinking about what he knew and what he intuited, wondering if he should trust his instincts here or if he should let Ike Ronson go his way. What did it hurt, a single rogue agent? Aurelio didn't have to chase Ronson all the way to Michigan, if that was where he was going. There was plenty for him to do in New York or DC. Hell, there was probably need for a Division agent right there in Harrisburg. Anywhere there were still people, there were still problems.

Aurelio took off his boots. Since the virus, he had realized that he could only really relax when his boots were off, because if he was secure enough to take them off that meant he didn't think any action would be called for in the immediate future. Right then, on the edge of a truck stop in Harrisburg, Pennsylvania, he felt that. There were going to be a lot of problems to solve in the morning, but he couldn't solve any of them right then.

What he could do right then was sleep, but sleep was a long time in coming. He lay on the bed, replaying the snippets of decoded conversation between Ike Ronson and the mysterious Mantis. Who was she? What group did she represent? What did they want?

And how had they lured Ike Ronson away from his oath to the Division?

Aurelio tried to check Ronson's location, but ISAC returned a last known location instead of a current location: still Stroudsburg. ISAC's coverage was spotty sometimes outside big cities. There were booster nodes in secure locations across the country, designed to ensure the stability of the network, but they didn't ensure perfect reliability in mountainous terrain or during electromagnetic storms. So maybe it was because of sunspots, or maybe Ronson was staying in Stroudsburg for some reason. What that reason might be, Aurelio could only imagine.

Was he looking for someone? That would account for the *left Manhattan… engage and assist* part of the communication. But there was nothing else to suggest who Ronson might be looking for, and the only lead he had on Ronson's destination was the possibility he was going to Michigan. But where in

Michigan? Detroit? Lansing? Aurelio couldn't think of any military installations in Michigan other than decommissioned air force bases up in the northern part of the state.

Sure would help if I knew who he was looking for, Aurelio thought. Because then I might be able to find out why that person was going to Michigan, and that would narrow the destination down. It occurred to him that Ike Ronson might not know why he was supposed to be looking for the target. He probably had more information than Aurelio did, but that wasn't a very high bar to clear.

He was drifting, getting sleepy even though his mind kept doggedly circling the few clues he had. It was time to let it all go for the night. In the morning maybe ISAC would have a current location on Ronson. Maybe Lieutenant Hendricks would call with more decrypted audio. Maybe, maybe, maybe.

Gotta put some miles behind me tomorrow, Aurelio thought. Get this done and get to DC.

But first he had to wind himself down and get to sleep.

CHAPTER 22

IKE

The JTF convoy he'd caught on with had only gone as far as Stroudsburg, where they were setting up logistical support for some kind of mission in the Delaware Water Gap. The field commander had asked Ike if he could come along and lend a hand, but Ike had begged off, citing a higher mission priority. Which was true, even if it wasn't an SHD-sanctioned mission.

"You sure?" The JTF officer was young and nervous. Ike had him pegged as a high school ROTC kid who'd ended up at one of the service academies but never seen any real fighting until the virus hit, and now he didn't know what to do. "We've got a terrorist group that's going to blow one of the I-80 bridges near here, and we need to find them fast. If I-80 is out of commission, our supply lines into New York get a lot longer. People are going to suffer."

Ike thought it over. "You have any idea where they are?" Maybe he could at least offer some advice.

The officer got out a map and spread it on the hood of a car, holding one corner down against the breeze. Ike put a hand on the other side. "They're somewhere in this area," the officer said, his fingertip tracing a rough circle that included a big swath of forestland around the Delaware River. "They attacked a convoy a month ago and got hold of some C-4. We went looking for it, and managed to learn about their plans, but the last team we sent out didn't come back."

Ike looked at the map, tracing hiking trails and noting places where the wilderness edged up against small towns. He also saw at least four bridges within ten miles of where they stood. The JTF force wasn't big enough to protect all of them, unless the group of terrorists was very small. They couldn't count on that. "Where was that team the last time you communicated with them?"

"Right there." The officer tapped a spot just north of I-80, where Old Mine Road passed a couple of small islands in the river.

In thirty-six hours Ike had to call in to Mantis. She would want to know what kind of progress he was making. On the other hand, if he bailed out on a mission like this, the JTF officer would gripe about it, and that might get back to other people who knew what had happened back in Manhattan. So far, the countermeasures he'd gotten from Mantis had stopped ISAC from tagging Ike as a rogue agent. His watch was still orange and he still had access to ISAC heads-up information. But a bad report on this, especially if someone did blow up the bridge, would have a lot of people looking at Ike.

Probably it was worth a brief side trip to avoid that. And if he could do some good along the way, well, so much the better.

"Okay," Ike said. "I'm going to need a few things."

Thirty minutes after sunset, Ike was moving fast through the woods that ran parallel to the Old Mine Road, headed for the spot the JTF officer had pointed out. He found it without much trouble. Scorch marks from explosions were still visible on the asphalt even in the fading light. Shell casings of several different calibers littered the road, and the cleared buffer on the forest side, but not the river side.

Ike headed into the woods, working steadily uphill in the dark. A fifteen-minute hike brought him to the Appalachian Trail, which ran north all the way to Maine and south all the way to Georgia. But he had a feeling the terrorists and their C-4 were a lot closer than that.

They wouldn't be on the road, because it was too easy to see them. They probably wouldn't be at one of the bigger campgrounds farther north in the park, because other people would be there, too, and it would be too difficult to keep their secret. But there were plenty of small, informal campsites just off the Appalachian Trail. Ike figured the terrorists would be at one of them, probably within a few miles of the bridge they were planning to blow.

If he was wrong, and couldn't find them by dawn, he would head back to the interstate, cut around the JTF base, and be on his way.

The top of Mount Tammany, just to the east, still caught the last light from the west, but beyond it the sky was dark, and on the trail it was nearly full dark. The bluffs dropping to the river were just to the south. Ike guessed north was the way to go.

He went slowly, pausing every twenty steps to listen and scan the surrounding woods for light. The trail rose to follow a ridge, and Ike paused before he crested the ridge. Night breeze rustled in the trees. Something small scampered through the brush to his left.

And up ahead, maybe two hundred yards distant, he heard people laughing.

Bingo, he thought, and got off the trail. He reckoned he'd traveled three miles or so. To his right was a slope down to a creek bed. He could hear the water and smell it.

He reached the top of the ridge and saw a fire ahead. Staying in the trees, he moved forward until he had a good look at the fire and the people around it. Before he started shooting, he wanted to be sure he had the right target.

He was looking at a clearing on the west side of the trail, framed by boulders and beyond them tall trees on a sharp slope back down toward the river. A big bonfire burned in the middle of the clearing, illuminating a cluster of tents—six of them—at the edge of the trail. Ike counted the people grouped around the fire. Thirteen. All white, all male. Several armed.

Ike took a look through a night-vision scope he'd gotten from the JTF officer. The fire was too bright to look at through the scope, but he could get a better idea of what things were like around the perimeter of the camp, beyond the brightest firelight. He saw a lot of small arms, several JTF issue. That marked this group as the killers of the JTF patrol, and therefore in all likelihood current possessors of stolen C-4. By the terms of Directive 51, Ike didn't have to do any of this. He could have just walked up and killed all of them. But he wasn't that kind of person. A certain kind of authoritarianism maybe was the best way to get a floundering society stood back up— that was why he was in contact with Mantis and her group—but that didn't mean Ike Ronson was going to go around killing people in case they were criminals or terrorists.

Hell, if he'd known the operation in Duane Park was going

to fall apart like that, he would have made another plan. Maybe another agent had gotten there in time to help those civilians. Ike hoped so.

He'd been having to make too many hard choices lately.

Luckily, the situation in front of him did not present a hard choice. Armed group in possession of stolen arms and probably explosives, with solid intel they were planning a terrorist attack. Ike put the night-vision scope away and let his eyes adjust again. Then he moved through the trees until he was across the trail from the campground. A swampy pond was behind him, lively with spring peepers and various insects.

The way Ike saw it, his best plan was to find a good firing position, introduce himself with a couple of grenades, then put the M4 to work. If some of them got away into the woods, that was probably all right. The important thing was to break the group and recover or destroy the C-4.

Which he had yet to find. It was possible that his grenades might find it, in which case the whole campground would probably go up in smoke. Ike considered this. C-4 was pretty stable. A gunshot wouldn't set it off, but a frag grenade might if it went off right next to a brick of the explosive. And if the C-4 did go off, and there were other people in the tents, maybe noncombatants…

He was a little bit gun-shy because of what had happened that morning in Manhattan. Best to be sure. He got out the night-vision scope again and scanned the edges of the campground. The JTF typically shipped C-4 in steel cases about the size of a carry-on suitcase, and as he scanned, Ike didn't see anything that matched that profile… until one of the people by the fire shifted and a metallic glint shone in between two of the tents, on the side of the campground closest to the trail.

There it was. Four cases. That was more than enough to bring down a bridge. Or erase the campground and everyone in it.

Ike decided to take the careful route. C-4 needed both heat and shock to detonate, so if he didn't put a grenade right on the cases, the chance of accidental detonation was pretty low. He picked a grenade off his belt and slung it sidearm across the trail so it skipped into the crowd of men on the side away from the semicircle of tents. As it hit the ground, he was already throwing another.

He hit the ground, watching from his belly. The clank of the grenade on a rock drew the attention of the closer men. But before any of them could say anything, it went off. Two seconds later, so did the other.

Ike ducked his head when his internal countdown got to zero, so the explosions didn't ruin his night vision. When he lifted his head again, he was sighting down the barrel of the M4 and wishing he had something a little more suited to sniper-style work. But he was only fifty yards away.

None of the men around the fire were still standing. Several of them were trying to get to their feet. Two of them were on fire because one of the grenades had blown the bonfire apart and showered them with embers. Ike ignored them. He saw one of them stagger upright and squeezed off a single shot, putting him right back down. Some of them were screaming warnings and orders. Others were just screaming. Ike saw a silhouette. Another one upright and moving. The M4 bucked against his shoulder, and the silhouette pitched over out of his field of view. He heard crashing in the trees, like someone was falling down the wooded slope. Two or three of the would-be terrorists had gotten their guns up and pointed generally in Ike's direction.

They'd figured out where the shots were coming from.

Ike dropped one of them. The others saw the muzzle flash and started blazing away at the spot Ike was already rolling away from. He angled down the slope, but not so far that he ended up in the swamp. Then he got low again and waited for his pursuers to appear at the top of the slope, where they would be nice and backlit by the glow of the fire.

He saw one of them first, and waited until he knew where both of them were. Then, as soon as he had them both in his field of fire, he chewed them up with a long burst.

Moving again, he went back the way he'd come, doubling back to the spot from where he'd first observed the campsite. There were still screams and moans, but Ike didn't see anyone else able-bodied. He stayed low, crossing the trail and approaching the campsite from behind the tents. He listened at each tent as he passed, pausing when he got to the cases of C-4 to make sure they were undamaged.

From inside the fourth tent he heard a baby crying.

God damn it, Ike thought.

He stepped lightly between that tent and the next, hovering at the edge of the firelight until he was certain there was no threat from any of the wounded. Probably he ought to put them out of their misery, but he decided he would let the JTF worry about that. None of them even saw him. They were either too busy dying or happened to be looking the other way.

The tent was a standard four-person camping dome with zipper doors. One of them was half-open. Ike ducked through it and saw the baby. It was lying on a sleeping bag, crying like… well, Ike didn't have much experience with babies. It didn't look hurt, so he assumed it was crying like babies cried when grenade explosions and gunshots woke them up. It lay on its back, eyes squeezed shut and toothless mouth wide open. A tiny life, spared by the randomness of shrapnel patterns.

The woman who might have soothed the baby was dead on the sleeping bag, one arm still curled under the baby's head. Shrapnel had punched through the side of her neck, just under the jaw. From the looks of it, she'd never known what hit her. Ike looked down at her for a long moment, wondering what had brought her to this place. Was she a captive? Had she loved one of the men he had just killed?

It didn't matter now. Ike's grenade had killed her. All that mattered was what came next.

Ike slung his M4 and wished that just for once a mission could be straightforward. Then he got over that moment of self-pity and looked around for a sling or pack or something he could use. Hiking three miles in the dark was no problem, but he'd never tried to do it holding a baby.

It was just after midnight when Ike got back to the JTF camp and found the officer exactly where he'd left him, next to the mobile command post. The officer looked up as Ike approached, and his eyes got big when he saw the baby cradled in Ike's left arm. It had stopped crying somewhere along the trail, maybe from the rocking motion of Ike's steady walk. Now it was asleep.

"Your C-4 is about three miles up the Appalachian Trail," Ike said. "Don't take the branch that goes down by the creek. I was going to detonate it in place, but I figured you might want it."

"You left it there?" The officer was looking back and forth from the baby to Ike's face. Confusion and irritation warred on his face.

"It was too heavy to carry," Ike said. "You don't have to worry about your terrorists running off with it."

"How can you be sure about that?"

"Tell you what," Ike said. "You send a patrol up there right now. Tell them to look for the campfire. It'll still be burning. They won't find anyone left to walk off with four cases of C-4." Minus five one-kilo bricks and a couple of detonators, he did not add. He'd stowed them in his pack. You never knew when you might need a little explosive in the field.

"I'll do that," the officer said. He was still looking at the baby.

"Good," Ike said. "Now, where can I find either a medic or a wet nurse?"

"I have to say, the last thing I expected was to see you coming back with a baby," the officer said.

"Yeah," Ike said. He looked down at the baby, sleeping with its mouth open and one tiny fist curled up at the side of its face. "It's been a day full of surprises."

CHAPTER 23

VIOLET

The weather stayed hot, and the kids were getting stir-crazy from not being able to roam anymore. Saeed and Amelia thought they should see how far they could go before an adult reeled them back in, and Violet decided to go along. The other kids stayed inside, not wanting to make anyone mad at them.

"Where do we go?" Amelia wondered. They were at the edge of the Castle grounds, on the south side.

"For sure not that way," Saeed said, pointing south. "That's where the weird chemical thing is."

"Plus the flood," Violet added.

"So around to the Mall, then," Amelia said, and she started walking.

Saeed stopped her. "Wait, no, not that way. Let's go around the other way. Stay far away from the Capitol." Amelia shrugged. "Okay, whatever."

They walked around the west side of the Castle and up to the Mall. A fire was burning somewhere down in the direction of the baseball stadium. Smoke curled out over the river. "Wonder what that is," Saeed said.

"Who cares," Violet said. "As long as it's not here."

Then she immediately felt bad, because someone was losing stuff in a fire or maybe dying and it wasn't right for her to not care. She did care. She just couldn't always stand how it felt to care.

"I mean, it's not that I don't care," she added. "It's just that it doesn't really matter to us what's burning since we don't know and we can't get over there to find out anyway."

A rumble in the sky drew their attention upward. "Hey, look," Saeed said. "A jet plane."

Stunned, they all watched it. None of them could remember seeing another jet since Black Friday, or right after it. Now, almost six months later, it was like seeing a dragon or a UFO.

A streak of smoke shot across the sky as they watched, and fire bloomed from the jet's side just behind its right wing. It angled sharply left and down, trailing smoke and fire. Behind it, the kids could see pieces of the jet tumbling through the sky, winking in the midday sun.

The jet tried to regain altitude, but one of the engines on the right wing broke off and spun crazily down toward the ground. The jet heeled over and disappeared behind some buildings on the other side of the city. A moment later, a column of smoke began to rise.

"Whoa," Amelia said. "Did somebody shoot that plane down?"

"I think so," Violet said. She traced the smoke trail from the missile, but it was so windy that she couldn't tell where the missile had come from.

"First jet we've seen since before Christmas, practically, and someone shoots it down," Saeed said. He sounded sad, like out of all the other violent things they'd seen, that one really mattered. Violet understood. To him, technology was like a sign of progress. A jet in the sky meant maybe things would be normal again someday. And then it all went down in flames.

Without really meaning to, they had wandered over to the carousel on the Mall, just in front of the Castle. They could see it from their window, and it was one of the places they tended to hang out when they were on the Mall. Today, it was kind of a test. The carousel was pretty close to the Castle, so maybe none of the adults would make them come back.

Amelia climbed up on the scaly blue "sea horse." It was her favorite, with a forked tail instead of back legs and a head that someone had told Violet looked like old Chinese drawings of horses. Saeed got up next to her. Why not, Violet thought. She climbed up, too, filling out the row. Her horse was also blue. Saeed's, in the middle, was white. Both of them looked kind of angry, it seemed to Violet. Maybe the carousel needed music to seem beautiful.

"Did you ever ride this when it worked?" Amelia asked.

Violet had. "A couple of times, yeah."

"I think we rode it once on a field trip or something," Saeed said. "Or maybe it was another carousel somewhere else. I don't really remember for sure."

"I wonder if somebody could fix it up," Violet said. "Get it working again. It'd be fun to have it there."

"It would be even better if there was, like, a party to go with it. We could invite everyone. Maybe they'd all get along better." Saeed was still glum. Since his comment about space the day before, Violet thought he'd been kind of sad all the time. He said optimistic things, but she was starting to think he didn't really mean them. Now the jet crashing had made it worse.

"That would be cool," she said, to be supportive. "Nobody can fight at a carousel."

They rocked back and forth on the horses, pretending they were moving. Maybe they were a little too old for that, but it made them happy to pretend. "I bet Shelby and Noah and Ivan wish they were out here," Saeed said. His mood seemed to brighten all of a sudden. "We should go get them."

"We could," Violet said, "but Wiley couldn't come out, could he? Maybe it's better that they're hanging out with him."

"Yeah, I guess." Saeed kept rocking his horse. Violet leaned forward on hers, resting her chin on top of its head. She'd never ridden a real horse. Maybe someday.

Amelia was looking out over the Mall. "Hey," she said. "There are people coming."

Saeed slid off his horse. "We better get out of here."

Violet and Amelia dropped down to the carousel platform, too. Should they run? The people didn't look threatening. They had guns, but almost everybody out in the open in DC had a gun. None of these people were pointing their guns at the kids. All of them seemed to have tattoos of the American flag, and they were dressed alike. Not quite in a uniform, but their clothes were all navy blue and khaki, with lots of pockets.

"Come on," Violet said. They started to walk back around the carousel, away from the group of strangers and toward the Castle. But when they got around the carousel, they saw the group had angled to meet them before they could get back home. "Uh-oh," Amelia said. "I'm scared."

"It's okay," Saeed said. "They can see us from the Castle."

"If they're looking," Violet said.

One of the men in the group—they were all men—called out

to them. "Hey, kids. Taking a horseback ride?" He smiled at them. It seemed genuine, but Violet was still nervous.

"We were just about to go back to the Castle," she said, making sure the men knew she and her friends belonged somewhere close.

"Is that right? You live there?"

"Yeah," Violet said. "We were over at another place, a hotel down by the river, but it flooded."

"Mmm. Bad season for floods." The man took another step closer to them. He had his hands in his pockets and his rifle slung over his shoulder. The other men hung back a little, not paying much attention. "Listen, who's in charge there?"

"Junie and Mike," Saeed volunteered.

"Okay. What are your names?"

The kids all introduced themselves, and the man nodded. "I'm Sebastian. So tell me about Junie and Mike. They married?"

"No, Junie was kind of the leader of the Castle from the beginning, and Mike was in charge of our group when we came over from the hotel," Amelia said. "So now they run things together, pretty much."

Looking at the Castle, Sebastian thought this over for a minute. "Okay. Good to know." He pushed his sunglasses up on his head and bent forward a little, hands on his knees, so his face was level with theirs. "Listen, you should be careful out here. There are a lot of bad people roaming around DC, and pretty soon we're going to have to clear them out. It might get... well, let's just say it's not going to be safe until we get things under control."

"I thought the JTF was here to do that," Saeed said.

A couple of the men in the group chuckled. To Violet, it wasn't a good sound. Sebastian held a hand back toward them and they quieted down. "The JTF is trying," he said. "But if they can't handle things, someone else might have to. Then things will be back to normal. Maybe better, who knows?"

"I wish," Amelia said.

"Me, too, Amelia. We all wish. But it takes hard work to make wishes come true." Sebastian straightened up. "Hey, you mind walking us over to the Castle? We'd like to talk to Junie and Mike about some of this stuff. Plus, you probably don't want to stand around talking to grown-ups when you've got cool kid stuff to do."

The kids looked at each other. They couldn't really say no. "Um, sure," Violet said. "Come on."

The Castle grounds were full of people working in the garden as Violet, Saeed, and Amelia led the group of men around to the Independence Avenue entrance. "Beautiful garden," Sebastian commented. "You're going to be eating well in a month or so."

Remembering Darryl and Dileep's conversation, Violet just said, "Yeah, we helped plant everything."

"Good," Sebastian said. "It's good for you to know how to do that. Plus, food tastes better when you know you helped make it."

Everyone in the gardens had stopped what they were doing to observe the group of armed strangers. Junie stepped out from behind a row of bean vines growing up a lattice that Violet had helped put up. The beans were already flowering. "Children, go on inside," she said.

"Hello, ma'am," Sebastian said. "My name is Sebastian. The kids here told us we should look for Mike or Junie."

"I'm Junie. What is it you want?"

Violet, Amelia, and Saeed moved toward the door, but they didn't go inside just yet. They saw some people up on the Castle's balconies, watching the strangers. She felt a lot of tension in the air, but she wasn't sure what it was about.

"Well, we'd like to talk," Sebastian said.

"You don't need eight men with rifles to talk."

Sebastian nodded. "That's true. But sometimes you need eight men with rifles to get to the place where you want to have a conversation."

"Huh," Junie said. "Well, you're here now. Would you like some water?"

"Thank you," Sebastian said. "It sure is hot. You mind if my men rest out here while we talk?"

"Of course not," Junie said. "Come on inside."

She gave Violet a look as she and Sebastian passed by on their way inside. Violet had no trouble interpreting the message: *We are going to talk about this once these strangers have gone, and your story better be good.*

Violet exchanged glances with Saeed and Amelia. "What were we supposed to do?" Amelia asked.

"I don't know," Violet said.

"I know what we should do now," Saeed said. "Stay way out of the way until Junie decides to come find us."

That seemed like a good idea. They went inside, straight up to their room, and told the whole story to the rest of the group. Then they played cards and backgammon and Chinese checkers for the rest of the day until it was time to go to dinner.

CHAPTER 24

AURELIO

The first thing Aurelio did in the morning was try to run Ike Ronson's location via ISAC again. *Last Known Location: Stroudsburg, PA.*

Damn it, Aurelio thought. Why wasn't ISAC tracking him? And why hadn't it processed his actions in Duane Park and marked him rogue? Calling in a false alarm that knowingly endangered a fellow agent, plus deliberately leaving civilians to be massacred, was more than enough to put a red circle on an agent.

Something else was going on, and Diaz not only didn't know what it was, he hadn't yet figured out what the right questions were to ask.

The day got even more confusing when ISAC notified him of an after-action report filed by the JTF garrison in Stroudsburg. A Division agent identifying himself as Ike Ronson had gone on a solo night mission to disrupt a band of terrorists who were plotting to destroy an interstate bridge with stolen C-4. The mission was successful, with eleven confirmed kills and all but a small amount of the C-4 recovered.

And along the way, he had saved a five-month-old baby girl

and brought her back to the garrison.

How did that square with what Ronson had done the day before in Manhattan?

He put a call in to the Post Office and got Lieutenant Hendricks on the line. She didn't sound happy to hear from him. "I was hoping you'd peeled back some more of the layers on that encrypted conversation," he said.

"Nope. The only reason we got as much as we did was that we had raw voice from a remote listening device we had in place to monitor that location. I haven't been able to do anything with the rest."

"What about Michigan? Anything in any internal briefings about something going on there that might have gotten his attention?"

Hendricks sighed. "I can do a search. But Michigan's a big place, and there's a heavy JTF presence in all the cities there, especially close to the Canadian border. Our friends up north got serious about border security when the virus hit. So it's going to be a lot of sorting, and I don't have a lot of time."

"How about the person Ronson is looking for? I'm thinking of the 'left Manhattan' bit."

"We don't even know for sure he's looking for anyone," Hendricks answered. "All we know is he's probably going to Michigan, and along the way he diverted to break up a terrorist plot and save a baby while he was at it. I have to tell you, Agent Diaz, I'm not convinced anymore that he's a bad guy."

"It's great that he saved a baby," Aurelio said. "That doesn't bring the people in that building down on Duane Street back to life. And it doesn't explain why he's trying to hide conversations with unknown parties whose orders he appears to be following."

"Directive 51," Hendricks said. "There's nothing I can do."

"You can keep monitoring his traffic. In fact, I'm asking you to do just that. Please."

"I'll do that as I can, Agent Diaz. But you have to understand, I do not have the operational bandwidth to run down possible wild-goose chases."

"I do understand. I appreciate any time you can put into it."

"I'll update you when I have more. Anything else?"

"Not right now. Thanks, Lieutenant."

Hendricks ended the call and Aurelio stifled the urge to shoot something just so he could vent his frustration. Instead he started walking. He already had the map in his head: Route 22, snaking up and over the mountains to catch 322, steadily bearing northwest to State College and then on to catch I-80 at Clearfield. That was about a hundred and thirty miles, with a lot of up and down along the way. Three days if he pushed hard.

Then it was another hundred and twenty miles to the Ohio state line, and maybe two hundred from there before he got to a city of any size in Michigan. Good thing the SHD issued excellent boots as part of each Division agent's gear.

On his way out of town Aurelio stuck his head into a convenience store to see what snacks might still be on its shelves. There wasn't much, but he did score a Washingtown Spears baseball cap. It was getting warmer and he didn't need a watch cap anymore. He spent a few minutes getting the brim curved to his preference, then settled it on his head and headed out.

He saw lots of deer and small animals along the road, but Aurelio didn't see another living human being until he was crossing the Susquehanna River and spotted a boat drifting with the current. A man and a young girl were fishing. Aurelio watched them for a while, wondering where they lived. How they lived. He'd been born and raised in Washington, DC, and spent his entire life there until the past three months in New York. He didn't know anything about life outside a big city, pandemic or no pandemic. Had the virus hit small towns as hard as big cities? It was easy to imagine that the countryside was depopulated, as people congregated in bigger cities following the failure of electricity and other infrastructure.

On the other hand, if you could make it through the winter and you had tools to fish and hunt, it might be easier to survive in the country. Grow a garden, learn to preserve what you grew and caught, and you could become something close to self-sufficient. At least until you had an accident or got sick, and the closest doctor was fifty miles away.

The boat drifted away around a bend in the river. Just before he lost sight of it, Aurelio saw the girl haul in a fish, its scales catching the sunlight as it thrashed on her line. Her dad leaned over to unhook it, and then they were gone. He kept walking.

By nightfall he'd seen only a few other people, and no groups larger than four or five. When the sun dropped behind the hills, he let himself into a farmhouse off the main road near a small river town called Port Royal. Once inside, he took a look around to make sure he wasn't intruding on someone. The house smelled dusty. Nobody had cooked in it recently, or lit a fire. The downstairs was empty.

Aurelio flicked on a small flashlight and went up a staircase from the foyer. He found a bathroom and three bedrooms. Two were unoccupied. In the third he found two bodies, one adult and one child. They were mostly skin and bones, partly worked over by animals, but Aurelio didn't see any weapons. It looked like they had died together, lying in the bed. Just one more sad story among millions.

Back downstairs, he looked through the kitchen cupboards and pantry. Mice had destroyed everything but the canned goods, which still stood in neat untouched rows. Aurelio opened himself a can of peaches and another of tuna. He ate them in the dark, looking out the window. Clouds blew across the night sky, covering and uncovering the stars. There was a half-moon.

Thirsty, he tried the faucet. Nothing. So he drank the last of his water and decided he would check out back for a well in the morning. Until then, there was nothing to do but stew over Ike Ronson and whatever he was planning to do in Michigan.

Sitting there looking at the moon, it occurred to Aurelio that he could do the Michigan search himself if he could get access to the JTF's mission logs. ISAC did not seem robust out here in the country, in the deep valleys of central Pennsylvania. But Aurelio went out on the farmhouse's long porch and tried to access those logs. No dice. He wasn't sure if the problem was access or bandwidth, so he settled for sending Lieutenant Hendricks a message asking her if she would mine the logs for mentions of Michigan.

If he hadn't heard from her by the time he got closer to Pittsburgh, Aurelio decided he would try to do the search himself. But he wasn't a trained forensic data analyst. Lieutenant Hendricks was. Also, she would have access to JTF operational and intel logs that Aurelio didn't even know existed. So all in all, it would be better if she did it.

He found a rocking chair and sat, feeling the day's miles in his feet and the small of his back. He took his boots off and stretched out his legs. His ankle was still swollen from the shoot-out at the

High Line, but it was hurting less. This would be a good time for a beer, he thought. The idea spurred him up out of the chair and back into the kitchen, where he was delighted to find two beers on the top shelf of the fridge. Ignoring the mold spreading across the bottom shelves and lining the crispers, he took one of them and went back out on the porch. He didn't recognize the brewery. Must have been local. But the beer tasted good, and he let its cold on his tongue turn into warmth in his belly.

It occurred to Aurelio that he didn't have to worry about anyone attacking him. No matter where he'd been in New York or DC since Black Friday, he'd lived with the constant knowledge that he had to be on his toes. Any relaxation of his guard could end up being fatal—to him and possibly to a lot of other people. But out here, he would see a light a mile away. Even if he was asleep, the sound of porch boards creaking would snap him awake in a split second.

He was safe. It was a strange feeling.

On the other hand, part of the reason he was safe was that everyone who had once lived around here was either dead or gone. If that was the trade-off, Aurelio guessed he would rather live with a little bit of constant danger. He wasn't cut out to be alone. He wanted other people around.

He wanted his children around. Graciela was gone, but he still had Ivan and Amelia. Every step he took west, away from them, felt like a step in the wrong direction.

But he had a duty. He'd sworn an oath. He would fulfill that duty and that oath, and then he would go to Washington. Right then Aurelio hated Ike Ronson, not because he had a full understanding of what Ronson had done but because Ronson was drawing him out into Pennsylvania and probably

Michigan, prolonging by weeks or months that day when Aurelio would finally be able to look after his children.

He couldn't protect them from here. That ate at him. He'd chosen to go to New York because there was a need, but now there was a need in DC, and instead of being there to help meet it Aurelio was in goddamn Port Royal, Pennsylvania, sitting in a dead man's rocking chair.

Who was he looking for? What was so important that a Division agent would go rogue and chase someone six hundred miles?

Those questions were still chewing at him when he got to Clearfield, three days after leaving Harrisburg. He hadn't heard back from Hendricks. In fact, he hadn't heard anything from New York. There seemed to be some kind of problem with ISAC. Comms were unreliable, and the HUD was useless. Aurelio saw people in Clearfield, most of them hanging around a restaurant called Dutch Pantry just off I-80. There were horse-drawn carriages in the parking lot.

Pennsylvania Dutch, he thought. This was Amish country, too. The Amish wouldn't have been as affected by the loss of electricity; they didn't use it anyway.

He looked at those wagons again, and had an idea.

CHAPTER 25

IKE

Seventy-two hours after presenting the baby to the JTF officer in Stroudsburg, Ike Ronson was in Ohio.

After filing an after-action report with the JTF officer, Ike caught four hours of sleep and was on his way the next morning. He'd asked the officer about a possible ride to Michigan and was told that their whole detachment was staying there until the situation with the I-80 bridge was definitively solved. Anything beyond that was above the officer's pay grade.

"Best I can do is get you down the road to Bloomsburg," the officer said. "We've got a truck running to pick up a load there."

"I'll take it," Ike said. "By the way, what happened to the baby?"

"We're looking for someone to take care of it in town here," the officer said. "Her, I mean. It was a little girl. Lots of people lost kids to the virus. I'm sure someone will take her in."

So that had Ike feeling a little better about himself as he climbed aboard the truck and headed west across bridges he had saved from being blown up. By oh eight hundred he was on foot, putting Bloomsburg behind him. Stroudsburg, Bloomsburg... Pittsburgh. Seemed like every town in Pennsylvania was Somethingburg. He stayed on I-80 as it rose and fell over the Appalachians—or was it the Poconos here? He wasn't an expert on geography. He did, however, know where Michigan was, so he started walking. By the time the sun went down and he had to look for a place to hole up for the night, he'd covered nearly forty miles.

He was on the outskirts of a town called Mackeyville and had seen fewer than a dozen other human beings since the JTF truck driver that morning. This sure wasn't New York. At midnight in New York, he would likely as not be on an operation, trying to contain the chaos and violence that seemed to erupt every time the Division turned its attention away from one location to focus on another. Part of that was the collective trauma everyone had experienced being ground zero of the virus. Part of it was the blockade, which had driven already stressed people around the bend. And part of it was the pure fact that without the constraints of law and civilization—or some kind of power greater than themselves—some people just turned into barbarians.

This was what had first made him open to Mantis's approach when she'd contacted him through an intermediary six weeks or so before. She was the voice of a new rising power, gathering itself outside the East Coast megalopolis. They saw the damage chaos was doing. They saw how the current government and the JTF weren't up to the task of restoring order and keeping people safe.

They saw another way. It would be a harder way, at least at first, but if Ike signed on he would be part of a new, stronger America. Was he interested?

Ike had lost his girlfriend and one of his children to the virus. His other two children and his ex-wife had been murdered by a group of lunatic arsonists called the Cleaners in early January. The JTF hadn't protected them. The Division hadn't, either. So, yeah, Ike was interested in something better.

Six weeks later, he still was, but he was getting jumpy because he still didn't know who led this group or what their specific plans were. He believed in their goals, so he had bought in, but he felt like it was about time they started telling him more about who they were and how he was going to fit into their plans. He'd turned his back on the Division for them, and he had civilian deaths on his conscience because of it. They owed him something for that.

Mantis saw it differently, as he found out when he pinged her the morning after he got to Mackeyville. It was forty-eight hours almost to the minute since she'd called him into action back in Manhattan.

"Mantis, this is Sentinel."

"Mantis here. What is your status, Sentinel?"

He updated her on his current location and the diversion to keep up his cover with the Division. "Probably a good idea, Sentinel," she said. "But do not divert again. Intercepting and assisting April Kelleher is your only mission now. Conclude it successfully and you will be in a position to take on greater responsibility."

"Understood, Mantis. Any update on her location?"

"One possible sighting in upstate New York west of Syracuse. Not deemed actionable at this point due to the unreliability of the source, but we are following up."

"Understood. Same question about what she's after."

"We suspect we know, but that intelligence is unconfirmed. Better for you to learn it from her rather than go into your first interactions with preconceptions."

Ike didn't like that, but there wasn't much he could do about it. "Understood, Mantis. Anything else?"

"That's all, Sentinel. Report again in forty-eight hours."

The call ended. Ike took a minute to get over his irritation that Mantis was still deliberately keeping secrets from him. Part of that was standard operational security, but opsec didn't demand that he do passive intel gathering without having any idea what he was trying to learn. This was a test. He was on the mission that would prove his bona fides to Mantis, and whatever shadowy figures stood behind her.

Fine, Ike thought. It wasn't the first time he'd had to prove himself.

He shrugged his pack onto his shoulders and started walking. If April Kelleher was going through upstate New York, he was ahead of her... unless she'd found a faster way to travel. Whatever her speed, from there she would end up in Buffalo, then follow the south shore of Lake Erie. Ike debated angling north to get to the lakeshore faster himself, and trying to track her down along that route. It was a dicey proposition, he thought, since he had no idea how fast she was going.

The safer bet would be to get to Cleveland as quickly as he could, try to wring some intel out of the local Division and JTF sources—assuming his cover held—and then move on past Toledo to Ann Arbor. He might be able to make contact with her anywhere along the way, but if not, he at least had to be in Ann Arbor a few days ahead of her so he could spread the word that the Division was looking for a certain redheaded woman.

All of that would change if Mantis or the JTF came through with some better intel, but Ike knew he had to plan as if he had only his eyes and ears and intuition to find her. So this was the best plan he could come up with under the circumstances. Time was of the essence. Therefore speed was of the essence.

Ike had an idea. He walked across the road to a large warehouse advertising a company that built sheds and other prefab structures. The door was locked, but Ike got in with no problem. He found the office, and in the office he found a phone book. Good thing some people were still old-fashioned enough to want phone books, he thought. Otherwise it would have taken him hours of searching before he was able to find the nearest bike shop… which was about five miles north of him, in a town by the name of Lock Haven.

One of the requirements of the Division was elite fitness, and Ike had logged thousands of hours on his bike over the last ten years. It was probably still hanging up in his apartment in Greenpoint. He'd done centuries plenty of times, and once a double century in Florida where the terrain was so flat you felt like you could go forever. But this was central Pennsylvania. The road out of Lock Haven rose steadily for the first twenty miles, then turned into a very steep climb for the next five or ten. Ike rested at the crest of the ridge, where there was a scenic turnout. He liked the bike he'd chosen. It was nicer than the one he'd had before Black Friday: light carbon frame, better components, racing tires. And it felt good to be on a bike, even though Ike's legs were burning at the end of the climb. He was in survival shape now, not distance-cycling shape.

But that was all right. He would get there.

He got back on the bike and kept going. By the end of the day, after two more punishing climbs, he was in Clearfield and his ass felt like someone had been hitting it with a hammer. He coasted down the exit ramp into a tangle of fast-food restaurants and convenience stores. One of them had a road atlas on a spinner rack, and from it Ike figured he was about three hundred miles from Toledo. He covered a third of that distance the next day, getting to the outskirts of Youngstown, Ohio.

In the morning he would check in with Mantis again. His watch was still orange. His cover was holding. ISAC had been more or less quiet during most of the past two days, since he was out of operational range of the bigger cities where most Division agents were deployed. Now, though, he was in an urbanized area that stretched from Youngstown and Canton up to Cleveland. Operational chatter from agents in those areas told him that things in the cities of the upper Midwest were a little better than they were in New York, largely because people here had easier access to food. By the time the virus had appeared out here, it was already apparent that big territorial blockades weren't going to help. New York's airports, roads, and train stations had done a superb job of spreading the virus before anyone started showing symptoms.

Even so, the agents in this part of the country seemed to be keeping busy. Ike figured they would notice his presence sooner or later, and he might well get a call to support an op. That would put him in a tough spot. He had direct orders from Mantis not to divert again, but...

Stop, he told himself. Deal with that problem if it comes up. Until then, stick to the mission.

Which was, in the end, to bring into being a new, stronger America. As Mantis had said, it was going to entail making some hard choices in the beginning, but Ike believed he was going to be a part of something better: a strong guiding hand to lead America out of its plague-stricken darkness and into the new light of the future.

CHAPTER 26

APRIL

It ended up taking eight days to make the trip because of a problem with one of the locks south of Rochester. Still, when April stepped off Sonia and Julia's barge for the last time in Tonawanda, New York, she felt like she'd made a good start to the trip. She still had a long way to go, but she'd covered nearly half the distance in eight days, and Sonia said there might be lakeshore boats that could get her to Michigan faster than the walk by way of Cleveland and Toledo.

As an added bonus, April had not heard a single gunshot during those eight days. The longer she was away from New York, the more she realized how different things were. She'd mentioned this to Sonia, who cautioned her against thinking that she'd left all her troubles behind in Manhattan. "The canal is pretty calm because people need it to survive," she said. "But I've heard some bad stories about stuff happening in little towns, just like the big cities. Doesn't take much to peel back the veneer of civilization, you know?"

April supposed she was right, but it still felt to her like the pressure cooker of Manhattan had created a situation worse than she would find out in the rest of the country. Even so, she took Sonia's advice to heart. She would have to stay alert.

"Before you go," Sonia said, "take this." She held out a tightly packed plastic bag, about the size of a five- pound bag of flour.

"What is it?" April took the bag and squeezed it. Whatever was inside, it made little crunching sounds.

"Tobacco," Sonia said. "Bring it out only when you need something really bad. It's more valuable than gold right now. Use it wisely, and don't tell people you have it. Seriously."

"You don't have to do this," April said. She tried to hand the bag back. "Really. If anything, I owe you."

Sonia waved the offer away. "You added a gun to the trip. Besides, you were good company. Be well, April.

I hope you find what you're looking for. And if you ever get back to the Albany area, I'll take you sailing on the river."

She turned away to oversee the unloading of the barge's remaining cargo, and April put the tobacco in her pack. Time to begin the next stage of the trip, finding her way around the southern shore of Lake Erie. If only she could go through Canada, but everyone she'd talked to had made it clear that was not happening. Canada had its own problems with the Dollar Bug, but they weren't nearly as bad as the collapse on the U.S. side of the border. It was practically impossible to get from the United States into Canada either by land or by sea.

So around Lake Erie it was. Erie, Cleveland, Toledo, then north to Ann Arbor. That was how April envisioned it in the map she carried in her head.

Unless Sonia was right and there were trading ships going along the lakeshore. To find that out, April started asking around among the dockworkers in Tonawanda's small port.

They pointed her to a group of sailors, who said that there were in fact lake ships, but they didn't come up to Tonawanda. "Current's too fast for them to get back to the lake," one of them said, pointing out at the bright blue Niagara River.

"Nobody has any access to fuel here, then?" April remembered Blake, and his mysterious sources. Someone must be getting fuel out here, at least once in a while.

"You can get it," another sailor said. "But hard to find, and when you do find it, it's real pricey. Easier to pay someone to haul your stuff up from Buffalo if you want to get it onto the canal."

"Where you trying to get to?" a third sailor asked.

"Michigan, eventually," April said.

"Huh." The sailors considered this. "Thing is," said the one who'd told her about the price of fuel, "there's sometimes trouble along the stretch between Buffalo and Erie." He nodded at April's gun. "If you know how to use that, though, you can probably get on a boat."

"Or," the first sailor said, "you can hoof it to Erie and save yourself the trouble."

"If you don't run into the Jamestown Aryans along the way," the third sailor said.

"What kind of trouble?" April asked.

"Pirates. There's thieves on land and thieves on the water."

"Okay. So if I go by water, there might be pirates, and if I go by land… the Jamestown Aryans?"

"Yeah, they're bad news. Pretty much everything between Buffalo and Erie, for ten or twenty miles inland, is all theirs. You're white, so they probably wouldn't kill you. But you run into them, you're liable to end up married," the first sailor said, using his fingers to put quote marks around the last word.

"Sounds like I should take my chances on the lake, then," April said.

The sailors agreed. "But a woman traveling alone, man, I'd sleep with one eye open and both hands on that gun," the first one said.

"I was in Manhattan when the quarantine happened," April said. "I can take care of myself."

"Manhattan? Damn. I guess you can. How'd you get out?"

April considered an honest answer. Oh, I found a reclusive scientist who wrote a book that predicted the Dollar Bug, and he called in a favor with an order of militant monks who showed me how to run the blockade and gave me a piece of priceless art to trade for a ride up to the far end of the Erie Canal.

But instead, she just said, "That's a long story. How far is it to the docks in Buffalo?"

It turned out to be about ten miles. April made the trip with a caravan of horse-drawn wagons bringing goods from the canal barges to either waiting lake boats or vendors in the marketplace that had sprung up on Buffalo's waterfront. She sat in the back of a wagon whose sides were still painted with advertisements for hayrides, going straight down Military Road and then the freeway spur that ran along the river. It started to rain, changing the river from bright blue to a steely gray, and by the time they got to the Buffalo waterfront, she was glad she had a good coat.

When she swung down from the wagon in the middle of the market, she was besieged by people trying to sell her everything from eggs to allergy pills. Kids ran back and forth, carrying vegetables or chickens. She almost ran into a young girl holding a stick with a dozen fish strung on it by their gills. "Fresh-caught walleye," the girl said with a hopeful smile.

"I wish," April said. She'd been eating mostly dried meats and fruit since she left New York. "But I'm traveling."

The girl went on, hawking her fish to the rest of the caravan. April went on, too, looking for a boat. Even without the threat of the Jamestown Aryans, walking from Buffalo to Ann Arbor would take her at least ten days. The slowest boat would save a lot of time over that.

As she passed through the market, April refilled her water bottles and traded an Ace bandage and a container of dental floss for a dozen hard-boiled eggs and a bundle of greenhouse carrots. Added to the venison jerky and cheese she'd picked up at stops along the canal, that would feed her for a good few days.

Then she got to the marina. Several sailboats and one paddlewheel steamboat were tied up, rocking in the waves kicked up by the rainstorm. She didn't see anyone on any of their decks, but smoke was coming from the steamboat's stack. That was interesting. How did they get fuel? Or had they retrofitted the boat so the boiler was fired with wood?

She walked over to the bottom of the gangplank and called out. "Hello! Anyone home? Permission to come aboard?"

An old man stuck his head out of the wheelhouse window, his hat falling off to reveal a liver-spotted expanse of scalp fringed with wild white hair. "What? Yeah. Who are you?"

Rather than shout back over the rain, April walked up the gangplank. She picked up his hat as he was coming out of the wheelhouse and handed it to him. "I'm hoping to get passage," she said.

"To where?"

"Ideally Toledo, but I'll take what I can get."

He got his hat settled on his head again and wiped rain from his face. "You carry that shooter just for show, or can you use it?"

"I don't like to, but I can."

"I'm going to Cleveland. That suit you?"

"That suits me fine."

"All right, then." He stuck out his hand and April shook. "Dirk Schuler. You are...?"

"April Kelleher."

"There's berths down below, April. Drop your pack." Schuler turned, beckoning her to follow. "But keep the gun handy. We leave in an hour, and the first part of the trip is always the worst."

He led her down belowdecks and showed her a bunk. "We got three other crew, and passengers. Should take about nine hours to get to Cleveland, depending on the wind. I'll even throw in dinner."

"Sounds good," April said. "What did you mean about the first part being the worst?"

"That's where we're most likely to run into the local pirates," Schuler said, heading back up to the deck. April followed. "Yeah, I heard about them. But the sailors up in Tonawanda said they weren't as bad as the

Jamestown Aryans."

"Nobody's as bad as the Jamestown Aryans," Schuler said. He looked up at the sky. The rain was clearing. "So that ain't much of a bar to clear."

The rest of the crew were coming up the gangplank, carrying satchels stuffed with goods from the market. Behind them came a dozen or so passengers. The stern deck was covered with cargo. "Where'd you find this boat?" April asked.

"It used to run tourists around on one of the lakes in upstate New York," Schuler said. "I forget which one. Some guy brought it down the canal right after they got the canal open, maybe in March, and then... well, what I said about the first part of the trip being the worst? I was on this boat the first time he fired it up to go over to Cleveland. He didn't live through the trip. After that it was my boat."

As he spoke, he was watching the crew stow their gear and lead the passengers into the cabin. Now he turned to April and his face was dead serious. "I meant what I said about keeping that gun handy."

CHAPTER 27

VIOLET

Three or four days after the kids had met Sebastian at the carousel, Junie led a group of adults on a trip over to the White House to talk to the JTF. They were gone all day, and when they came back, they called a meeting for after dinner. "Everyone," Junie said.

"Kids, too?" Mike asked.

"Kids, too. They need to hear this."

Dinner was quieter than usual that evening. Everyone knew something big was going on, but only a few of them knew what it was, and Junie had asked them not to say anything until she'd spoken. It was strange, too, because the food was better than what they'd had the past couple of weeks. The garden had started to produce, and there were fresh green beans along with striped bass, which were running in the rivers. Mike had found a spot to fish down by where the Anacostia River ran into the Potomac. It was far enough away from the center of DC that nobody wanted to fight over it. At least not yet.

Eventually almost everyone was done except the really slow eaters, and Junie stood. She tapped a spoon against a glass, and

195

the conversations in the room quieted. "I know that's supposed to be a wedding thing," she said, "but I couldn't think of another way to get y'all's attention. We have a serious thing to decide."

Mike stood next to her and added, "Really. Everyone. Listen up. We're not talking about how to assign chores here. This is... well, it might be life or death."

That got people's attention. It sure got Violet's. She looked around at the other kids. As usual they were all in a group together. Sometimes one of the other kids in the Castle group would join them, if they'd been playing a game or something together that day, but usually those kids stayed with their families. Violet and her friends didn't have families.

Well, she thought, Ivan and Amelia had their dad. If he was still alive.

Junie was talking again. "A few days ago we were approached by one of the organized militia groups here in DC. You've all seen them. This one is maybe better than some of the others. They're not apocalyptic maniacs, at least. But they are what they are. They believe power comes from the barrel of a gun, and they believe their ideas are better because they have more guns. I don't believe that. I believe that we stand or fall together, and that right and power usually don't have anything to do with each other." She paused as someone in the room made a rude noise. Violet couldn't tell who. Junie looked in the direction of the noise for a long moment before going on. "But that's philosophy, and this is the real world. The short version is this: They offered us a deal. We join up with them, and they'll offer us protection against all the other groups fighting to control this city and this country."

"In return for tribute," Mike interjected.

An angry murmur rose in the room, but fell again as Junie

raised both of her hands. "Please. We might not have known it until just now, but we're in the middle of a battle that's coming, and the stakes are what kind of country we're going to live in from here on out. The virus took away the America we had. Now the question is what kind of America we're going to have.

"Those men up in the Capitol—and they're in the Smithsonian museums, too; they're close to taking over everything to the east and south of us—they have a vision that I don't agree with. But I also have a responsibility to every man, woman, and child here in the Castle. So I have a question to put to all of you. I'm going to lay out the stakes, and then we're going to vote, and we're going to live with the results of that vote no matter what. That's democracy. That's the ideal we all believe in, or at least I hope we do."

Every man, woman, and child, Violet thought. Were the kids really going to get a vote? Would anyone care what they thought? Something about that man Sebastian scared Violet. She knew Amelia and Saeed felt the same way. There was something about the way he'd walked up to them on the carousel. She didn't know the word for it. Something about his smile didn't seem real. She didn't trust him, and she was glad to see Junie didn't seem to, either.

"So after they came to talk to us, I did what I thought was the responsible thing," Junie went on. "I went and talked to the JTF. I told them what these men said, and asked the JTF what they really thought about what this city and this country were going to look like in the next year. The JTF people were courteous and caring, as they always are. But they're also realists. They know the resources they have, and the things they can and cannot do.

"Here's what the JTF told me: They are understaffed and overwhelmed. They're trying as hard as they can to keep things safe for us and for the other settlements, at Ford's Theatre and wherever else. But they know other groups are trying to take control of DC. They also know that the government can't do anything about it. President Ellis is doing everything he can to keep things together, but... well, you see what it's like out there."

Someone broke in here. "Ellis? What happened to Mendez?" Eliezer Mendez had been vice president when the virus struck, and ascended to the Oval Office when President Waller had caught the Green Poison and died in January. At least that was the official story. None of them knew what had really happened.

"They wouldn't tell me that, but he seems to have died," Junie said. "So that made Andrew Ellis next in line."

There was grumbling in the crowd here. Ellis had not been popular in DC. "I didn't vote for him," a man sitting near the children muttered.

"None of us did," Junie answered. "I'm not even sure what state he's from. But he's the president now because that's how the succession works, until we can have another election. We have to choose. Do we believe in the institutions we had before, or are we going to let those go and be part of this new reality going forward? Do we ally ourselves with those men who occupy the Capitol Building, or do we hang on to what we had before and what we might have again?"

"Wait," a woman at the far end of Junie's table said. "You didn't tell us the rest about what the JTF said."

"They said this. We need to fortify the Castle and be ready for a storm. They'll try to help, but if that storm comes they can't promise they'll be ready to keep us from being blown away." Junie sighed. "After talking to those men who are occupying the Castle, I think the JTF is probably right.

There's a battle coming, and we want to stay out of it. The best way to do that is hunker down and try to protect ourselves until it's over."

"What if we do that and those people in the Capitol win?" a woman called out from the far side of the room. Violet recognized her. She had been a cop somewhere in Virginia. "They're going to think we sided with the JTF."

"And they would be right," Junie said. "If you believe the United States of America still exists, you just about have to side with the JTF. If you don't believe that... well, we all remember what Abe Lincoln said, right? A house divided against itself cannot stand. We've got a choice to make. Which future are we going to believe in? I know what I believe."

"Believing isn't going to save us if they decide to come kill us all," the former cop said.

"No, it won't," Junie agreed. "But if we give up before the battle even happens, we've decided we don't believe in the United States anymore. We don't believe in the Constitution anymore. Are we ready to say that?"

People were uneasy, muttering to themselves and the people next to them. Junie looked over them, then glanced over at Mike. He nodded, in what Violet thought was an encouraging way. Then he stood up next to Junie.

"I get it," he said. "You're worried that when push comes to shove, the JTF won't be able to protect us. We're worried about that, too. But I don't trust those people over in the Capitol to protect us, either. They see us as a foreign element in territory they believe is theirs. Is that what you want to be? Or do we want to be American citizens? I say we go with the JTF plan for now. If things change in the next month or so, we can reconsider, but we're okay right now. If we invite an armed rebel group into the Castle, we're putting ourselves right in the crosshairs when the fight comes."

"Think on it," Junie said. "Sleep on it. If we want to have a vote, we'll do that, but we'll do it tomorrow."

She sat back down. Mike did, too. The only sounds in the room were people shuffling their feet and shifting their weight. Then people started to get up and go about the business of clearing the dishes and cleaning up. Nobody had much to say.

Later that night, when the kids were all in their room and just about to blow out the candles and go to sleep, Junie tapped at their door and came in. "We need to talk," she said.

"We didn't ask those people to come to the Castle," Amelia said right away. "They came up to us, and…"

"And we were scared," Violet said.

"Yeah. We wanted to get home, but they asked to come along, and we couldn't say no." Saeed was buried in blankets, only his head visible.

"I understand why you did that, but you should know you can't trust those people." Junie settled herself on an empty couch. "I'm not sure you can trust anyone except the JTF to do the right thing. There are groups all over this city, and every one of them thinks they can take it all. They're like hungry dogs fighting over a scrap of meat."

"That makes us the scrap of meat," Wiley said.

"That's what we're trying to avoid," Junie said. "As long as we stick together, it'll be all right."

"Will it?" Shelby's voice was small, coming out of the corner under the window where she liked to sleep.

"It will. Keep believing. That's how you make things happen, children." Junie got up and blew out the last candle. "Now, you get some sleep. We're going to have a lot of work to do these next few days."

CHAPTER 28

AURELIO

Aurelio had imagined a number of different possible ways to get across Pennsylvania and Ohio, but riding on an Amish version of the Pony Express had not been one of them. Yet here he was, on the fifth leg of the journey. He'd picked up the first ride back in Clearfield, then switched in Clarion, Slippery Rock, Salem, and Orrville. Before the last couple of days he'd never even heard of any of those towns. He'd never spoken to an Amish person. In fact, he'd considered the Amish semimythical, like cowboys or mountain men. Instead he found them—at least the men who drove their wagons over long distances—to be practical, taciturn, a bit standoffish, but generous in their way. The plague hadn't affected them that much because they rejected most twentieth-century technologies anyway. Lucas, the man currently sitting in the driver's seat of the wagon next to Aurelio, had a theory that their rejection of modern life had helped them survive the virus. "So you had how many dead there in New York? Seven of ten? Eight of ten?"

"Not quite that many, I don't think," Aurelio said. "But it might be close."

"We had three of ten in our community," Lucas informed him. "The Lord watches his own."

Aurelio wasn't a religious man, but he didn't want to argue about it. "Could be," he said.

"Is," Lucas said.

They were coming into Willard, Ohio. It looked to Aurelio like a typical little town out in the middle of nowhere: a strip of stores on the main drag, some franchises and some local, surrounded by a few blocks of houses and then two-lane roads spoking off into the flat expanses of farmland in all directions. In the parking lot of a farm equipment dealership, the local Amish had set up a trading post. Lucas halted the wagon next to a row of similar-looking wagons and got out.

Aurelio followed, glad to be standing up again, even if it was only for a few minutes. A group of teenage boys started swapping bags and boxes from the back of Lucas's wagon to an empty one nearby. Lucas approached the driver, who nodded a greeting.

"This English here, he's going to Toledo," Lucas said, indicating Aurelio, who even after a few days still found it strange that they referred to him as English. Apparently it was what they called anyone who wasn't Amish.

"Well, I'm not going to Toledo," the other man said. "Headed up to Sandusky to trade for some fish."

Lucas looked at Aurelio. "Where's Sandusky?" Aurelio asked.

The two Amish men looked at each other. "Forty, fifty miles from Toledo?" Lucas suggested.

"Closer to fifty, I think," the other man said. To Aurelio he added, "Right on the lake."

"Well," Aurelio said, "that's closer than I am now. I'd be grateful for the ride."

The Amish took off his hat, swiped a sleeve across his brow, and put the hat back on. He stuck out a hand. "Frank Rentschler." He was about fifty, with salt-and-pepper hair and beard, a sharp contrast between the white of his forehead and the sunbaked brown of his cheeks. When they shook hands, Aurelio could feel the strength of a man who spent his time outside.

He helped Frank finish loading the wagon and then they headed out, following a county road more or less due north. "How long do you think it'll take to get there?"

"Six, seven hours," Frank said, keeping his eyes on the horses. "Depends on if there's trouble at the turnpike."

"What kind of trouble would that be?"

"Bandits sometimes." Frank nodded down at the seat between them, and Aurelio saw a sawed-off shotgun leaning against it, its muzzle next to Frank's right foot.

When they got closer to the turnpike on Route 99, Aurelio saw that the road went straight ahead under the highway, but there was also a side approach to a turnpike interchange with Highway 4. "That's the main road into Sandusky," Frank said. "If you want to deal with the bandits." He nodded straight ahead. "This way takes a little longer, but it's usually less trouble."

A few hundred yards from the turnpike underpass, Frank added, "Never been on the turnpike in my life. Just a big road, right?"

"I haven't, either," said Aurelio. "I grew up in Washington, DC. But, yeah, it's just a big road. Six lanes."

"Rode in a car a few times during my Rumspringa. Then I came back home, and now here we are thirty years later, and the rest of the world came back to us. Not too many people in cars now, are there?"

"Not too many, no," Aurelio said. He saw heads pop up over the bridge railing on the turnpike. "Looks like someone's watching us."

"Huh," Frank commented. "Best to get through quick." He flicked the reins and the horses started to trot.

"Hey, Amish!" one of the men on the bridge shouted when they drew close enough to hear. He jabbed an arm off to their left, where the Highway 4 interchange was. "All traffic through there onto Route 4!"

Aurelio swung the G36 up and slipped the safety off, keeping it low enough that it would stay out of sight to anyone up on the bridge. "You don't want to go through the interchange, right?"

Frank moved his head maybe an inch side to side. "Nope." He kept the horses at a trot.

"What do you think they're going to do about it?"

"Hard telling."

In the shadows under the bridge, Aurelio saw motion. Then four men appeared. Two had handguns, one an AR-15. "It's not going to go well if we stop, right?"

Another tiny shake of Frank's head. The man under the bridge brought up the AR-15. Two of the other men held up their hands, palms out.

"When I shoot," Aurelio said, "I need you to find out how fast these horses can go."

Frank nodded. "Problem isn't the horses. It's the wagon."

They were forty yards away. Thirty.

At twenty, Aurelio raised the G36 and fired.

Shooting a moving target was hard. Shooting a stationary target from a moving vehicle was also hard, especially when your field of fire was constrained by the heads of two horses right in front of you. Aurelio's first burst missed. The bandit with the AR flinched away rather than returning fire, though, which not only told Aurelio they were dealing with amateurs but gave him time to shoot again.

This time he hit the target, somewhere in the legs. At the same time, Frank shouted, "Hyaahh!" and lashed the reins across the horses' backs. They surged forward, scattering the men under the bridge.

Except one, who turned and ran away straight in front of them. Then, as the wagon passed, he leaped and caught hold of the right-hand horse's tack. He swung a leg up onto the yoke holding them in harness and drew a gun.

Frank was shouting something, but Aurelio didn't hear it. They were already under the bridge and out into the sunlight on the other side, but if this guy shot the horses they were going to have the whole gang of bandits on them in minutes. And if Aurelio tried to shoot him from that angle, he was pretty likely to take out one of the horses himself.

He dropped the G36 on the floor and vaulted over the front of the wagon onto the horse's back. With one hand he grabbed onto its harness, and with the other he chopped down hard on the bandit's forearm. The gun went off, but the bandit dropped it to clatter away under the wagon. Aurelio had never ridden a horse before, and it was all he could do to stay on its back. He threw a punch at the bandit, but couldn't get much behind it.

The bandit drew a knife and slashed at Aurelio, who caught his arm and tried to twist it away. But he had no leverage without letting go of the horse's harness, and if he did that he was going to end up down between the horses and then under the wagon. The bandit wasn't much better off. They were in a stalemate. Behind them Aurelio heard gunshots, but the wagon kept barreling down the road.

The bandit whipped his arm in a tight circle, breaking Aurelio's grasp. An old trick, but one that worked every time when your opponent didn't have the leverage to move. Then he thrust the knife low, straight at Aurelio's belly.

There was no choice. Aurelio swiveled to one side and clamped his elbow on the bandit's arm, trapping it against his rib cage. Already losing his balance on the horse, he let go of the harness and grabbed onto the bandit's shirt. If he was going, they both were going.

The horse bounced him off, and he pulled the bandit with him. Aurelio tried to turn in midair so he would land on the bandit instead of the pavement. He was half-successful. The bandit hit the road first, flat on his back. A split second later, Aurelio's right shoulder came down on his sternum. A split second after that, carried forward by the horses' momentum, the side of Aurelio's head hit the pavement. He sprawled away from the bandit, rolled, and came to a halt facedown on the gravel shoulder of the road. He heard sounds, but they sounded far away, and he wasn't quite sure where his hands were. When he lifted his head, he had trouble focusing his eyes.

A few yards away, the bandit was curled up on his side, gasping for breath. Aurelio got slowly to his hands and knees, then tried to stand. He couldn't quite do it. He sat there on the gravel, taking deep breaths.

A shadow fell over him and he looked up to see Frank. "Got my bell rung when I hit the road," he managed to say.

"I can tell," Frank said. "You're bleeding pretty good."

Aurelio hadn't noticed, but now that Frank mentioned it, he

could feel the blood on the side of his face.

"Come on," Frank said, and he helped Aurelio to his feet. "We can't stop here."

He got Aurelio back into the wagon and they kept going at a trot. Aurelio was starting to get his head together again. He felt the side of his face and found two cuts, one at the outer edge of his eyebrow and another on his cheekbone. That was what those bones were designed to do, he thought. At least I still have my eye.

"I thank you, Mr. Diaz," Frank said. "Those men would have taken everything I own, and might have killed me. They've done it to others."

"Happy to help," Aurelio said. Then the motion of the wagon finally got to him and he threw up over the side.

When he was done, Frank said, "You got a pretty good concussion there, I bet."

"I might," Aurelio agreed. His vision had resolved, and he wasn't having any cognitive troubles. Who was president? Andrew Ellis. What month was it? May.

He swished some water around in his mouth and spit it out onto the road. Back in New York, he might have taken a day off to make sure the symptoms didn't stick around and indicate an actual brain injury. Out here, though, he didn't have those kinds of resources, and he didn't have that kind of time. He had to find Ike Ronson.

A few miles down the road, Frank reined the horses back to a walk.

"They'll be coming after us, won't they?" Aurelio asked. His shoulder was killing him. He was pretty sure he'd separated it, but it wasn't popping out of joint when he moved it, so with any luck it would heal with rest.

Not that he had time to rest.

"Might be," Frank said. "But I can't afford to hurt my horses. Hurt 'em more, I should say."

At first Aurelio wasn't sure what he meant, but when he took a closer look at the horses he saw one of them was bleeding. Frank brought them to a halt and they got out. Aurelio watched back down the road for pursuit while Frank checked on the horse. His eye was starting to swell. "Lucky," Frank said after a minute. "Looks like it just peeled away some skin."

Aurelio came around to see. The bandit's bullet had plowed a furrow about six inches long on the horse's rib cage. But there was no exposed bone. "If you have to get shot, that's the way to do it," Aurelio said.

Frank patted the horse's forehead. "I guess," he said and climbed back into the wagon. "Let's get on to Sandusky before it gets dark. I can stitch you up there."

CHAPTER 29

APRIL

The steamer's first stop was in Erie, a fact that Captain Schuler had neglected to mention to April when she got on board. "I thought we were going to Cleveland," she said.

"We are, after we go to Erie." He started shouting instructions at the crew. April leaned against the outside wall of the wheelhouse, fuming as the steamer eased through the channel from the lake into Presque Isle Bay. Before that moment, she had never given Erie, Pennsylvania, a single thought, but the harbor setting was picturesque. Probably it had been a nice small city before the Dollar Bug. Hard to tell what it was like now, though the waterfront just this side of the channel was bustling. She even saw uniformed police officers. A row of small windmills spun in the shore breeze at the far end of the harbor, and somewhere along the docks she heard the unmistakable rattle of a generator. Did they have electricity here? How much?

It was becoming clearer to April that the effects of the virus varied pretty widely. Some places seemed completely depopulated, but in others people seemed to have reestablished something like an equilibrium. For every burned-out ruin she'd seen, there was another place where people had pulled together, survived, and maybe begun to thrive again. For every territory controlled by the Jamestown Aryans, there was a town like Erie, where people of every color seemed to be working together toward the common goal of getting through the day.

New York wasn't the whole world. That was good to know.

Still, she was irritated with Schuler for not being completely truthful about their itinerary. Also for making it sound like they were going to be under attack during the entire trip. They had only seen three other boats the whole trip, largely because they'd stayed out of sight of land. The lake was calm in the aftermath of the brief rainstorm, and Schuler held a course straight across to Erie instead of hugging the shore.

"Sometimes we ride the Canadian border the whole way until we're due north of Erie, then cut down," one of the crew had told her when they were about halfway there. He was soaked with sweat from stoking the boiler and had come up on deck to take a break and cool off. Ash speckled his dreadlocks. "The Canadian Coast Guard will yell at you to get away from the border, but they also usually help out if you get in trouble."

"Usually?"

"Can't always count on anybody," the stoker said. He'd drunk two liters of water since coming up on the deck. He untied the bandanna holding his locs, shook them out, and retied them. "Two hours to Erie, give or take," he said and went back below. April watched the southern horizon, waiting until land came into view again.

Erie? April went to find Schuler.

* * *

Now there they were, waiting to take on firewood and offload a few passengers. Nobody else got on. After ninety minutes and a fierce negotiation between Schuler and the dockworkers who loaded the wood, they chugged back out the channel onto the lake again, making the turn around Presque Isle and angling southwest toward Cleveland.

April went up into the wheelhouse and found Schuler steering the boat around a wrecked freighter that lay half-sunk in the shallows. "We'll be in Cleveland by tonight," he said.

"Okay. Doesn't seem to be much trouble out on the water." April watched the wreck slide by. It seemed to have run aground, and then the winter had already begun to break it apart. She wondered if the crew had died of the virus and left the ship to drift.

"Not yet. We've been lucky so far." Schuler glanced over at her. "But don't let your guard down."

"I spent five months in Manhattan. I'm not sure I could let my guard down even if I wanted to."

"Is that right," Schuler said. "What's it like there? It looked pretty bad on TV before the power went out." "It was pretty bad. It's a little better now."

"But not so good that you wanted to stay. I mean, you must really have wanted to get the hell out of there to risk heading out by yourself."

"I wanted to see the rest of the country," she said. "It's interesting how different things are. Every twenty miles things change."

"So you ran the blockade to be a tourist." Schuler's tone told April he didn't believe her.

"No, I'm looking for someone," she said. It was true in a way. She was looking to complete her final picture of Bill, his life and death.

"Uh-huh." With the wrecked freighter behind them, Schuler called down the old-fashioned voice tube to the boiler room. "Full steam."

"Full steam, aye, aye," a voice floated back up.

A minute or so later, the paddlewheel started to dig harder into the lake, and April felt the boat accelerate. It was kind of a thrill. She hadn't been on any kind of motorized transportation since the first week of December. It lifted her mood, just like seeing those windmills had lifted her mood. People were hanging on. And if the BSAV was real, and the government hung together long enough to help distribute it, maybe things really were about to start getting better.

Her good mood held all the way to Cleveland, which announced itself from miles across the lake with the unmistakable glow of electric light in the sky. "My God," April said. "Does the whole city have electricity there?"

"Oh, no," Schuler said. "Not hardly. Just a couple of areas down near the water. JTF has things settled down enough that they've got some big generators wired up, and I think some windmills, too, down the shore."

They slowed and cruised into a container port next to a lakefront airfield. When they had the boat moored, April said, "Sure you're not going any farther?"

"Yep," Schuler answered. "We're picking up cargo and passengers, getting a good night's sleep, and heading back to Buffalo."

"All right, then," April said. "Thanks for the ride."

"You're welcome. Glad you didn't have to show me you know how to use the shotgun there. You're about a hundred miles from Toledo if you stay on Route 2 along the lake."

"Good to know. Any idea what it's like along the way?"

"Nope," Schuler said. "But there's a JTF base over at the football stadium." He pointed west, and April saw the stadium looming on the lakeshore. It was one of the places that had power. "You might try there."

"I will. Good luck with those pirates," April said.

"Consider yourself lucky you missed them," Schuler shot back. He went belowdecks to yell at the stokers, and April walked around the glass pyramids of the Rock and Roll Hall of Fame in the direction of the stadium. She passed crews loading and unloading other boats. Again it struck her how different things were here than back in Manhattan. Without a blockade to deal with, people were trading here, keeping themselves alive. She wondered what would happen if the blockade on Manhattan was lifted. Would the island export its troubles to Brooklyn and Queens and the Bronx, or would the situation stabilize as people found themselves able to get the things they needed without engaging smugglers and black-market middlemen?

If she ever went back, maybe she would find out.

That thought had never occurred to her before. She didn't have to go back. It was a little too big to wrestle with right then, so she just let it sit in the back of her mind while she walked around the Great Lakes Science Center toward the open eastern end of the football stadium. A perimeter of Jersey barriers extended a hundred yards from the entrance, with a fortified JTF checkpoint at its only gate. She walked up, careful to keep her hands in view and the shotgun slung over her back.

"Hold on," the sentry said. "Identify yourself."

"My name is April Kelleher. I'm looking for a way to get to Ann Arbor, Michigan, and I'm wondering if you can help."

"Help how? Give you a ride? I don't see that happening."

"I'd settle for some advice. What's the situation like between here and there?"

The sentry pushed his helmet back. He was maybe twenty years old. "What are you going to do, walk?"

"If there's no other way to get there, yeah."

"Forgive me saying so, ma'am, but that's nuts."

"Maybe." You should hear about some of the stuff I've already done, April thought. Then you'd really think it was nuts.

"Well, the suburbs out to the west are pretty much emptied out," the sentry said after a pause. "If you go that way, I'd stay real close to the lake, especially when you get out by the old steelworks. We've had trouble there. Past that, jeez, I don't know. It's pretty much country from there to Toledo, except right around Sandusky."

"Thanks," April said. "That's the kind of information I was looking for. Do you mind if I refill my water before I go on?"

"Be my guest." The sentry stood aside and pointed at a tanker truck sitting just past the checkpoint inside the security perimeter.

April filled both of her water bottles, then drained one and refilled it again. Plenty of times along the trip she'd drunk from a stream, and her stomach was used to it now, but she wasn't sure it was a good idea so close to the city. Even with industry shut down, there were enough toxins left in those rivers to be washing out for decades.

She had just gotten her pack resettled on her back when a voice behind her said, "Excuse me."

She turned and saw a Division agent. Lean, with dark skin and eyes, suspicious set to his face. He cradled a FN SCAR assault rifle. "Hi," she said.

"You mind telling me where you got that pack? And the Super 90?"

Looking him right in the eye, she said, "I recovered them from the body of a Division agent named Doug Sutton, who died saving my life."

"Is that so," he said.

"It is," she said. "I was being held hostage, along with some friends of mine, by a violent gang. He found us."

"Where was this?"

"New York."

"New York?" the agent echoed. "What the hell are you doing in Ohio?"

"Passing through as fast as I can," April said.

He looked at her for a long time. She had a feeling he was already receiving information from the Division's comms system about whether or not there was an agent in New York named Doug Sutton, and what they knew about the circumstances of his death. "Listen, a word of advice. There are a lot of agents who would not give you the benefit of the doubt the way I did," he said.

"What exactly do you mean by that?" April asked, even though she was pretty sure she knew.

"I mean quite a few agents tend to shoot first and ask questions later when they see a civilian wearing Division gear. Nine times out of ten the person wearing it is the person who killed the agent. Only reason I didn't put you down is you were already inside a JTF perimeter and I didn't figure you'd be dumb enough to start anything in here."

One other time an agent had noticed her Division gear and spoken to her about it. That was right before she'd gone into the Dark Zone for the first time. He hadn't said anything about agents killing people who scavenged Division gear. Maybe it was a new thing. Or maybe not every agent did it.

"Well, thank you for the consideration, Agent," April said. "I'm going to go now. I have a long trip ahead of me."

"To where?"

"Ann Arbor."

"What's in Ann Arbor?"

"Answers about who killed my husband, if I'm lucky," she said. Already the partial truth had come to seem natural. Soon, if she got to Ann Arbor, she would have to start asking about SBGx and the broad-spectrum antiviral... but she wasn't going to just yet.

"All right." The agent was giving her a hard look, but he wasn't pointing his gun at her just yet. "ISAC tells me your story about Agent Sutton checks out. You're free to go, but I'm telling you, it's not smart to be wearing our gear if you're not one of us."

"I appreciate the heads-up, Agent," April said.

He turned away, and she got the hell out of there.

The sun was getting low, but she wanted to get out of Cleveland into the rural areas where she would be less likely to run into other agents. Now that she had the warning in mind, April realized that she couldn't count on Division agents to help her. They had their own code of honor, and to a lot of them, apprehending her—or worse— would be a way of upholding it.

So she had to move, and move fast.

Around the other side of the stadium was a large undeveloped area covered with vehicles. Most of them were horse- or ox-drawn, but April heard engines running, and smelled... french fries? She hunted through the rows of trucks and wagons until she came to an idling flatbed with two men standing in the bed lashing down sections of steel scaffolding. At the back of the cab stood two large plastic barrels filled with what could only be fryer oil. The smell was intense, and it filled April with nostalgia for fast food, which she had rarely eaten before the virus.

She'd heard of people doing conversions on cars and trucks to run on vegetable oil, but this was the first time she'd ever seen one of them. "Excuse me," she said. "Where are you going?"

"Out by the airport," one of the men said.

"Which way is that?"

He pointed west.

"I have a favor to ask you," she said, "and an offer to make." He stood up, finished with the scaffolding, and said, "What?"

April dropped her pack and got out the plastic bag Sonia had given her at the end of the canal trip. She pinched a tiny tear in the bag and held it up. "Smell that."

He bent his face to the tear and inhaled. His eyes got wide.

"Five pounds of tobacco," April said. "Half of it's yours if you give me a ride to Michigan right now."

"Where in Michigan?"

"Ann Arbor."

He thought it over. "Don't have the fuel to get there and back. But I'll get you to Toledo."

"Deal," April said. She climbed onto the bed of the truck and settled herself next to the barrels. Patting the bag of tobacco, she added, "Can we go now?"

CHAPTER 30

IKE

The next time Ike checked in with Mantis, from inside a huge outdoors and camping store in Dundee, Michigan, he got a big surprise.

"We have an important update for you, Sentinel: April Kelleher was in Cleveland twelve hours ago."

"She was?" Twelve hours ago Ike had rolled into the vast parking lot in front of this store. Then he'd had a little trouble with locals who took exception with him going into the store, but he'd taken care of them, no fuss no muss. Then he'd passed the night in a brand-new sleeping bag from the camping section, and this morning he felt ready to take on the world.

"A Division agent called her out for wearing SHD gear," Mantis said. "He let her go after she explained where she got it, but he reported the interaction and it was entered in SHD operational logs."

She was lucky, Ike thought. He would probably have knocked her out and taken her in for a more forceful interrogation. A lot of agents would have. But without knowing the whole circumstance, he wasn't going to judge. The whole point of the

Division was agents had the discretion to assess a situation. The agent in Cleveland had the same training Ike had; for all Ike knew, he would have done the same, although his instinct would have been to assume she was hostile.

"So if she was in Cleveland twelve hours ago…" Ike calculated. Walking, she would be close to Toledo by now.

"The surveilling agent reported that she confirmed her destination as Ann Arbor. Proceed there immediately, Sentinel."

"Probably better if I intercept her before she gets there, Mantis," Ike answered. "That will give me more time to gain trust."

"We have considered that, Sentinel. Our judgment is that it is not worth the risk of having her reach her objective before you contact her. Imperative that you make contact before she does that."

"Understood, Mantis. It would be easier if you told me what you know about where she's going."

Mantis paused. This was the moment where they decided how much they were going to trust him, Ike knew. And based on their decision, he was going to know more about how much he could trust them.

"Our assessment is that her likely destination is the North Campus of the University of Michigan," Mantis said.

"That's useful," Ike said. "It would be more useful if—"

"That's all we're going to share at this point, Sentinel. Proceed to Ann Arbor. Intercept and assist April Kelleher while ascertaining her objective. Those are your orders. Is that understood?"

"Understood."

Mantis ended the transmission.

Ike was maybe ninety minutes by bike from Ann Arbor, if he kept a lively pace. He looked outside. The weather was holding for now, but there were clouds in the west. He kicked through the looted ruin of the store for a while, hoping to turn up something he could use, but the people of Dundee had been thorough. Other than new socks and underwear, he came up empty.

Still, that was something. He got changed and wheeled the bike outside, mapping April Kelleher's potential routes in his head. If she was on foot, she would have to go through Toledo, and then common sense dictated she would come up U.S. 23, which ran straight north from Toledo to the east side of Ann Arbor. Ike could see it from the parking lot of the store as he checked his tires.

The wild card was Lake Erie. Ike had largely avoided unnecessary human contact on his trip across Ohio, but going through Toledo he'd seen a lot of boat traffic on the river, and some vessels headed out onto the lake. Before the automobile, boats had been a lot faster than land travel. It was by and large the same now, for people who weren't going to do a hundred miles a day on a bike. Ike wasn't going to do that for much longer. He was eating like a horse to keep up his energy, but even so, he didn't have access to the kind of calorie intake necessary to ride that hard. Once he got to Ann Arbor, he was going to leave the bike behind for a while.

If he succeeded in the mission, he had a feeling he wouldn't need it. Mantis's group had access to a lot of hardware, including vehicles. He knew that from her recruitment pitch, and he believed it because it fit with her access to advanced technologies—like the ISAC countermeasure that was still keeping his watch face orange and his name out of ISAC's rogue agent roster.

Ike felt he was close. Close to understanding who Mantis's people were, and close to becoming part of their project.

All he had to do was get to Ann Arbor before April Kelleher, and then make sure not to miss her when she arrived.

Which brought him back around to the lake. If she went by boat, it would probably take her up to Detroit, so she would be coming toward Ann Arbor from the east along Interstate 94. That highway intersected U.S. 23 just on the edge of Ann Arbor. Ike used ISAC to pull up a more detailed map of Ann Arbor. The University of Michigan's North Campus was also off U.S. 23, but farther north than the I-94 interchange. If Kelleher knew to go there, and she was coming from the east, she might enter Ann Arbor from farther north.

This was a tricky problem. Kelleher could be within a couple miles of his location right now, or she could still be approaching Toledo, or she could be on a boat somewhere in Lake Erie.

He ran through the possibilities one more time and decided that, whether she was going by land or water, she was going to be coming into Ann Arbor from the east. So his first task was to get there. He would figure out the rest of it from there.

He reached the I-94 interchange at around oh nine hundred and looked around. There wasn't much to see, just miles of empty roadway and a few abandoned buildings sitting in acres of weedy parking lot. A movie theater; what looked like a self-storage place with rows of aluminum sheds. To the south was mostly parkland.

Farther north, Ike came to another interchange, where Washtenaw Avenue crossed under the highway. A large shopping center sprawled just to the west, and in the parking lot there was a JTF field base. He circled down the ramp and approached. If April Kelleher had already arrived, she might have checked in with the JTF to ask questions. Or she might not have. One problem Ike had was that he didn't know how much she knew. It was possible she was going to make a beeline directly for a particular location, with a specific goal in mind. It was also possible she was in more or less the same situation he was, with an objective in mind but a lot of uncertainty surrounding the final steps toward achieving it.

The sentries at the JTF base hailed him and he waved back as he dismounted and walked his bike up to the checkpoint. "Where you coming from?" one of them asked, just making conversation. They looked well rested and calm. They even had recent haircuts.

"I've been on the road a while," Ike said. "I'm looking for someone, wondering if she might have checked in here."

"Most passing civilians don't," the other guard said. "Unless there's some kind of problem. Which there hasn't been much in this area. Most of the people left in Ann Arbor are down by the football stadium. That's where the main JTF base is. It's on the south side of town, over that way." He pointed.

Ike filed that away. If the main JTF presence was on the south side of the city, and his operational objective was to the north, that was good. Less chance of a problem when he found out what Kelleher was after and the time came for action. "You have ISAC interface here?"

The first guard nodded back at the mobile command post. "Sure. But most of the SHD stuff is concentrated in Detroit and Lansing. When we see you guys around here, it's usually guarding stuff around campus."

"Well, North Campus," the other one said.

"Where's that?"

The first guard pointed west. "Quickest way to get there from here is to take Huron Parkway. You'll find it about a mile up Washtenaw. Go north; when you cross the river you'll see Fuller Road. Take a left and you'll see the signs. Probably four or five miles from here."

"Thanks," Ike said. "What if the person I'm looking for was coming from Detroit? Which way would she take to get there?"

"Probably the same way, since she'd be coming out 94," the second guard said. "But if she was coming on M-14—"

"Why would she do that?"

"Like if she took a wrong turn and ended up—"

"Don't listen to him," the first guard said. "If she's coming from Detroit, she's coming out 94 or Michigan Avenue. Either one goes right through Ypsi. That's Ypsilanti, the next town east. Then she'd end up either right here on Washtenaw, or she would go up 23 just like you did and get off by the river. Then, just like I said, up Fuller Road."

Ike was struck by how mundane this conversation was. Two guys arguing about directions. He got sentimental for a moment, imagining a United States in which the guys arguing about directions weren't also carrying M16s and trying to maintain the social order.

That, in the end, was why he was doing what he was doing.

"Listen," he said. "I need to ask you a favor. This woman I'm looking for. She's about five-seven, white, has red hair, and is probably carrying a Division-issue backpack. Her name is April Kelleher."

Telling these guys her name was a bit of a risk, but Ike figured she was already on the JTF and SHD radars because of her interaction in Cleveland. So he probably wasn't giving away anything he shouldn't.

Also, the information was having its intended effect, which was to get the JTF guards engaged. A lot of them saw Division agents as commando superheroes, and if a little hero worship could get Ike what he wanted, that was fine.

"So she's one of yours?" the second sentry asked.

"No," Ike said. "That's one reason I need to talk to her." That wasn't exactly true, but the implication that April Kelleher was some kind of dangerous fugitive would also hook the JTF sentries. "If you see her, don't give her a hard time. Raise me via ISAC. I'm Ike Ronson."

"Will do, Agent Ronson," they said in unison.

"Thanks, guys." Ike raised a hand and pedaled away, feeling fairly certain that the sentries would spread the word to other JTF elements in their area. If Kelleher came in from the east, someone would notice and alert Ike.

That meant he could cover the southern approach. Riding back down 23, Ike settled on a railroad bridge in a town by the name of Milan. Just to his north was a small prison, just to the south an abandoned auto parts plant. The presence of the prison set alarm bells ringing in Ike's mind. He'd tangled with the gang formed from escaped prisoners of Rikers Island, and there was no reason to believe a bunch of angry men with no prospects or family ties would behave differently here. So if Kelleher was going to run into trouble along the way, this was a likely spot. Engage and assist, he thought.

There were lights burning in the town as the sun went down. Most of them were concentrated in the small downtown just to the west, but Ike saw people on the factory grounds, too. Other signs of human presence were visible in the cluster of machine shops and auto repair places across the highway from the factory.

If Kelleher was walking, she would still be at least a day away. But she'd clearly found ways to travel faster between New York and Cleveland, so Ike wanted to be ready immediately. He would hunker down in this spot and watch until by his calculations she would already have passed at a walking pace. If he hadn't seen her by then, he would go back to Ann Arbor and start putting plan B into action... whatever plan B turned out to be.

He had thirty-six hours before his next report to Mantis. With any luck the whole mission would be wrapped up by then.

CHAPTER 31

VIOLET

The day after the dinner meeting, the Castle was like an anthill. People in a hurry everywhere, breaking up into teams with different jobs that to Violet seemed to spend a lot of time getting in each other's way. They'd voted by a big margin to place their trust in the JTF, so they were doing what the JTF suggested: fortifying the Castle.

Junie and Mike decided they should establish a barrier around the whole block including the Castle and the two museums surrounding its garden grounds to the south. So one team was making trips to nearby streets, breaking into cars and pushing them into a line that stretched from Twelfth Street past the Sackler Gallery over to the corner of the Arts and Industries Building. Another team was building walls, from plywood, scrap lumber, and scaffolding taken from construction sites, to cover the gaps between the Castle and the two flanking buildings. Those walls were done pretty fast, before lunch, and by early afternoon a line of cars stretched along Independence Avenue, with a gap right in the middle so people could get in and out. "We'll start setting guards here at the entrance," Mike said as he helped get the last car into line. "If we have time, we'll also get a scaffolding wall up behind these cars."

If we have time, Violet thought. She was watching from behind the line of cars. Were they going to be attacked? She heard hammers pounding all over the place, as other grown-ups put plywood sheathing up over the ground-floor windows of the Castle and the other two museums. Violet hated to lose the light inside the Castle, but she had to trust that the adults knew what they were doing.

Other crews were barricading the ground-floor doors of all three buildings, making sure the only approach to the Castle was through the south entrance. They spent the whole day working, and that night the kids were so nervous none of them could sleep. Junie didn't come to visit them, like she often did when she knew they were scared, and that made things even worse. Probably she was still busy with stuff, but Violet wanted to be one of the things Junie was busy with. Most of the day, their only interactions with adults had been running to get things and being told to stay out of the way.

At dinner that night, Mike and Junie had given everyone an update on the progress. The ground floor of the Castle was fairly secure, and so were the spaces between the Castle and the other two buildings. In the morning they would finish covering the windows on the ground floors of the other two buildings— "hardening" them, in Mike's words.

All of the kids had seen gun battles in the months since the virus. Now, up in their room in the dark, they were all wondering whether they were going to live through another one. "You know who's going to help?" Ivan said. "The Division."

"They will," Amelia agreed. "They always do."

They sure had over at the pond, Violet thought. But nearly too late. Still, everything had turned out all right. If only there was a number you could call to make sure the Division was coming.

Of course, then there would have to be phones. And only the JTF and the Division seemed to have any kind of phones or technology anymore.

"The JTF can see us from the White House," Noah said. "If anything bad happens, they'll be right here. It's going to be okay."

"But where do we go if it isn't? We need a plan," Shelby said. For such a little kid—Violet thought she had just turned nine—Shelby was really hung up on plans. Maybe they made her feel more secure. Violet, on the other hand, felt more secure when she felt like nobody was lying to her. Sometimes making a plan was like telling yourself a lie, if you didn't really have any way to make the plan work.

"We should go to sleep," Wiley said. "I'm tired. I got shot, remember?"

"Wiley got shot, everybody," Saeed said.

"I guess it makes you tired," Amelia joked.

Some of them laughed. Some of them were too jumpy to find anything funny. Violet just wished she could go to sleep and wake up in a world that looked like it had before Black Friday.

The next day, bright and early, they were back to work. The adults kept them so busy it was hard to find the time to worry about anything. Junie made sure everyone had extra to eat if they wanted it, breaking into some of their stores of canned treasures like fruit cocktail and spaghetti with meatballs.

Then, in the middle of the afternoon, Sebastian returned.

This time he was alone. Violet and the other kids were carrying stuff for the adults shoring up the line of cars. Even Wiley was feeling better enough to help carry scrap lumber and pull nails out so the wall crew could reuse them. Violet saw Sebastian approach the entrance to the grounds, between a big black SUV on one side and an older white SUV on the other. He knocked on the hood of the black SUV. "Hello? Mike or Junie around?"

He saw Violet and said, "I believe I recognize you from the carousel."

It took all of her courage, but Violet said, "Hello."

"Can you get either Mike or Junie for me? I'll wait right here." He leaned casually against the black SUV's fender and Violet hurried into the Castle.

She found Mike helping to haul a bookshelf from the library over to a window in the other side of the building. "That man from the other day, the one with the flag tattoos," she said. "Sebastian. He's here."

Mike nodded. He looked grim. "Okay, Violet. Thanks. Is anyone else with him?"

"No, he's alone." Violet walked with Mike out the door.

He put a hand on her shoulder. "You go find the other kids, okay? Keep them away in case there's trouble."

"He's all by himself," Violet reminded Mike.

"Maybe he is, and maybe he isn't," Mike said. "He could have a dozen people with him around the corner. Just do what I told you, okay?"

Violet veered away to where Wiley and Amelia were pulling nails from lumber, down by the Sackler Gallery. "That guy Sebastian from the carousel is back," she said. All three of them crept up along the line of cars until they were close enough to see and hear what was happening, but still far enough away that Mike wouldn't stop what he was doing and tell them to leave.

"This isn't the response I was hoping for after our last conversation, Mike," Sebastian was saying as they came within earshot.

"There are a lot of threats in this city, Sebastian," Mike answered. "We had one of our kids almost killed by roaming thugs not even two weeks ago. Now we're hearing there's a group over on Roosevelt Island that's some kind of cult trying to spread the virus all over again? We want to stay out of it. All of it. We're going to grow our gardens, and keep ourselves safe, and hope that everything returns to normal."

"Nice idea," Sebastian said. "Not really doable in the current situation, though. Sooner or later, everyone's going to have to choose a side. The government's got one foot in the grave and the other on a banana peel. The JTF is overwhelmed and can't even keep order half a mile from the White House. Nobody's coming from outside to help. If you're relying on those institutions to help you, you're already out of luck."

He was still leaning on the SUV, and Violet noticed he was doing something with his finger on the hood. It looked like he was doodling some kind of image, but maybe she was just imagining it.

"That's a hell of a sales pitch," Mike said.

Sebastian shrugged and grinned. "Facts are facts, Mike. We're the only people in Washington, DC, who can keep order. Without order in Washington, DC, there's no order in the United States of America. Without order in the United States of America, those states aren't united anymore. If we don't hold things together, by any means necessary, the American experiment is over. Plain and simple. And I don't know about you, but I refuse to let that happen."

"Agreed," Mike said. "I don't want it to happen, either."

"Then you need to reconsider some of your choices." Sebastian dropped his sunglasses back into place. "I sure don't begrudge you the right to self-defense, Mike. For yourself and all the people under your care. But you might consider—and consider carefully— who you think you're protecting yourself from. Because once you decide you're protecting yourself from someone, that person has no choice but to consider you an enemy."

He rubbed his fingertips together and then rapped his knuckles on the hood of the car. "Guess that was kind of a long speech. Anyway, you take a few days to think about it. I'll come back by and we can continue this conversation when you're not so busy."

Sebastian strolled off down Independence. Mike watched him go. Then he turned and saw all of the people working along the line of cars looking at him. "Better get back to it," he said. "I'm not sure how much time we have."

Everyone got back to work. Wiley and Amelia returned to their pile of lumber. Before she went to join them, Violet had to know what Sebastian was doodling. She stepped out between the two SUVs and stood on her tiptoes to get a better view.

Drawn in the dust on the hood of the SUV was a crude sketch of an American flag.

CHAPTER 32

AURELIO

Aurelio had meant to get up in the morning and keep going after Frank stitched him up and found him a place to stay in Sandusky, but his head had other ideas. When he fell asleep, he didn't wake up for nearly sixteen hours. By then it was early evening, too late to hit the road again, so he had lost an entire day. The fisherman who had offered him a place to sleep was gone, out on the lake. His daughter and another woman who Aurelio took to be a family friend were eating dinner as Aurelio came out of the back room in the fisheries research center where they now lived. Several other people occupied different parts of the building, on Sandusky's small harbor with marinas on either side and a ferry pier a block to the west.

Aurelio remembered the woman's name—Jackie—but not the girl's. "You hungry?" Jackie asked him. "I bet you are, the way you slept."

There was a big platter of fried fish on the table. Aurelio sat and thanked her. He ate and got his thoughts together, wondering how far April had gotten while he'd been recovering. His head still hurt, and his eye was swollen, but Aurelio didn't think he had any cognitive problems. If he had a concussion, it wasn't a bad one. Or if it was, he wasn't feeling all the lingering symptoms yet.

"Riley ought to be back soon," Jackie said. "Me and Maddie are going to go mend some nets. We'll be right outside. You relax."

Aurelio nodded. He finished his fish and checked on his weapons and gear. Jackie didn't strike him as a thief, but it paid to be careful, and it was always possible that he'd lost something during the fight under the turnpike bridge. Better to know now than go looking for it later and find it gone.

Everything seemed to be there. He packed it all up again and set the pack by the door, along with the G36. He still had a sidearm. As he walked outside, smelling the sharp clean air off the lake, his HUD lit up with an incoming call. "Agent Diaz."

"Lieutenant Hendricks," he answered, surprised to hear from her.

"You were out of signal range for a while," she said. "ISAC has been compromised. We're not sure how, but we believe one of the booster towers has been destroyed. For the foreseeable future, you should count on a reliable signal only in areas where there is a strong JTF presence and signal overlap."

"Understood," Aurelio said. Here in Sandusky, he was probably in the effective ranges of JTF bases in Cleveland, Detroit, probably Toledo and Ann Arbor. "Glad to hear from you."

"You might not be when you hear what I'm about to say," she said. "The short version is this: Ike Ronson is looking for a woman named April Kelleher. She is on her way to Ann Arbor, and she was in Cleveland twenty- four hours ago."

Aurelio did the math. If she was on foot and pushing her pace, she was probably passing somewhere very close to

Sandusky right now. But if she had gotten from New York to Cleveland in ten days, she was probably finding ways to travel faster than walking.

He had to assume she was ahead of him.

"Okay," he said. "April Kelleher. Do you know anything about her? Like why she's going to Ann Arbor?"

"We know more than you would expect from a random civilian," Hendricks said. "But we do not know why she's going to Ann Arbor. Here's what we do know. We intercepted another conversation between Ike Ronson and his handlers, and managed to decrypt part of it. That's where we got her name and her destination. At about the same time, we received a report from an agent in Cleveland recording an interaction with a civilian carrying Division gear. From his description of her, and his recorded statement that she identified herself and gave her destination as Ann Arbor, we consider it highly likely they are the same person."

Highly likely, Aurelio thought. Intel officers could never just come right out and be certain. He was out on the pier now, watching Jackie and the girl mending nets as the afternoon sun lit up Sandusky Bay in orange and gold. "Makes sense to me," he said.

"Here's where we take an operational interest. I ran the name April Kelleher through our systems, and we've got recorded contacts between her and a scientist by the name of Roger Koopman, who has done some consulting and research for the JTF scientific wing."

That name rang a bell. "Koopman. He's got some kind of hideout in the Dark Zone, doesn't he?"

"That's him, yes."

"I'll be damned," Aurelio said. "This woman is white, a redhead, carrying some SHD gear?"

"That's what the agent in Cleveland reported."

"I saw her in the Dark Zone three or four days before Ronson bailed on the city hall op," Aurelio said.

"Then you probably saw her around the time she last talked to Koopman. Whatever he told her, it set her off on this trip to Michigan." Hendricks paused and Aurelio heard rustling in the background, as if she was shuffling files around. "Kelleher's husband, Bill, was a biotech researcher working for a company called SBGx. He was murdered shortly after Black Friday, possibly because part of his work involved the synthesis of a class of drugs known as broad-spectrum antivirals. Koopman has access to that information, and also was kept abreast of our own research into a vaccine or treatment against Amherst's virus. Our team, led by Dr. Jessica Kandel, had successfully modeled a potential treatment, but they were unable to synthesize it. They did, however, transmit their models to a facility in Ann Arbor. Is this all coming together for you, Agent Diaz?"

It was. "So someone thinks Kelleher knows about a possible vaccine, and that someone sent Ike Ronson after her."

"That's what it looks like from here." Again Lieutenant Hendricks paused and shuffled through papers. "We're not certain, but we consider this evidence more than sufficient to suggest a course of action to you— knowing, of course, that under Directive 51 you are free to do as you see fit."

"And what would that suggestion be?"

"Whatever Ike Ronson is after, whatever April Kelleher knows, it is our assessment that he should not be permitted to communicate it to his handlers," Hendricks said.

"That would be my assessment, too, Lieutenant Hendricks," Aurelio said.

"Where are you now? I'm seeing Sandusky, Ohio, but as I said, ISAC has been less reliable over distances these past few days."

"ISAC has that right. I'm in Sandusky, but one way or another I'll be in Ann Arbor tomorrow," Aurelio said. "Do you have Ike Ronson's location? I can't find him."

"ISAC has a last-known of Toledo, but we can't pin him down."

Aurelio had been monitoring ISAC as she spoke, and he was getting the same result.

"I looked a little harder at the encryption on those transmissions," Lieutenant Hendricks continued, "and it seems he's got some kind of countermeasure that's interfering with ISAC."

"That's some high-end gear," Aurelio said.

"Indeed it is," she agreed. "Whoever he's working for, they've got top-end tech and they are not aligned with the goals of the SHD and the JTF. This mission just got a lot more important, Agent Diaz."

Not to me, Aurelio thought. To me it was important from the beginning.

"Understood, Lieutenant. I better get moving."

"Agreed. Good luck, Agent."

Aurelio broke off the transmission and took a moment to process what he'd learned. First, there was possibly a vaccine against the Green Poison. That was astonishing all by itself. Everything he'd done as a Division agent had always happened under the cloud of the potential that the virus would mutate and return. But a real vaccine would end that threat. It would mean a true stable rebuilding of America could begin.

And this April Kelleher, whoever she was, might be leading a corrupted Division agent straight to it.

He walked out to the end of the pier. He was more than a hundred miles from Ann Arbor. Two long days on foot. And he needed to get there faster. "Jackie," he said.

She paused in the middle of tying a knot. The girl looked up, too. Aurelio was a little embarrassed that he still couldn't remember her name, but he had more pressing things on his mind.

Aurelio gestured over at the ferry terminal. "That ferry. Where did it go?"

"Used to go up to Pelee Island, on the Canadian side of the lake," she said. "But the boat's been gone since winter, and nobody can go to Canada anymore. The whole border, land and water, is sealed up tight."

"Okay," Aurelio said. "But are there any other ferries? There must be lake traffic, right? Since hardly anyone has cars anymore."

Jackie stood up and stretched, then started rubbing her hands. "Sure. You go out to Cedar Point, there's a couple of ferries that run along the lakeshore there."

She pointed across the bay, and Aurelio noticed the towers of roller coasters and other amusement park rides, glowing in the late afternoon sun. The amusement park was on a barrier island. Aurelio followed the dark line of the land against the water, around to the east, where a causeway connected it to mainland Sandusky a mile or so from where he stood.

"I know they go over to Cleveland and Toledo from there. Might even go to Detroit if the weather's good," she said.

* * *

Aurelio said his good-byes to Jackie and got across the causeway and out to Cedar Point before it was fully dark. The landscape of towering steel frames, swooping and curling back on themselves in the twilight, was eerie and sad, recalling the time when people had the safety and leisure to do things like take their kids to amusement parks. It would happen again, Aurelio thought. He would do his part to help.

He navigated through the park, looking for the shoreline. On the open-water side of the island was a long, empty beach with a few boats run aground. They weren't going to help him.

On the other side, facing the bay, he found a large marina. Dozens of boats lay sunken by winter storms at their moorings, but out at the end of the longer docks a few larger boats were tied up. Aurelio walked past a boathouse and restaurant, smelling fried fish. A group of people inside were eating and talking. He saw other human figures on the boats and decided to go there first. They would have the information he needed.

"Hello," he called when he got close to the end of the dock. There were three boats moored bow to stern, facing to the left, where a channel to the bay was visible between two breakwaters.

A deckhand on one of the boats stopped coiling ropes. He was in his thirties, wearing only canvas shorts. Sandy hair curling down over permanently sunburned shoulders, sleeve tattoos. He leaned on the boat's gunwale and said, "What's up?"

"I was told there are ferries here," Aurelio said. "I need to get to Michigan fast, like yesterday. You know who I can ask?"

"Ain't nobody going to take you tonight," the sailor said. "I'm going to Toledo tomorrow if that'll suit you."

"I need to get to Ann Arbor. And I don't mean to seem melodramatic, but there are lives at stake."

"I've seen you guys before," the sailor said. "I didn't figure it was a pleasure cruise. Listen, I got to go to Toledo tomorrow, but that boat there belongs to a woman by the name of Bryn. She's inside. If you've got something she wants, she'll take you to Detroit first thing."

"Bryn," Aurelio repeated. "Got it. Thanks."

"Rock on," the sailor said. He went back to his ropes and Aurelio went into the restaurant.

There were only four women in the group gathered around a long table with bottles of whiskey and plates of fish bones. The entire group looked up when Aurelio came in. They clocked his gun and his gear and they got quiet. "I'm looking for Bryn," he said.

A stocky woman with a gray crew cut paused in the middle of taking a sip of whiskey. "You found her," she said.

"Mind if we talk for a minute?" Aurelio asked.

She knocked back the whiskey, poured herself another, and said, "Sure."

Bryn wanted to help, but she also had herself to take care of, so to avoid a long negotiation Aurelio made her an offer he didn't figure she would refuse. "You get me to Detroit in the morning," he said, "and I'll give you this."

From his pack he pulled a Glock 19, careful to move slowly so she could see he was holding it by the barrel. He dropped the magazine out and ejected the round from the chamber. "Practically new," he said. "I kept it as a spare, but it's yours, with two full clips, if we can get going before sunrise."

"You got yourself a deal," she said, and the next morning, with dawn just beginning to glow in the east, Bryn was casting off with Aurelio standing in the stern. Her boat was maybe forty feet long, an old wooden beauty with a retrofitted engine that burned coal. "I don't know if you saw the coal docks over in the harbor," she said. "When the virus hit, everything shut down, and there was all this coal sitting there. I got together with some friends and we spent part of the winter working on the old *March Hare* here. Now I got a living, as long as the coal holds out."

"With any luck, things will be getting better by then," Aurelio said. He wondered why she'd named the boat *March Hare* but didn't ask.

"I got a feeling things aren't getting better," Bryn said. Black smoke pumped out of makeshift exhaust stacks cut into the stern. Aurelio moved away from them. They got out into the lake, and Bryn accelerated. "We'll be in Detroit in six hours unless the weather comes up," she said.

That would make it eleven o'clock. Then it was fifty miles or so from the Detroit waterfront to Ann Arbor. Aurelio didn't like that schedule, but he didn't see any way around it. He would just have to hope April Kelleher was on foot, and Ike Ronson hadn't found her. ISAC wasn't telling him anything about Ronson other than a more recent last known location: in southern Michigan, north of Toledo but south of Ann Arbor. Briefly Aurelio wondered what had happened to ISAC. Something was definitely wrong. Real-time tracking was gone; battlefield HUD was gone. At least Aurelio still had map assist and static database access.

Bryn steered directly northwest, and soon they were out of sight of land. The lake was a little choppy, but not bad, and as the sun got higher the dawn breezes calmed. It was a beautiful day to be on a boat, Aurelio thought, wishing he could enjoy it. But the press of his mission—and behind it the ever-present anxiety to get back to DC and be closer to Ivan and Amelia—made it difficult to think of anything else. Bryn kept up a steady stream of conversation, ranging from fish to the political situation in Sandusky to conspiracy theories about military convoys she'd heard about, passing through Ohio on their way east. This last caught Aurelio's attention, but when he asked about it she didn't have any details. "Just something I keep hearing about," she said. "Probably your people."

Could be, Aurelio thought. He let it go and watched the lake.

After about three hours they could see Michigan. "We're making good time," Bryn said. "Might be in Detroit in five hours instead of six."

That was better, but it still put Aurelio in Ann Arbor well after midnight, and exhausted from a fifty-mile forced march. Not a good way to go into a potential combat situation with another trained Division agent, if that was where things were headed.

As they got closer to the shore, he spotted a river mouth, with a golf course on one side and a swampy expanse of open land on the other. Bryn angled the boat more directly north, toward the broad opening of the Detroit River. "Gonna be a little slower now because we have to fight the current," she said. The boat chugged ahead.

Aurelio saw a boat ramp and landing near the golf course. "Bryn," he said. "Can you drop me there?"

"Depends on the water," she said. "I doubt anyone's been dredging the channel. Better to go on up to Detroit."

Aurelio's watch spawned a regional map. If he got off here, he was thirty-seven miles from Ann Arbor. That cut two or three hours off the foot march, plus more than an hour off the boat time. "Please take a look," he said. "There are a lot of lives depending on me getting to Ann Arbor fast."

She looked doubtful, but she eased the boat in closer to the shore. "Don't think so," she said. "I can't risk running aground."

Angling back north again, they passed a small group of houses along the river. Then Aurelio spotted a marina. "Hey. There," he said. "There's a channel."

Bryn slowed down. "That's a tight squeeze, but okay. What I'll do is ease right up to the mouth of the channel. I'm not going in there, though. No telling if other boats have sunk, and by the time we find out it'd be too late."

"Works for me," Aurelio said. "As long as I can jump."

She slowed the boat to barely a walking pace, working it close to the mouth of the marina channel where an open picnic area faced dense woods on the other side. The engine growled as she nosed into the channel, getting the boat momentarily out of the current flowing out of the Detroit River just to the north.

The minute the boat was close enough to the edge of the channel, Aurelio jumped. His boots crunched on gravel and he turned to face Bryn. "Appreciate it," he said. "You still going up to Detroit?"

"I came all this way," she said. "Might as well see if I can make the trip pay for itself. Plus, there's still coal in some of the piles up at River Rouge. Take it easy, Agent Diaz."

"You, too, Bryn."

She reversed the boat out of the channel mouth and chugged away north into the main flow of the Detroit River.

It was a little before nine in the morning, and Aurelio was thirty-seven miles from Ann Arbor.

CHAPTER 33

APRIL

S he spent the night in Sylvania, a suburb right on the Michigan state line, north of Toledo. The truck driver hadn't wanted to leave her in the city. "Around the river, it's pretty rough," he said. "I know you got a gun and all, but still. You get out to Sylvania, you'll have the whole place to yourself. Then you walk straight up 23 to Ann Arbor."

She'd taken his advice, holing up in a patch of woods between a golf course and the highway. She didn't sleep well, but she slept some, and then she was up with the birds and walking. She had food and water enough to get where she was going, and she set a brisk pace. This close to the goal, April could feel the momentum building toward finally understanding the truth about Bill. And maybe—was it possible?—maybe she was going to find out whether the BSAV existed.

May was a beautiful time of year. April couldn't help thinking it was more beautiful without smokestacks and car exhaust choking out the smells of growing things on the breeze. That was maybe the opposite of survivor's guilt, this impulse to look on the bright side of a pandemic that had killed millions of people just in the United States. She wished she knew how things were in the rest of the world, but over the past months it had been all she could do to stay alive herself. Maybe now that things were getting a little better—at least in some places—she would have the space in her head to wonder about things beyond her next meal and next place to sleep.

She saw groups of people in the fields on either side of the highway, planting crops by hand or plowing with horses. Life went on. If the BSAV was real, and the Dollar Bug could be exterminated, it would keep going on. The survivors of the pandemic had a second chance, a clean slate.

If, that is, some kind of government still existed to keep people from breaking apart into a thousand different factions fighting over territory and resources. That was still an open question. Every town she passed through, she saw a few people going about their business. Some of them saw her, too, but none of them bothered her. Maybe they were scared off by the Super 90, or maybe they just didn't wake up in the morning with bad intentions. Either way, by the early afternoon, making pretty good time, she got to a town called Milan. On the edge of the highway, a sign warned

PRISON AREA
DO NOT PICK UP HITCHHIKERS

Good advice, April thought. But she was more likely to be a hitchhiker than pick one up. All the same, she started watching her surroundings more carefully and she carried the Super 90 in her hands instead of slung over her shoulder. She'd seen what the Rikers gang had done in New York, and if there was going to be trouble here, April was going to be ready.

She was between a soda bottling plant on the left and an auto parts factory on the right when she heard a sharp whistle from the direction of the factory. Not a wolf whistle; a signal. She looked in that direction and saw three men standing on the roof of the factory, pointing at her.

Then she looked in the other direction and saw three more men coming out of the bottling plant. They cut across the brushy margin between the parking lot and the highway toward her. April kept walking, not wanting to be between the two groups of men when either one of them got close. The men coming from the bottling plant broke into a run. They were maybe fifty yards away.

When they got out onto the pavement, April turned to face them and leveled the Super 90. "Now, hold on, sweetheart," one of them said. The other two sidestepped, like they were trying to get around behind her.

"I shoot people who call me sweetheart," April said. "Back off."

His eyes shifted away from her, to something over her shoulder. With chilling certainty she understood he was making eye contact with someone behind her.

April pulled the trigger, bracing herself against the Super 90's kick. At less than twenty yards away, the load of buckshot punched holes in him from collarbone to navel. The other two men with him dodged away to the side and April ran north, looking to her right to see who was coming from the factory side.

Bad news. There were at least six of them. Not close enough for the Super 90 to be effective, either. She planted her feet and fired three times at the closest of the men on the bottling plant side. He went down, but the other one was angling across the road to join the factory group. Safety in numbers… and she only had four shots left.

There was no way she would be able to get all of them before they were on her.

She turned and ran again. April was pretty fast, but she wasn't going to be able to outrun a group of men while carrying her pack and gear. The idea behind running was to draw them into a closer group. Ten steps down the road, she spun around and unloaded the last four shells into the group of pursuers. She saw blood flying, but she didn't stop to count the bodies. She dropped the Super 90 and ran.

One of the worst things she noticed in the split second before she turned and ran again was that one of her pursuers had an AR-15. If they'd wanted to kill her, they already could have.

That meant they weren't planning to kill her.

You'll end up married, the sailor back in Buffalo had said about the Jamestown Aryans.

Hell I will, April thought. She had a knife. As she ran, passing under a bridge, she unsnapped its sheath and drew it out.

Another hundred yards ahead of her was a railroad trestle, and just to the right of it a farmhouse. The house was empty. There was no one in sight.

Wait. She saw someone moving at the side of the railroad trestle, skidding down the embankment toward the level of the highway. She saw a gun.

Before she had a chance to see more, someone tackled her from behind. It was a perfect football tackle, both arms around her thighs. She went down hard on the asphalt, but before the man could get his weight on her, April spun around and drove the knife underhand into his ribs. A sound partly cough and partly groan came out of his mouth and he let her go. April scrambled back away from him. Three more men were almost on her, including the guy with the AR-15. He held it pointed at her.

"No more running," he panted.

Then she heard a gunshot and his knees buckled. He hit the pavement on his knees and pitched over forward. One of the other men picked up the gun, but he didn't know where the shot had come from.

In her peripheral vision, April saw something moving. She stepped to one side, away from the motion, and a man exploded into view. April caught an orange circle and the ISAC brick on his pack.

A Division agent.

He went in low as the shooter fired over his head, the barrel of the AR-15 kicking up. Using some kind of judo move, the agent wrenched the shooter over and planted him face-first in the ground. Somehow in the same motion he produced a gun. "Wait," April said, but by the time the word left her mouth he'd shot her attacker twice in the back of the head.

The other one, the last of her pursuers, backed away as the agent walked up to him with the gun leveled. "Hold on, man, we weren't—"

The agent shot him in the chest, and again in the head when he hit the ground.

Then he looked back down the road. April saw bodies back there, and also some men still moving. One was up and limping back in the direction of the factory.

"Pretty good work," the agent said, looking back toward April. "Looks like you had three KIA and four or five wounded by the time I got here."

He walked over to the dead man with April's knife stuck in his left armpit. Rocking the knife back out, he wiped it on the dead man's back. Then he walked over to April, flipped the knife over so he was holding it by the blade, and held it out to her. "If I didn't know better, I'd say you were one of us. But you don't have a watch, and I don't see the lenses. So maybe you should explain where that pack and the Benelli came from."

When she gripped the knife, he let it go. She cleaned it again before she sheathed it. Then she walked past him, back down the road to where she had dropped her gun. "His name was Doug Sutton," she said as she passed. "He died saving my life."

She picked up the gun and turned around. He was right there. Tall, dark haired, with a short beard against pale skin, lean like a distance runner but with a bit more muscle.

"I was about to say you guys are like superheroes," she said as she reloaded the Super 90. After this load, she only had a dozen more shells. "But you killed those guys even though you had them down."

"I don't see a jail anywhere around here," the agent said. "Actually, that's not true. There's a jail just up the road. But what I meant was there's no correctional facility where I could safely convey a violent criminal. So, you know." He shrugged. "Plus, they were going to kill you. Sooner or later."

He stuck out his hand. "Name's Ike. Ike Ronson."

She shook. "April Kelleher." Then she noticed her right hand was covered in the dead man's blood.

"Where you going, April?" Ike asked as April scrubbed her hand on roadside weeds and then on the leg of her pants.

"Ann Arbor."

"Huh." Ronson looked her over. Not like a guy checking her out, but more like he was appraising her fitness for some kind of task. "Why Ann Arbor?"

She thought of all kinds of lies she could tell him and then decided to tell him the truth, or at least part of it. "Mostly to find out who killed my husband."

"Huh," he said again. "You're coming from…"

"New York."

"So even though phone networks have been down since December, you heard about your husband getting killed in Ann Arbor, and now you're going there to find out why."

"No, he was killed in New York. I saw it happen. I've been looking for his killers since then, and I think the answer is in Ann Arbor." She was starting to feel the pressure of her lie of omission. What if she told him about the BSAV? He was a Division agent, right? They were supposed to help, and this Ike Ronson had just saved her life.

On the other hand, she remembered one of the first clues she'd teased out of Roger Koopman's book: *There are divisions in the Division.*

"I can go with you if you'd like," Ike said. "Seems like you shouldn't be traveling alone."

"I got this far," she said, a little defensively. Maybe she wasn't a Division agent or a commando or anything like that, but she'd survived the Dollar Bug and now she'd made it, what, almost six hundred miles out of New York by herself.

"You did," the agent agreed. "On the other hand, no offense, but I don't think you were going to get much farther."

This was fair, even though she didn't want to admit it.

Ike was watching her, like he could see her think. "If you want to come along," April said, "I'd be glad for the company. You sure you don't have another mission or something?"

"I've got other things to do in Ann Arbor anyway," Ike said with a grin. "We go together, I'm killing two birds with one stone."

CHAPTER 34

VIOLET

The day after Sebastian visited, Junie gathered all the kids and said they were going on a trip. "Where?" Amelia asked.

"We're going to see some other people," Junie said. "Some of them left the same hotel you did when the floods came in, but now they're settled farther away from the men at the Capitol Building. So we're going to see what their situation is like."

It had the air of a field trip at first, with Junie as their chaperone. She led them to the Smithsonian Metro stop, with four armed men escorting them. The men came with them down into the Metro stop to make sure they wouldn't run into any trouble. "It's getting harder to go anywhere on the surface," Junie said. "So we're going to take the Metro. Only we're going to do it a whole new way, without using a train."

The floodwaters were starting to recede, but the tracks at the Smithsonian station were still underwater. Junie had made sure all of the kids brought flashlights. Now she said, "Okay. Single file. Stay off to the side where the ground is a little higher. We ought to be able to keep dry that way."

They walked to the end of the platform and then climbed down onto the track bed. Violet was between Ivan and Shelby. They both wanted to hold her hand, so she put her flashlight away and relied on theirs to see where she was going. The tunnel stretched out ahead of them, perfectly straight, receding into the dark.

Junie was in front. "Come on," she said. "We're only going two stops. Won't take us more than fifteen or twenty minutes even if we go slow."

On the tunnel walls, Violet could see the stain of the floodwater. At its highest it had been over her head here. Now there was only water and silt on the tracks. If they stayed off to the side, their shoes barely got wet. The next station they passed was Federal Triangle, and then a few minutes later they got to Metro Center. A couple of different lines intersected here, so it was a bigger station, with platforms and overhangs and escalators frozen in place. Junie kept going, and the kids followed her. They hadn't seen any people down in the tunnels or the stations. Violet wondered why. It seemed like it might be a good place to hide out from the weather if you were scared of people up on the street level. But maybe there was something she didn't know.

She didn't have a chance to ask Junie about it because they were climbing an escalator, and then they came up onto the street across from a Macy's. They walked past a stretch of abandoned stores and restaurants, no longer single file but in a bunch again. When they got to Tenth Street, they turned down past the big cathedral and walked two blocks until they got to Ford's Theatre. Like every other DC schoolkid, Violet recognized it. She'd seen it on a field trip. Across the street was the house where Abraham Lincoln had died after… "Saeed," she said. "Who shot Lincoln?"

"John Wilkes Booth," he answered right away. Then his face

lit up as he figured out where they were. "Oh, this is right by the spy museum," he said. "Can we go?"

"Maybe another time," Junie said.

She led them to a makeshift gate set between Ford's Theatre and the bigger building at the end of the block, which had a glitzy bar and a bunch of condos in it. Two big men with shotguns were at the gate. Junie nodded at them. They nodded back. "Thomas," Junie said to one of them. "These are the kids."

Violet heard sounds from above and looked up. At this angle she couldn't see much, but it seemed like there were a lot of people on the roof of the condo building next to Ford's Theatre, and more people on the roof of the theater itself.

"Yeah," Thomas said. "JTF said you might be coming by. But I thought we were going to talk about this before you just showed up with a bunch of kids."

"Time is not on our side, Thomas," Junie said. "If we didn't come today, I wasn't sure we'd get another chance."

Thomas was having trouble looking Junie in the eye, and Violet could tell he was trying hard to avoid looking at her or any of the kids. "Well," he said. "We haven't really had time to talk about this."

"We had it sorted out with the JTF," Junie said. "They told us you were good."

"I don't know what they told you or didn't tell you." Thomas finally mustered the courage to look her in the eye. "But we haven't talked about it here."

"Here? We're here, Thomas. I brought these kids here. What do I do now?"

"Look, when the JTF first suggested it to us, it seemed like a good idea, but... it's just not going to work out. Too many mouths, not enough room. And if we start taking in more… He shook his head. "Also, we heard you got a visit from Sebastian and those guys. You know the people behind him? They're not afraid to kill people to make a point. If you got on their wrong side, and then we take in some of your people, how does that look?"

"We're talking about children," Junie said.

Violet realized this wasn't just a trip. Junie hadn't brought them here to meet other people.

She was looking for a new place for them to live… and Thomas was turning her down.

"No. Junie, no," Shelby said. Tears filled her eyes. Amelia and Violet scooted close to her.

"It's all right," Amelia said. "We'll stick together. We'll be all right."

Junie squatted down in front of them. They clustered around her, each of them wanting to touch her. They knew they were orphans. They knew they didn't really have parents anymore—except for Ivan and Amelia, and their dad could be anywhere. So for all of them, Junie was the closest thing they had to a parent. Why would she send them away?

"Listen," she said. "It's only until this business between the JTF and the flag-tattoo people gets settled."

"But what if…" They all looked at Noah, but he couldn't finish the question. Violet thought she knew what

he was going to say, though: *What if you get killed? What if we can never go back?*

That was the question on her mind, too.

"Junie," Thomas said. "Look. Go on home, and we'll get this sorted out. But we can't take seven children right now. We just can't."

"So you haven't talked about it, or you did talk about it and decided no, and you just don't have the guts to tell me face-to-face?" Junie stood defiant with the kids all around her, daring Thomas to turn them away, and Violet already knew how it was going to play out. Adults thought kids were blind to lots of things, but the truth was, kids saw through most of the charades adults had convinced themselves were real. Violet watched the two of them talking to each other, and she knew two things:

One, Junie thought she needed to get the kids out of the Castle because something bad was going to happen.

Two, Thomas wasn't going to let it happen. Not today, not ever.

"Look, Junie," Thomas said. "We're just trying to get through until this is all over."

"Us, too," Junie said. "Only we're already in the crosshairs." It wasn't like her to let slip something like that in front of the kids. Violet saw a different Junie in that moment, frightened and trying to do what she could to make the best of a bad situation.

Be ready, Violet told herself. If they can't protect us, we'll have to protect ourselves. How they would do that, and what it would mean, she didn't know. But she could tell from the conversation that a time was coming when she and the rest of the orphaned kids in the group might be on their own. They had to know that, and be ready for it.

"Just stay put another week," Thomas said. "See how things are going. We'll talk about it then."

There wasn't much to say after that. Junie and all of the kids could tell there was no help for them at Ford's Theatre. "Another week," Junie said, her voice heavy with scorn. "Might as well say next year."

She turned away, ignoring whatever Thomas might have said,

and led the kids back to the Metro Center station.

On the way back through the Metro tunnels, the kids were pretty subdued until right at the end, when they were sticking to the sides of the flooded part near the Smithsonian stop. "You wanted us to go somewhere else," Ivan said out of nowhere.

Junie stopped and turned to him. "No," she said. "No, I didn't. I want you here. Hell, I want you back with your parents, each and every one of you. Just like I want my own children with me. But they're not. And your parents aren't. And in a week, none of us might be, either. We'll see. I'm trying to keep you safe. Until yesterday, I thought the best way to do that was to keep you at the Castle. Now I'm not so sure. But now it doesn't matter. We're going to be at the Castle, and we're going to get through whatever comes. Together."

She walked toward the stairs to the street at the Smithsonian stop, and Violet was reminded how she'd thought it was going to be like a field trip when they left. It hadn't turned out that way at all.

They came back out into the sunlight on Independence Avenue. "We're going to stick it out where we are. That's it," Junie said as they walked down the block and the Castle came into view. She sounded defeated, and that made Violet worry more than just about anything she'd seen since her parents died. "Nothing more to say about it."

Because Junie had said that, they believed it, and none of them said anything as they walked back to the Castle. But Violet knew there was a lot more to say. She had a feeling something bad was coming, and the adults knew they were powerless to stop it.

That meant the kids were going to have to figure things out on their own.

CHAPTER 35

APRIL

April had walked more than forty miles that day by the time they got to Ann Arbor, and she'd had a huge adrenaline rush and crash in the middle of the day. She was exhausted. But she had a lead on where to go, at least.

Like any big college town, Ann Arbor was plastered with signs directing visitors and students to various campus locations. She also resorted to the old-fashioned trick of looking at maps. The North Campus, home to most of the university's engineering research labs, was across the Huron River from downtown. By the time they figured that out, they were already on the edge of the main campus, having walked in along a road Ike pointed out. April couldn't keep the name in her head. It went past a small JTF base, then an endless stretch of abandoned stores, and then stately old houses repurposed as campus offices of fraternities. Ahead of them loomed the immense University of Michigan Hospital, practically a city unto itself. Lights burned in some of its windows, and they could see JTF patrols and checkpoints on the road—Washtenaw, that was the name—as it curved past the hospital.

Ann Arbor looked like it had seen some rough times. Many

of the fraternity houses had burned, and the strip of bars and restaurants along the south edge of the main campus showed bullet holes and broken windows. They got off Washtenaw and walked through the campus. "The main JTF base here is down by the football stadium," Ike said. "On the south side of the city."

Bill had been a big college football fan, and April remembered seeing pictures of that stadium, with its big yellow Block M on the fifty-yard line. The players' helmets had three stripes that Bill had once told her were supposed to look like a wolverine's claws. Funny how little details like that floated back into your head when you were practically too tired to stand.

A campus bus stop helped them narrow down their probable destination even more. "Huh," April said, reading it with the help of a flashlight. "There's a biomedical research building right on the edge of North Campus." From where they stood, it was maybe two or three miles.

"You a biomedical engineer?" Ike asked.

"No, but my husband was a genetic engineer and worked on medical projects," April said. "I think the person I'm looking for probably works in that building. Or did. Either way, it's the place to start the search."

"Makes sense to me," Ike said. "You want to go over there now?"

She did, but she was also dead on her feet. After so many months, being so close to the truth about Bill had April paradoxically reluctant to take the final steps. What if Koopman was wrong and nobody here knew anything about Bill? Or, for that matter, the BSAV? She couldn't work through how she felt about that. Fatigue was singing its high whine in her head. She'd killed three people that day, and almost died herself, and walked for thirteen hours. Even if she found someone who knew Bill, she knew she was too exhausted to ask coherent questions.

"No," she said. "I'm beat, Ike. It's been quite a day."

"Sure has." He looked around, from the electric glow of the JTF checkpoints by the hospital to the silent darkness of the main campus quad. Another random tidbit floated through April's head. It was called the Diag. "Probably best not to show up when it's getting dark. That's a time when people tend to be suspicious."

"Yeah," she said.

"So let's hole up for the night. I saw a decent spot back down the block."

The spot he chose was a rooftop café, upstairs from a small deli. The stairs creaked under their feet and on the second floor they found a hookah bar. A glass counter with displays of different kinds of tobacco was smashed and empty. Same with the glass-front cooler on the wall. Empty bottles littered the floor, but there was no sign anyone was squatting there.

"Stinks in here," April said.

Ike nodded. "I don't mind sleeping outside. It's a nice night."

It was. They went out onto the roof. April noted an exterior stairway that led down into an alley behind the row of buildings. She also saw bullet holes in the walls and spent shell casings lying in the gaps between deck boards. But whatever battle had happened here, it was long over. The whole street was quiet.

"Hey, a fire pit," Ike said. It was one of the cast-iron kind, for having contained fires in a yard... or on a deck. He broke apart two wooden benches sitting on the balcony by the rear stairway and shaved some tinder into the bottom of it. Then he arranged some boards over it and produced a disposable lighter.

April had eight or ten of them in the bottom of her pack.

She'd traded others for food at different times over the winter. The ability to make fire on demand was a lifesaver. As long as she lived, April would never be without a lighter.

The fire was cheery. April dragged a wicker couch over close to it and stretched out her legs. Ike was in a chair on the other side. "Well," he said. "Here we are."

"Yeah. But you don't have to be. You got me here. Don't you have other missions calling?"

"Directive 51," Ike said. "I'll get you where you're going, and then I'll see who needs me here."

Something about the way he phrased that caught April's attention. Hadn't he said he had another reason for being in Ann Arbor? "Here? Are you usually somewhere else?"

Ike chuckled. "I've been all over Ohio, Michigan, Pennsylvania... I try to go where there's need."

"Well, I'm glad you were there when I needed you." April was getting sleepy. "Why were you there, anyway?"

"Trouble tends to come out of towns where there were prisons before the pandemic," Ike said. "I like to know where those towns are and keep an eye on them. Just so happened you were passing through."

"Lucky," April said. She yawned. "Now if I can only get lucky again tomorrow."

"What would that look like?" Ike's face was serious. April liked him. Not just because he'd saved her life. He was easy to talk to.

"That would look like... me walking into that biomedical engineering building tomorrow and finding someone who knew Bill. Then me asking that person why he was murdered, and getting an answer. Then..."

She stopped. She'd been about to add something about finding out whether Bill's work had helped to create a vaccine that would end the threat of a resurgent Dollar Bug once and for all. It had become a reflex to only tell part of the story, from New York up to Albany and then all the way here. But she didn't need to do it anymore, April realized. She could tell Ike. He was a Division agent, and even if she knew some Division agents had gone rogue, she also knew their watches turned red when that happened. There was some kind of AI system that tracked them. Ike Ronson's watch was orange.

And he'd saved her life. April Kelleher was no damsel in distress. She'd gotten herself out of more than a few tough spots in the months since Black Friday. But the two times she'd really been in over her head, a Division agent had been there. First Doug Sutton, now Ike Ronson.

"So there's another reason, too," she said. Already she was feeling a rush of relief about finally being able to tell someone. "Did I tell you I came from New York?"

Ike raised an eyebrow. "You mentioned your husband was killed there. Were you in Manhattan?"

April nodded. "Yeah."

"How'd you get past the quarantine? There's a blockade still, right?"

"I had a friend who called in a favor," April said. "Actually I thought it would be harder than it was, but it turns out there are places where you can practically walk out, as long as you know when the patrols are going to be there. I went on a railroad bridge over the Harlem River."

"They didn't have it alarmed or anything? That's not much of a blockade."

"They did. My guide showed me how to climb along the bridge girders so we stayed clear of the alarms. Then I caught a ride on a boat up to Albany. This is the part that doesn't seem real to me. I rode on the Erie Canal all the way to Buffalo, like it was 1840 or something."

"I guess for a lot of people it is," Ike commented.

"That's true." April had a little second wind now that she'd started talking about the journey, and given herself permission to tell the whole story. "The man who told me how to get out is a scientist. He... well, I'm not sure he knew Bill, but he knew Bill's work because they were in related fields. I found him because I thought he might be able to help me understand why Bill was murdered. And he did, sort of, but the way he explained it gave me a whole new set of... not just questions, but..." She was rambling and she knew it. She shifted on the couch so she was a little more upright, leaning against one arm with her legs still outstretched. "Let me put it this way. What I learned there gave me something like a quest."

Now she paused, because on the brink of telling Ike about the BSAV April realized it might just make her sound crazy.

"For...?" Ike prompted.

Both of them froze as they heard footsteps on the deck. Ike's hand dropped to his sidearm and April swung around to get her feet on the floor. The Super 90 was leaning against the other arm of the couch. Reflexively she reached for it.

Then she paused as another Division agent stepped into the firelight. He was compact and light on his feet, like he was made of springs. In the firelight, his features looked Mayan: sharp nose, broad cheekbones, heavy-lidded soulful eyes under the brim of a baseball cap. He looked from April to Ike, seemingly unworried about the hands both of them had on their guns. Then a broad grin broke over his face and he said, "Hey, sorry, didn't mean to scare anyone. You're Ike Ronson, right?"

CHAPTER 36

AURELIO

According to ISAC, Ike was still somewhere south of Ann Arbor when Aurelio got there in the early evening. But when he checked in with the JTF base in the parking lot of a shopping center with the whimsical sixties-callback name Arborland, he learned that they had flagged a woman matching April Kelleher's description passing by late that afternoon, going west on Washtenaw. Aurelio had followed that path, and after several hours searching the campus area, he'd spotted the small rooftop fire on South University.

After he circled around the block and found the alley, Aurelio had come slowly up the stairs. When he had visual on Ronson and Kelleher, he watched them for fifteen minutes or so. Before he made himself known, he wanted to get a sense of whether he was treating her like a captive, a coconspirator, or an ordinary civilian. It didn't take too long for him to see that she didn't consider herself a captive, and since she was talking more than he was, the conversation didn't seem like the two of them were scheming. From this he inferred that Ronson didn't know what Kelleher was after, and Kelleher didn't know Ronson was corrupt.

Therefore the most straightforward approach was probably the best. Ronson couldn't draw down on Aurelio without ruining the trust he was developing with Kelleher, and he couldn't shoot her because he still didn't know what she was after.

So when Aurelio stepped out onto the roof deck and said hello, he figured Ronson would be boxed in and would have to play along... and as it turned out, he was right. "Yeah," Ronson said. "I'm Ike. Who are you?"

Aurelio introduced himself. "I've had a couple of pings about a civilian in the area with SHD gear, so I was out looking around. And here you are," he said to April. "How did you happen to come by that gear?"

"I took it from an agent who saved my life back in February," she said. "He was dead, and I needed it."

I might have saved your life, too, Aurelio thought. The jackals in the Fifth Avenue church would have turned her into an art exhibit. "Fair enough," he said. "Ike, you taking the night off?"

Ronson met Aurelio's gaze, his face giving nothing away. He probably didn't know Aurelio was the agent who had responded to his bogus SOS back in Manhattan, but he was also probably suspicious of the coincidence of another Division agent finding him so soon after he had located Kelleher. Also, if he had access to ISAC, he could learn Aurelio's last operational locations anytime he wanted. "I ran into April on the road south of here, when she was encountering the local version of the Rikers gang. She was doing all right, but I gave her a hand."

No wonder she was so relaxed around him, Aurelio thought. He'd made just about the best first impression you can make.

"Now I'm listening to her story," Ike continued. "It was just about to get good."

"It's true," she said. "Now that you're here, you can hear the story, too. Then I'm going to sleep."

Aurelio dragged a chair over close to the fire and sat, making a roughly equilateral triangle with Kelleher and Ronson. "I'm all ears," he said.

"Then I'll cut to the chase." April was sitting up now, elbows on her knees and hands loosely clasped. She looked into the fire as she spoke. "In New York I learned that my husband, Bill, might have been involved in research on a new class of antivirals that could provide a treatment for the Black Friday virus. I also learned that a team in a lab here in Ann Arbor might have completed a sample of that drug. It's called a broad-spectrum antiviral, but this is a specific one tailored to the way the Dollar Bug can mutate. If that drug exists, and if Bill was involved…" She took a moment to compose herself. "I saw him shot down in the street by strangers, and if I knew something of his work had survived to help make sure this never happens again… It would really help me to know that."

She wiped her eyes with her sleeve and fell silent. Aurelio's mind went into overdrive trying to fit this new revelation in with what he already knew. Kelleher had heard about the antiviral. Someone had sent Ike Ronson after her. Therefore that someone also knew about the antiviral, and Ronson considered that someone more deserving of loyalty than the Division.

Without the checks of accountability and transparency, whoever controlled the manufacture and distribution of the antiviral would be in a position of unassailable power. If the virus mutated and came back, the next plague wouldn't touch them. They could use access to it as the ultimate leverage over anyone. Aurelio didn't look at Ronson. He knew Ronson was working through a different version of the same train of thought. Whether Ronson had known about the antiviral before now, and was just waiting for Kelleher to confirm it, that Aurelio didn't know. He suspected Ronson was just as surprised as he was. This was a shocking revelation.

The question was, what were they going to do about it?

Aurelio understood his duty. If the antiviral existed, he had a paramount responsibility to see that it got into the hands of the people who would do the most good with it. To his mind, that meant the government, for all its weaknesses and imperfections. The remaining members of the executive and legislative branches were trying to keep the United States of America alive. Aurelio had pledged himself to that goal as well, and a viable treatment for Amherst's virus would be a cornerstone of any sustained rebuilding.

Ike Ronson's masters probably had different ideas if they had suborned his betrayal of the Division.

By any understanding of Directive 51, Aurelio had the right to put a bullet in Ronson's head right then and there. The problem was, Ronson was a trained Division agent just like Aurelio was, and he was certainly watching Aurelio out of the corner of his eye just like Aurelio was watching him. The outcome of a fight was far from predetermined, and there was also Kelleher's welfare to consider. Ronson now had the crucial bit of intel that either he had lacked before or he'd needed to confirm. He didn't need April Kelleher anymore, and that meant Aurelio had to keep her alive whenever Ronson decided to tie up his loose ends and make his decisive move.

So despite his impulse to take Ronson out, Aurelio played it cool. "That's a hell of a thing to find out," he said. "How sure are you that this drug really exists?"

"You mean how sure was the guy who told me?" April sat up straighter and rubbed her face. "He thought it was true, but he didn't have direct confirmation, and he also didn't have any way to contact the lab here and find out. They're apparently working in conjunction with the JTF science wing, but they're not JTF."

"Then we better find out," Ike said. Now Aurelio did look at him. He saw a challenge in Ike's eyes, but also something else. Reading Ike's expression, Aurelio thought he was making some kind of appeal. To what? Their shared bond as Division agents? Ronson had severed that back on Duane Street.

Telling that final bit of her story seemed to have sapped the last of April's energy. She stretched out on the wicker couch and said, "We'll find out tomorrow." Her eyes closed and she was asleep inside a minute.

A long silence passed before Ronson spoke. "She's tough, man. Coming all the way from New York by herself."

Aurelio nodded. "Yeah, it's a long trip. A lot can go wrong. But you know that."

Ronson absorbed this and thought it over. He put two more pieces of wood on the fire. Then he pushed his chair back and lay on the deck, looking up into the night sky with his hands behind his head. "I'm going to say two things," he said. "One. You don't know everything you think you know about me."

"Okay," Aurelio said. "What's two?"

"I'm going to go to sleep," Ronson said. He closed his eyes. "You want to punch my ticket, that's your call. You don't, wake me up in four hours and I'll take second watch."

CHAPTER 37

IKE

When Ike woke up it was nearly dawn. He sat up, half expecting to see Diaz and Kelleher gone, but April was still asleep on the couch and Diaz was leaning against the deck railing, looking eastward toward the glow of impending sunrise over the leafy neighborhood to the east of the campus.

Ike stood and stretched. "I meant what I said about waking me up."

"I got hit in the head three days ago. Haven't been sleeping well since then anyway." Diaz didn't look at him. Ike had an urge to explain himself. He hadn't meant for those people squatting across from Duane Park to die. It was just an op gone bad. No way he would convince Diaz of that, though. Just like there was no way he would ever be able to convince Diaz that he believed he was doing the right thing by leading Mantis to the antiviral.

He'd made the decision right away. The government was crippled, the JTF barely hanging on. Bringing something that could save the world to people who couldn't do anything with it would be pretty much the same as pouring it out on the sidewalk.

Glancing back over at April, Ike was struck again by both

her courage and her trust. Chasing the dream of the truth six hundred miles, that was something. In a strange way he was proud to have helped her along the way. Whatever was going to happen by the end of the day, she was going to be alive to get her answers because Ike had stepped in at the right moment down in Milan. For a while he had worried that she might not want to tell him why she was going to Ann Arbor. He didn't want to have to beat it out of her. In fact, he wasn't sure he would have been able to make himself do it. But in the end he hadn't had to. He got her talking, and it just happened. Ike had never trained as an interrogator, but he'd read that the best way to get information out of someone wasn't to beat it out of them, but just to keep them talking, and keep them convinced that you were listening and interested. Build a rapport. Lo and behold, it had worked. And it hadn't hurt that she was fatigued and grateful.

It was a little after oh six hundred. "I'm gonna take a leak," he said. Diaz didn't respond.

Ike went down the alley stairway and strolled along the edge of an unfinished construction project. It looked like this whole part of the city had been in the process of remaking itself from three- and four-story buildings to monumental concrete towers. Not your father's college town.

As soon as he was out of earshot, he called in to Mantis. Right on schedule, forty-eight hours since their last conversation. But this time he wouldn't be the one asking questions. "Mantis, Sentinel here."

She answered right away. "This is Mantis."

"I'm going to make this quick." Ike looked back toward the stairway as he spoke, keeping his voice down. He didn't see Diaz, and Kelleher would probably sleep until noon if they let her. "Have made contact with April Kelleher. Have learned her objective. She is chasing a rumor that someone in Ann Arbor has created an antiviral drug that will cure Amherst's virus. The rumor is considered credible by the JTF. Today we are going to the likely location where the drug is being produced."

"Superb work, Sentinel. We will send a team to capture the product and extract you."

That might complicate things, Ike thought. He had to make sure he laid eyes on the sample before Mantis flooded the area with commandos. Otherwise he might not end up delivering on the promise, and he wouldn't get another shot to prove himself.

Also, he had enough of a heart to want to make sure Kelleher—and sure, even Diaz—was out of the way before the shooting started. Ike might have betrayed the Division, but he had his reasons, and he didn't have any desire to get agents killed. "ETA?" he asked.

"Team will deploy immediately to a staging area near Ann Arbor, and move in once you have confirmed the presence of the product. Send one word: Stampede."

That solved the problem, Ike thought. "Confirm signal: Stampede."

"Mantis out."

Everything was set in motion. All that remained was to find the lab and see if this miracle drug actually existed.

When he got back up onto the deck, April was stirring. Diaz hadn't moved. April sat up and said, "I dreamed about coffee."

Diaz laughed. "I probably dream about coffee every night. I had an uncle who worked on a coffee plantation in Guatemala. My mom used to roast beans at home. I think I'm made partly of coffee."

"That where you're from, Guatemala?" Ike asked. He had never gotten the taste for coffee.

"No, man, I was born in DC. But my parents were from Guatemala. Acatenango Valley, right down the hill from a volcano. They came to the States after it erupted in 1972."

"Better story than I have," Ike said. "I'm from New Jersey."

They broke out food and ate. When they were done, Ike poured water over the fire and stirred the ashes. He'd been a Boy Scout once. A long time ago.

"Big day today," Diaz said. "Where do we go?"

"North Campus," April said. "I forget what the building is called, but if we can find Fuller Road it'll take us right there."

They found Fuller Road after skirting the edge of the campus and going down a hill past the hospital. It curved to the east, with overgrown soccer fields and a public pool on their left and the hospital looming at the top of the hill on their right. Just past the soccer fields, they crossed the river and saw signs for a VA hospital and North Campus.

A few minutes later, the campus came into view. Several of the buildings were fortified with Jersey barriers and razor wire, and JTF soldiers were visible in firing emplacements at intervals along the secure perimeter. "Well," Diaz said. "Looks like we found something someone thinks is important, anyway."

He led the way across a parking lot toward the closest checkpoint. Gesturing back at April and Ike, he said, "Agent Ronson and I have a civilian with some important information. We need to be directed to one of your lead researchers."

As usual, their Division gear got them answers. "You're going to want to talk to Dr. Chandrasekhar." The gate guard pointed at the nearest of five buildings behind the security perimeter.

Its front walls were mostly glass, with a trapezoidal awning extending out over the main entrance. Inside the building, Ike could see lights and people moving. "She's kind of the manager of all the projects, as far as I know," the guard added.

They went inside and asked around. Their third inquiry led them to an office deeper inside the building, away from the fancy glass entrance. Here the doors and halls were more utilitarian, the windows smaller. Their tight rectangles revealed laboratories and equipment rooms.

Kavita Chandrasekhar was maybe five foot three, her gray hair pulled back in a practical barrette. One pair of glasses rode high on her forehead and another on the bridge of her nose. She was in a small office with diagrams of complex molecules all over the walls and a laptop open on a desk piled with scientific journals. Its single window, half-open to let in the spring breeze, looked out to the east, directly at the Gerald Ford Presidential Library. When Ike, Diaz, and April appeared in her doorway she switched glasses and said, "What can I do for you?"

"We're sorry to bother you, Professor," Diaz said. "But we're hoping to ask you a few questions." Indicating April, he added, "Actually, she is."

April extended a hand. "April Kelleher," she said.

"Oh," she said, shaking April's hand. "Until recently I was working on a project with a team in New York, one of whom was also named Kelleher. Is it a common name?"

"Honestly, I don't know," April said. "But I'm guessing that particular Kelleher was my husband."

CHAPTER 38

APRIL

The more she talked about it, the easier it got.

That had been true the night before, when she started opening up first to Ike and then to Aurelio, too. It was true this morning when Professor Chandrasekhar said, "Really? William Gibson Kelleher? He was your husband?" April couldn't remember the last time she'd heard someone say Bill's full name, which he only used on professional research articles. People often took his first two names as a science fiction fan's homage to the writer by that name, but Bill had always said his middle name was his father's tribute, as a lifelong Los Angeles Dodgers fan, to 1988 World Series hero Kirk Gibson.

"Yes," she said. Then, for the fifth or sixth time since she'd left New York, she told the story.

When she was done, Professor Chandrasekhar looked at Ike and Aurelio. "It's okay to tell her?"

Ike didn't say anything. Aurelio said, "Fine by me."

"Well," Professor Chandrasekhar said. "When the virus began to spread and it was clear we had a pandemic on our hands, authorities here took steps to protect this laboratory and some others nearby. The JTF, when it was formed, stepped in, and we have had the aid of several Division agents as well. All so we could continue to have the power and facilities to do our work. In New York, of course, the original samples of the virus were easiest to obtain. It was already mutating by the time it began to spread here and elsewhere in the country. So we followed closely the work of Dr. Kandel and others there, and offered our own insights as they occurred. At several points during the course of these experiments we referred to the work of Bill Kelleher. As well as many other scientists. Communications began to fail very soon after Black Friday, and I had no idea Bill Kelleher had been killed. I am very sorry to hear it. We never corresponded, or met, but reading his work I felt I knew him a little."

Koopman was right, April thought. And I was right to come here. Maybe it was crazy to set out on this trek all by myself, but it was also right. A tangle of feelings left her speechless for a long moment: sadness, regret, satisfaction, pride in both Bill and herself.

"It's good to know that he helped," April said. "But I wish I knew more about why he was killed."

Across the room, she heard Ike say, "Stampede."

Professor Chandrasekhar looked over at him. "I beg your pardon?"

"It's going to be a stampede whenever this drug gets produced and people figure out where," Ike said. "Listen, if there's a sample of it, we should get it somewhere safe. Like, Fort Knox safe."

"Oh, there is a sample," Professor Chandrasekhar said. "An entire batch, twenty-four doses. We did all the sequencing and splicing right here, made it in another lab a few hundred yards away, and sent it out a week ago to Washington, DC. A scientific

274

adviser to President Ellis should have the samples by now. A year or so from now, it should be widely available." She smiled at the thought.

"Wait," Ike said. "It's not here?"

That was the first time April had heard him sound ruffled by anything. To her, it was enough to know that the BSAV existed, and that Bill had played a role in its creation. He had done good work and died for it. She had done her own good work.

"No," Professor Chandrasekhar said. "President Ellis's adviser requested specifically that we send all synthesized antiviral serum to him for secure handling in Washington, DC. We will continue to research and develop variations of it here, but the first broad-spectrum antiviral treatment for Amherst's virus is complete and… well, it should be in the hands of government officials in Washington." Ike's concern registered with her and she added, "Should we be concerned that something has gone wrong?"

"Like you said, communication lines have been tricky lately," Aurelio said. "And none of us has been to DC in a while. I live there, and I haven't seen it since February."

"I should follow up with the officials I have been talking to." Professor Chandrasekhar scribbled a note on a legal pad by her laptop. "Now, as I have been saying, there is more work to do. If I can help you with anything else…?"

"Just one more question," April said. "A man named Koopman, I don't know if you know him? He's in New York, too?" Chandrasekhar shook her head. "Okay. He said that a number of scientists working in this field were killed right after Black Friday, when the virus was released. He speculated that this was because Amherst had to release the virus sooner than he wanted, maybe because he feared being discovered. So he hadn't had time to perfect certain parts of it, specifically its defenses against antiviral drugs."

"I see where you are going," Chandrasekhar said. "So Amherst had people killed who were working in those fields, to delay research that would eventually combat his virus."

"Either Amherst or other people who had learned of his project and wanted to use it for their own ends," April said. "That's the wrinkle Koopman added."

"I hate to think there are such people," Chandrasekhar said. "But I know they do in fact exist."

April noticed neither Ike nor Aurelio had anything to say. She glanced in Aurelio's direction again and saw his watch face light up. He glanced down at it, then stepped out into the hall.

"Listen, if the drug's not here, we should get moving," Ike said. "Aurelio and I, we've got things we could be doing. April, you planning to stay here now that you walked all this way, or what are you going to do?"

"Hold on," she said. This was going to be her one chance to get a complete picture of the forces that had combined to produce the men in black suits who had killed her husband. She wasn't going to miss it. "Professor. How do you know there are other people trying to use the virus?"

"Facilities like this one are very rare right now," she said. "Many were destroyed and looted; others are abandoned. We had some foresight to try to protect this lab, but we also had some luck to be successful. So we are occasionally contacted by groups who wish us to synthesize something for them. We refuse, naturally. On occasion the JTF and sometimes the Division are required to emphasize that refusal, if you take my meaning."

This fit with what Koopman had said, at least in broad

strokes. If those groups had already been active when the virus was released, what did that mean? Had they known in advance about Amherst's insane project, and started to make plans about how they could turn it to their advantage? What kind of lunatic would do that?

The kind who valued power, was the answer. All of them would have a rationale, but the truth was, those rationales existed only to excuse the pursuit of power. People like that had no problem killing to serve their vision.

So those were the people who had murdered Bill, she thought. Because through his work, whether he knew it or not, he had helped make possible a future where a single lunatic could not end millions of lives and devastate millions more. They did not want that future. They wanted another one, where they alone controlled who lived or died.

Maybe that was melodramatic, but it fit the facts. And it gave April the consolation of knowing that Bill's work had survived him to help give rise to the treatment that would offer a new future to the people who had survived. She was surprised by how much that meant to her. After all, Bill was still dead.

But having seen so much meaningless death, so many people suffering and breathing their last with no one to care or even notice... being able to believe that Bill's death had meaning gave April hope. It closed a circle, demarcated a boundary between her past and her future. She wouldn't get him back, but that just made her one of millions who had lost someone they loved.

All of them had to live for tomorrow now.

That was the thought in her mind when she saw Aurelio come back into Professor Chandrasekhar's office.

CHAPTER 39

AURELIO

The thing that made Aurelio especially angry was that he'd been starting to second-guess his assessment of Ike Ronson. Was it worth the deaths of fourteen people to make sure the world knew that help was coming? That the Black Friday virus, the Dollar Bug, the Green Poison, was soon going to be a bad memory, built over by the rising future of a new America? That wasn't a call Aurelio could make. He wasn't sure it was a call Ike could make. But that was the problem. He'd been sure in Manhattan. He'd been sure all the way across Pennsylvania and Ohio and Lake Erie and Michigan. He'd even been sure last night.

Now, this morning, he wasn't. Maybe he'd misjudged Ike. After all, he had protected April and made sure she got here.

The only thing hanging Aurelio up was the question of who Ike was talking to. Was it a rogue element inside the SHD? Was it another government agency that didn't trust the SHD? Or was it an outside actor—and if so, what did they want?

Without answers to any of those questions, Aurelio had only his eyes and his ears and his gut to go on, and they were telling him that Ike Ronson was sincere.

The problem was, Ike's sincerity didn't make those fourteen people in the elevator lobby by Duane Park any less dead. There was still something Aurelio didn't know, a critical piece of information without which he could not in good conscience act.

Lieutenant Hendricks provided it. She pinged him while April was talking to the professor, and he went out into the hall. "Diaz."

"Agent Diaz, consider this an armor-piercing warning to get the hell out of wherever you are if that place is within a mile of Ike Ronson."

"That's quite a greeting, Lieutenant."

"I've been working the problem of Ronson's encrypted conversations. Every sample gives me a little more to work with, and this morning at about oh six twenty he contacted his handler, by the name of Mantis. Listen close, Agent Diaz, because you don't have time to ask me to repeat it. He fed her Kelleher, the drug, the location. Mantis is sending in a team to, and I'm quoting here, 'capture the product and extract you'— 'you' meaning Ronson."

I should have shot that son of a bitch right when I saw him, Aurelio thought. "Go on," he said.

"That's it," Lieutenant Hendricks said. "Except for these two final pieces of possibly redundant advice. One, you should be ready for that location to get very hot very soon. And two, we recommend you neutralize Ike Ronson immediately."

She broke off the call and Aurelio counted slowly backward from ten, getting his breathing and his fury under control.

Then, as casually as he could manage, he walked back into the lab. The professor and April were talking. Ike was leaning against the wall just inside the door, to Aurelio's right. He caught Aurelio's eye and nodded. Aurelio nodded back.

Then he pivoted and knocked Ronson out cold with a left hook that carried all his vengeful anger about everything Ronson had already done, and everything his actions were about to cause. The punch banged Ronson's head off the door frame and he dropped without a sound.

"My God, Aurelio," April said. The professor stood at her desk, eyes wide and one hand over her mouth.

"Get me something to tie him up with," Aurelio said. "Then I'll explain."

Ike began to stir after two or three minutes, but by that time Aurelio had found three extension cords in a supply closet and used them to tie Ike's hands around the back of a chair in Chandrasekhar's office. The professor stood back, staying out of the conflict, but April got right in his face. "What are you doing? I wouldn't be here if it wasn't for him."

"I believe you," Aurelio said. "But ask yourself why an agent out of Manhattan just happened to be waiting to escort you the last twenty miles to Ann Arbor."

He saw the implications of this register with April. "Wait," she said. "He told me he was deployed around Ohio and Pennsylvania."

"When he said that, it was true. But he left Manhattan three days after you did, with specific orders to find you."

"Orders from who?"

"That's what I'm hoping to find out when he wakes up," Aurelio said. "You should also know that when he got the call to follow you—'engage and assist' was the specific order—he bailed out in the middle of a firefight after calling in a bogus SOS. How do I know that? Because I was the agent who responded. I finished the job he quit on, and I was the one who had to count the bodies of the civilians who got killed because he ran out on them."

The shocked expression on April's face told Aurelio he needed to throttle back a little. "Look," he said, more calmly, "I know this is a lot for you to take in. Ike did save your life. He did some other good things along the way, too. But he's also a double agent, and according to a call I just got from JTF intel, he's called in a strike team on this location."

This got Professor Chandrasekhar's attention. "He has what?"

"You need to get your people out of here, Professor," Aurelio said. "And whatever research you can carry, take that with you. If I had to guess, I'd say by tonight this building won't still be standing."

The professor got moving. She was already shouting orders when she got into the hallway, and her voice echoed away back toward the glassed-in side of the building.

"You're probably right about that," Ike said.

Aurelio took a step back as Ike lifted his head and added, "You hit hard, Aurelio. Even if it was a sucker punch."

"You play people for suckers, sooner or later you get sucker-punched," Aurelio said. "Who's Mantis?"

Ike smiled. Aurelio could tell it hurt. "I don't know," Ike said. "And before you ask, I don't know the name of the group she's working with, either. I'm supposed to find all that out later today, after…" He angled his head back and forth, taking in the room and by extension the building, their mission, all of it. Aurelio noted that his speech was a little slurred, probably because his jaw wasn't working right from the punch. "After all this is over," Ike finished.

"How'd they get you on board?" Aurelio asked. "How'd they get you to run out on a bunch of kids in New York?"

"That wasn't supposed to happen," Ike said. "I drew the DPF out thinking I would get them riled up and shooting, and use that as cover to get out of town. I didn't know there were people in the building until it was too late. That's… that's on me. It was a bad mistake."

"But you still ran out."

"Yeah. I did. Because there was one chance to be part of this, and that was it. If these people can save a million lives, and those people had to die to make it happen… Look, Aurelio. You want me to be a turncoat, some kind of villain, fine. Like I said last night, punch my ticket. It's your call." Aurelio felt April shift and out of the corner of his eye he saw her looking at him. She hadn't known about that conversation until just now, and right about now she would be figuring out that Aurelio hadn't arrived by chance in Ann Arbor any more than Ike had just happened to be passing through Milan at the right time.

"Both of you were looking for me?" she said. "And neither one of you could tell me. What am I, a goddamn chess piece?"

"We're all chess pieces," Ike said. "Some of us are just clearer about what side we're playing. Me, I know that things are going to get uglier before they get better. You saw DC, Aurelio. Nobody's in control there. You tell me, who do people turn to when they need to know what to do? Who's leading this country right now? Nobody. And somebody has to. In the end, you and I—you, too, April, and probably the professor, too—we all have the same vision. We want things back the way they were, only maybe a little better. I tried the Division way. It's not working. So now I'm trying another way."

"I see you had a lot of time to work on your rationalizations while you were following me," April said. She was flexing her fingers, the way people did when they were so angry the primitive part of their brain was about to take over. Aurelio shifted a little closer to her, so he could intercept if she went after Ike. He might deserve whatever he got, but Aurelio wasn't going to be part of beating a bound man.

"Maybe they are rationalizations," Ike said. "But I could have cut your story out of you yesterday down in Milan, or last night on that roof deck. I didn't. And the JTF doesn't go around wearing white gloves, either. You heard what happened with the quarantine down in DC, right, Aurelio? How many people died because of that? Same thing happened in other places, too. Our hands aren't clean."

"No," Aurelio said. "We've all got blood on our hands. But we choose whose blood."

"Yeah, we do. Like you said, I lost those people in New York. That was bad. But..." Ike wriggled in the chair, trying to shift his weight and get his blood moving. "Listen, man, either shoot me or leave me alone. I'm done trying to justify myself, and you're not listening anyway."

Aurelio went around behind the chair. He saw Ike tense, but Aurelio wasn't going to hurt him. He squatted and unbuckled Ike's SHD watch. Its circle was still orange. "You won't be needing this," he said. "Or this," he added, picking a grenade from Ike's belt.

"Wait," April said. "You're not going to shoot him."

"No, I'm not going to shoot him." Aurelio was looking at Ike as he spoke even though the words were addressed to April. "I'm going to leave him right here, and we are going to help all the white coats around here evacuate. Then we're going to call in an armor-piercing SOS to Detroit, and hope we're still breathing when the cavalry arrives."

"Better move fast," Ike said. "Mantis's people are. Couple of weeks from now, they're going to seize fuel supplies up and down the East Coast. They've got it all planned out. South Portland, New London... I can't remember all of them. And a couple weeks after that... Well, I'll be honest. They haven't told me any more than that. But things are going to get real different."

Seizing fuel supplies meant only one thing: Mantis's people had large numbers of vehicles. That in turn meant they were a much more organized force than the run-of-the-mill militias scattered all over the country. And if Mantis's people controlled fuel supplies, that was fuel the JTF wouldn't have.

"You know what that means, right?" Ike grinned again through the pain in his jaw. "Yeah, you do. Mobility wins wars, Aurelio. This war is already won, whether I'm around to see it or not." His eyes went out of focus for a moment, then he blinked and came back. "You hit hard. Did I tell you that already?"

No wonder he's talking so much, Ike thought. He's concussed and his inhibitions are down. That's why he was slurring, too.

He would have pressed Ike for more information, but a sound drifting through the open window caught Aurelio's attention and tied a cold knot in the pit of his stomach. In the distance, but coming closer, was the unmistakable thump of helicopters.

CHAPTER 40

APRIL

Aurelio hustled April back outside. The calm atmosphere of the building had been shattered by Professor Chandrasekhar's alert—just like that beautiful glass facade was going to be shattered as soon as the shooting started. Aurelio felt sorry in advance for anyone caught on that side of the building.

"You're just leaving Ike there?" April had heard Ike's confession, but she still was having trouble squaring it with how she had seen him act.

"He'll be free inside twenty minutes, is my guess," Aurelio said. "You can't keep someone tied up if they have the use of their hands and they can find something sharp."

April imagined Ike scooting the chair around the office until he found… what, a pair of scissors? "And what if he doesn't? Or what if that's not enough time?"

"That's his problem," Aurelio said. "I cut him a break already. He's still breathing."

Outside, the JTF garrison was scrambling into defensive posture. They could hear the chopper blades, too, and one of them was pointing toward the northeast.

"If Mantis's people have helicopters and pilots, plus fuel, this is going to be a problem," Aurelio said.

"I don't understand why they're attacking even though the samples are gone." They were at the perimeter fence now. Aurelio scanned the sky.

"They don't know the samples are gone," Aurelio said. "And by the time they find out, we need to be a long way from here."

She saw him wrestling with conflicting mission objectives. Help the people here in a fight they were likely to lose, or get out and make sure news of the BSAV got to the right people. Whoever they were.

Small-arms fire from the south tore into the fence and ricocheted off the Jersey barriers. As she ducked, April glanced that way and saw black-clad soldiers weaving among the cars in the parking lot off Fuller Road. The JTF returned fire.

Three helicopters came into view over the trees to the east. "Black Hawks," Aurelio said. "Don't see any missile pods. My guess is, they're carrying more troops. Together with the force in the parking lot, we're looking at maybe fifty hostiles, with close air support."

Watching the helicopters, April said, "Translate that into civilian."

"We're cooked," Aurelio said.

He tapped his watch face and then his ear. "This is Division agent Aurelio Diaz, current location Ann Arbor near intersection of Fuller Road and Beal Avenue. JTF position here under assault from platoon-strength paramilitary force with helicopter air support. Request immediate fire support, all agents and all available assets."

He listened for a few seconds. "Yeah, I did say helicopter air support," he said, raising his voice over the approaching helicopters and the escalating firefight in the direction of the parking lot. "No, I am not kidding. You can hear them, right?"

Another pause to listen. "Well, you better hurry. If it takes that long, none of us are going to be around."

Glass shattered behind them as stray rounds started to find the building's front walls. Aurelio popped up over the fence and fired two quick bursts. "See what we can do here," he said, mostly to himself.

April felt useless. Her shotgun wasn't much use in this combat environment, and if fifty men made it inside the walls, she had a feeling it wouldn't help then, either.

Two of the Black Hawks swung around to the south. The third stayed behind, holding its position several hundred yards away. "I'm going to touch base with the local commander," Aurelio said. "See if he happens to have a roomful of RPGs somewhere."

He ran off, keeping his head low and staying close to the wall. After he ducked behind a shorter wall of sandbags, April lost track of him. She could see some of the approaching soldiers hopscotching among the cars in the parking lot. They popped up to fire, then ducked away as the JTF defenders fired back. Frustrated and scared in equal measure, April stayed at one corner of the barrier, keeping her head down and wondering where Aurelio had gone. She couldn't hit any of the soldiers attacking the gate or the JTF emplacements over toward the Beal side of the building. She also couldn't get out. All she could do was sit tight and wait for a chance to either fight or run.

One of the two approaching helicopters reached a spot about a hundred yards due south of the building entrance and hovered there, a hundred feet in the air. A heavy machine gun mounted in its side door opened up, chewing through the wooden walls of the JTF positions. The second chopper came around behind it, easing down until it hovered less than three feet off the ground, about halfway between the main entrance and April's corner. She saw soldiers clustered in the door, their feet hanging over the side, with others standing behind them.

Finally April saw an opportunity to do something. She rested the Super 90's barrel on a Jersey barrier and braced herself. As the chopper's skids touched the ground, April unloaded its full magazine, eight loads of buckshot, at the open door. The helicopter was fifty yards away, so there was a lot of scatter in the loads, but she saw some of the black-uniformed soldiers drop to the ground. Others dodged away from the door as sparks flew from the Black Hawk's fuselage.

Unfortunately her fire drew attention from the other helicopter. Its machine gun swung in her direction. April pressed herself against the Jersey barrier and got as low as she could. Bullets hammered into the concrete, stinging her with flying shards, but the chopper couldn't quite get an angle on her. It wouldn't be long, though. She had to move.

When the machine gun's fire swept on to another target, April scrambled to her feet and ran around the west side of the building, pinning herself to the wall just past the corner, where she could still see part of what was going on. From the roof just over her head, she heard rifle fire. Impact stars bloomed all over the windshield of the closest helicopter. Other JTF soldiers concentrated their fire on the same helicopter, and eventually it heeled over and took up a position farther away to the southeast. Now its machine guns raked the front of the building, turning the two-story windows into a waterfall of glass shards.

Shooting around the gate intensified, and something exploded under one of the JTF firing platforms. A moment later four of the black-uniformed soldiers got through the gate. JTF defenders cut them down, but the helicopters opened up on them. Seconds later, another group in black came through. This time they got halfway to the building entrance before Aurelio popped up on the other side of the security gate and shot three of them. The other one returned fire, but Aurelio was off and running, weaving past generators and stacks of crates and even using a large iron sculpture as a momentary shelter to reload. He sprinted out from behind it, firing as he ran, and disappeared from April's view.

If any of the soldiers found her now, she was dead. She had a knife and that was it. It occurred to her that maybe her best hope was for Ike Ronson to find her, but that was a slim hope indeed, because if Ronson did find her, April intended to stab him. He wouldn't be much of an ally after that.

The third helicopter had been out of her field of vision for a while, but now it loomed directly overhead. It hovered over the lab building, its downdraft beating on April as it unloaded its complement of soldiers onto the building's roof.

Aurelio came hustling around the far corner, staying close to the wall. Halfway to April, he stopped and raised his rifle. Instinctively she hit the ground, and Aurelio fired over her. She rolled back to her feet and saw one of the soldiers in black pitching forward face-first onto the grass.

When he got to her, Aurelio leaned in close. "They've got men on the roof. It's game over. We have to get out." He tapped his ear. "SHD agent Diaz here," he said, shouting over the rotor downdraft from the helicopter still hovering overhead. "Position overrun. Urgently need tactical support. I am extracting with a valuable human asset."

He winced as a flare of white noise loud enough for April to hear crackled out of his earpiece. "Shit," Aurelio said. "There goes ISAC."

"ISAC?"

"Our comms network. It's been unreliable for days now, but I think it just fried out. I still have some database and voice comms, but everything else is toast. Anyway, never mind. We have to get you out of here."

"What makes me a valuable human asset?" April asked.

"I'll tell you when we're not under fire." Aurelio looked around and then up. The third helicopter eased forward, out of sight. "They're in the building now. JTF is completely overrun. All we can do now is put some distance between us and Ike before he tells them who they should be looking for."

To the west were a couple of smaller buildings and a large solar panel array. Beyond it, more campus buildings. To the north, the same. East was out, and so was south. At least, that was what April was thinking, but Aurelio said, "Okay. We're going to go northwest." He pointed. "And I mean running. As soon as we get past those first buildings, we cut back south. There's woods on the other side of the VA hospital, and if we can get into them, we'll be all right. Sound good?"

"As good as anything else," April said.

"Oh, one more thing." Aurelio ran to the body of the soldier he'd shot and recovered his weapon. He handed it to April. "You might want this later."

Only then did she realize she'd left the Super 90 behind when she ran from the helicopter. But there was no going back for it now. She followed Aurelio along the building wall to its northwest corner. Then he said, "On three. One... two..."

They ran.

CHAPTER 41

AURELIO

They made it past the solar panel array and through a low swampy patch between two ponds with no trouble. The attacking force was completely focused on the laboratory building. "So far, so good," Aurelio said. They were crouched in the brush on the south side of one of the ponds, catching their breath before they started the next stage of their breakout dash. Just across Fuller Road, the VA hospital loomed. A JTF force, not nearly enough to turn the tide of the battle, was heading out across the road toward the combat zone. Some of the attacking force took up positions in the parking lot to meet them.

"Now's a good time," Aurelio said.

He broke from the brush and headed across the road. April ran with him. She looked over her shoulder as they got across to the hospital parking lot.

Six men in black uniforms were breaking away from the coming shoot-out in the parking lot. "They're following us," April panted.

Aurelio glanced back. "Looks like we're not *into* the woods yet," he said. Even in the middle of a life-or- death situation,

April took a moment to roll her eyes at the terrible joke.

"Dad jokes survived the plague, huh?" she needled lightly as they dodged behind a commuter bus abandoned in the lot.

"Once you're a dad, it's like a latent gene comes to life," Aurelio said. This gave April pause. She hadn't known he had kids.

He peeked around the front of the bus, drawing fire. Their pursuit had slowed and broken into three-man teams, one angling between them and the hospital entrance while the other came straight toward the bus. "Pin those guys down for a minute," Aurelio said, pointing toward the entrance. "And keep your feet right by the front tire."

April did as she was told, waiting until the three men appeared in the drop-off circle in front of the hospital.

She sprayed a burst in their direction and they took cover.

Perfect, Aurelio thought. He unhooked a grenade from his belt. "Thanks, Ike," he said. He pulled the pin and skipped it under the bus sidearm, like he was skipping a rock. Then he stepped behind the bus's rear tires.

The grenade blast blew out most of the bus's windows. Aurelio heard a thunk down by his feet, which must have been shrapnel hitting the tire. He glanced over and saw April looking down, too. Then he sidestepped around the back of the bus. The grenade had laid out two of the three attackers. The third was just then scrambling out from behind a pillar in a parking garage by the hospital. Aurelio dropped him. He heard April firing and looked over to see one of the trio in the drop-off circle stagger as the others exposed themselves to get a shot at Aurelio. A second later he heard a rapid click. April was out of ammo.

Aurelio came back around the rear of the bus at a dead run. "Now's our chance. Go!" he shouted. He sprinted around the access road circling the hospital grounds, April right behind him. The sounds of machine-gun fire and helicopter rotors followed them into the woods.

They cut straight south, around the edge of a big apartment complex. Then they came out on the riverbank, sooner than Aurelio had expected. "Not good," he said. They were both carrying too much to swim, and besides that, swimming would make them easy targets if there was still going to be pursuit. Aurelio had a brief vision of a Black Hawk catching them in the middle of the river.

"No, look," April said.

He looked where she was pointing, not even a hundred feet upstream. A footbridge crossed the river, disappearing into the trees on the other side.

"I take it back," Aurelio said. "Good."

They got across the path, and on the other side of the river they found that they were on the Gallup Park Pathway, which ran between the river and railroad tracks. Aurelio kept them moving fast for more than an hour, staying on the railroad tracks after the path ended. They finally stopped at an old dam, with the remains of a paper mill across the river. Nobody seemed to be around. Their arrival startled a heron, which lifted away from the riverbank and soared over their heads to the south. "I think this is the next town over," Aurelio said. "Ypsilanti. We should get something to eat and then keep moving. Once Ike's handlers figure out the samples are gone, they'll be looking for us."

April was quiet as Aurelio handed her an MRE. It was one of his last. They would both be foraging for the foreseeable future unless they decided to head for a JTF garrison. "We should have stayed to fight," she said.

"I get it," Aurelio said. "But the minute those Black Hawks showed up it wasn't really a fight anymore. Also, if we're dead we can't share the intel we picked up."

"Is that what you meant when you said I was a valuable human asset? Because I'll tell you the truth, Aurelio. I don't feel too valuable right now. I feel like I led Ike Ronson right to all those people, and now they're dead."

"Listen, I'm right there with you," Aurelio said. "If I'd taken him out last night, none of this would have happened. So we can do one of two things. We can sit around wallowing in survivor's guilt, or we can make sure we tell people what's about to happen so more people don't die."

She was quiet for a long time. Then she said, "You're a hard-ass, Aurelio."

"These are hard-ass times. People have died because of things you did, people have died because of things I did. But put the blame where it belongs. Ike Ronson sold us both out." Aurelio finished his MRE and wiped his fork on his pants before stowing it in his pack. "I wish there was time for commiserating, but there isn't."

"Okay," April said. She took a deep breath, held it, let it slowly out. "So what do we do next?"

"Here's how I see it." Aurelio held out a hand. "Give me the clip from that M16."

It took April a minute to figure out how to release the magazine, and Aurelio didn't help. She was going to need to know how to do that once they separated. When she found the release switch, she handed it over, and he reloaded it as he went on. Good thing the G36 and M16 used the same ammunition, he thought.

"Here's what makes you valuable. Professor Chandrasekhar

probably won't make it through the day. Neither will anyone else in there who knows they already sent the antiviral samples to someone in DC. That means you and me and Ike Ronson are the only three people with that knowledge. He's going to tell his friends. We have to tell ours."

"So back to New York," April said. "I'll be honest, I was hoping to never go back there."

"Well, you don't have to. At least not yet. What you need to do is go to DC. That's where the samples were headed, so that's where the intel needs to go first. ISAC is on the fritz, so I have no long-range comms right now, or I would let them know you're coming." He did still have local area information and static database access, but that was probably from local signals in Detroit. ISAC wasn't quite blind, but it was definitely myopic.

"DC," she said. "I don't know anyone in DC. I mean, I did have a friend there. Her name's Mirabelle. We were pretty close in college. But I doubt she's still alive. And anyway, shouldn't you do that?"

"I have to get to one of the petroleum storage facilities Ike was listing. If an assault is coming, the JTF needs to know about it and beef up their defenses. So I'm headed to New London, Connecticut. Ike named it, and it's a lot closer than Maine." Aurelio handed her back the magazine and she clicked it into place. Then he handed her a box of shells. "That's all I can spare."

"I hope I won't need any of it." April looked haunted. "I was a design manager, Aurelio. I did sketches and spreadsheets. Now I've..." She closed her eyes. "I don't even know how many people I've killed."

Join the club, Aurelio thought. But it was tougher on her. She hadn't trained for the possibility. "You haven't killed anyone who didn't have it coming," he said. "They chose their side."

"My head knows that," April said.

"But you still feel bad. That's good. If you didn't feel a little bad, you'd be emotionally dead. The world put you in a tough spot. You're making the best of it."

He stood up and stretched, then shouldered his pack and slung his rifle. "We shouldn't stay in one place too long. They might still be looking for us."

Late that day they got into Detroit, navigating by word of mouth to a trading post and port on Zug Island, where the Rouge flowed into the Detroit River. Looking across the river at Canada, maybe a thousand yards away, Aurelio wondered how things were over there. Maybe someday he would find out. The next morning they found passage to Cleveland, and after restocking at the JTF base there, it was time to part ways. Aurelio had put in a word for April with the JTF, and they had agreed to help her get at least as far as Pittsburgh. The JTF officers there would have a better idea how to get her to DC.

"When you get there," Aurelio said, "find a Division agent. Show them this." He handed her Ike's watch. "That'll get their attention. Then tell them exactly everything you learned out here. Give them my name. A lot of agents in DC know me. Remember, we have to assume that nobody on earth except Ike Ronson's bosses and maybe a couple of people in back offices somewhere know the BSAV is real. Get word of that to the Division agents in DC. Tell them that's what they're fighting for."

She put the watch in her pack. "Seems weird that I'm going to DC, when that's where you're from."

"Yeah," Aurelio said. "But that's how it is sometimes. Can I ask you a favor?"

"Of course."

"I have two kids. Amelia and Ivan. They were in a refugee camp at the Mandarin Oriental Hotel, but then most of the people there were moved out to another camp at the Smithsonian Castle. You ever been there?"

She nodded. "I've seen the sights in DC, yeah."

"I went up to New York because that's where I was needed, but I was planning to head back down to DC when all this with Ronson went down. And now I'm going to Connecticut. So if you could maybe see if my kids are okay..." He was getting choked up. April reached out and put a hand on his shoulder.

"I'd be happy to, Aurelio. You said Amelia and Ivan?" He nodded. April patted him and said, "I'll do that first thing."

"No, get the intel about the BSAV to an agent first."

"I'll make you a deal," April said. "If I see an agent before I get to the Smithsonian Castle, I'll do that. But if not, I'll check on your kids. Then I'll tell the agent to get word to you."

His throat was still tight. Aurelio nodded his thanks. "Tell them I'm okay," he said.

"I will." A horn honked. April looked over at the staging area by the football stadium, where she was supposed to meet the driver for her ride to Pittsburgh. "I think that's my ride."

"Sounds like it," Aurelio said. "Listen, one more thing."

Half-turned away, she stopped to listen.

"I know it's hard to look past all the bad things that happened the last couple of days," Aurelio said. "But I hope you at least got a little peace out of learning about your husband."

April smiled. A melancholy smile, but still a smile. "I did, yeah," she said. "Thank you for reminding me of that. I hope I can give you a little peace when I get to DC." She lifted a hand in farewell and walked off toward the waiting truck.

Me, too, Aurelio thought. Me, too.

CHAPTER 42

VIOLET

The attack, when it finally came, started at midnight. Violet thrashed awake at the sounds of gunfire and bullets hitting the Castle walls. Before having a conscious thought, she was already diving out of bed to hit the floor. She lay there panting as the other kids in the room did the same, lying flat or huddling in the corners. Shelby started to scream. Saeed was closest to her. He gathered her up in a hug and just held on to her while the bullets pounded into the walls. They heard glass breaking down on the lower floors, and adults shouting.

Then the Castle people started to fight back.

In the past week, they had done a lot of work. The walls around the grounds were up and fortified. The windows were sealed. On the upper floors of the Castle and both museums, Junie and Mike had directed the construction of sandbag-walled firing positions. Sentries kept watch twenty-four hours a day.

Even so, Violet was terrified. Shelby was starting to calm down, but even though Violet was gulping air, she couldn't seem to get her breath.

At first the bullets all seemed to be hitting lower floors, but now they climbed the building. The sounds of shattering glass echoed down the stone hallways. One of the last windows to be shot out was the kids' bedroom window facing the Mall. The bullets that blew it in punched into the drywall ceiling, and one of them ricocheted back down off the stone roof above, punching through the door.

The firing stopped. People were still shouting on the lower floors, but nobody was shooting back from the Castle.

A moment later Violet heard Sebastian's voice, booming across the Mall. He was using a megaphone. "Hello, Smithsonian Castle!" he called. "This is a hint. A warning, a shot across the bow, as it were. We've been very patient with you, but that patience does not appear to be getting results. So it's time to take some more decisive action."

Violet wanted to get to the window and see him. Somehow that seemed less scary than just listening to his voice without knowing where he was. But there was broken glass all over the floor and the couches by the window and she didn't have shoes on. So she had to stay put and hear the rest.

"We're going to be back tomorrow. I'll even tell you when we're coming. Let's say... I was going to suggest early in the morning, but I know I've interrupted your sleep. So let's say noon. We'll come back at noon, and I dearly hope for your sake that your gate on Independence Avenue is open. Junie? Mike? I hope you're hearing me. Sleep tight, everyone."

There was a pop as the megaphone cut out. For a long while after that, the only sound in the room was Violet and the other children breathing. Eventually Amelia said, "What do we do?"

* * *

They didn't sleep that night. Junie came up an hour or so after Sebastian had made his speech. "We knew it might come to this," she said. "We're going to have to fight. But all we have to do is hold them off until the JTF comes to help. And all you have to do is stay out of the way and safe. Come on."

She led them down to the second floor, where there was a room with no windows just off the bigger space they used as a kitchen. "Go get anything you'll need for the next few days," Junie said. "We'll find you some blankets and things that don't have glass in them. Okay? Be quick. I'll wait here."

They ran upstairs, gathered the few things they owned—a stuffed animal here, a parent's wallet with pictures, other odds and ends—and were back down in the new room in a few minutes. "Okay," Junie said. "I'm going to leave the door open. You'll see when it's light. We'll have breakfast and we'll figure out what to do next."

When she was gone, Violet said, "I think we should do our plan."

"You sure?" Amelia said. "Maybe she's right. We just have to hold on until the JTF comes."

Saeed was shaking his head. "I bet they won't come. Sebastian will know we're waiting for them. He'll stop them from coming."

This thought hadn't occurred to Violet. Her chest got tight again and she forced herself to breathe.

"You don't know that," Amelia said. Ivan was nodding, taking sides with his big sister.

"What would you do?" Saeed asked. "I mean, if you were going to attack us. Would you do it if you knew the JTF was going to come to the rescue?"

None of them could answer that.

"I think we should do our plan," Violet said again.

* * *

Nobody had much time for the kids that morning. Junie and Mike were overseeing further defensive preparations. They were also sending people to the rooftops of the two museum buildings next to the Castle with binoculars... and rifles. Most of the broken glass was swept up, and some of the shot-out windows were boarded over. Some of them were now firing slits, just big enough for a rifle barrel and a narrow view of the outside.

Violet and Noah were able to get into the kitchen and get some food. They ate lunch, and then took some of the extra food with them back to the windowless room. It was eleven o'clock. They packed up the food in case they had to do the plan.

The week before, after they'd gone up to Ford's Theatre and been turned away, Violet had gathered all of the kids together and told them they needed to figure out their own plan for getting away if things got bad at the Castle. They'd argued over the details for a while, but eventually they had settled it.

Violet had the idea to gather stuff and get out, all together, without saying anything to the grown-ups. She wasn't sure how to do it, though, and that was where Saeed and Ivan came in. "You didn't know about the tunnels?" Ivan said.

"Yeah," Saeed said. "There's steam tunnels going out of the basement."

"Where do they go?" Amelia asked. "And what were you doing down there anyway?"

"Exploring," Ivan said. "We couldn't do it outside..."

"So we did it inside," Shelby finished with a bright smile. She'd just lost another tooth.

"You knew about this, too?" Violet was surprised. Shelby wasn't usually the sort to go in for adventure.

"Yeah. We were bored."

Violet looked at Noah and Wiley.

"We didn't know about it," Wiley said. "At least, I didn't."

"Me, neither. I've been stuck upstairs taking care of my stupid brother," Noah said.

"Okay, guys. So there are steam tunnels. Where do they go?" Maybe this would work, Violet thought. If the tunnels weren't flooded or something.

"Well, we only went to the end of one of the short ones. It goes over to the basement of the Sackler Gallery." That was the museum on the southwest corner of the Castle grounds. "There's a long one that goes across the Mall, but we didn't go too far into it because we got to a branch and then we were worried about getting lost."

Just like that, they had a plan. If things got bad, they could get out under the ground... as long as they knew they weren't going to end up somewhere terrible. Saeed and Ivan and Shelby held out for the long tunnel, but Violet worried they would get to a place that was locked up, and then they wouldn't be able to come back to the Castle. So they decided to check through the shorter tunnel to the gallery and see if they could get through.

It turned out they could... once Noah and Wiley and Saeed had broken a lock off an old door in the Sackler Gallery's basement. Actually it was the third basement level, way underground. Most of the museum was underground, something the kids had just found out when they started exploring to see where the tunnels went.

Upstairs an adult yelled, "Hell's going on down there?"

"Nothing!" they all yelled at once.

That had been a few days before, when they still had a little optimism. Now, with Sebastian's men about to attack, they didn't have much optimism, but they did have a plan.

The shooting actually started a little before noon. Knowing they were going to have to fight, the Castle's defenders decided not to wait for Sebastian's men to show up and start the fight on their terms. So when the first groups of Sebastian's men showed up, strolling down Independence Avenue like they owned the city, Castle snipers on top of the Freer Gallery and the Castle itself began firing. The approaching soldiers scattered in disarray. Another group appeared on the Mall, and people with rifles on the towers and turrets of the Castle started shooting at them. None of them believed Sebastian would spare them if they opened the gate. So none of them believed they had anything to lose.

Mike stopped by the windowless room. "Kids," he said. "It's starting. I don't know what to tell you other than stay out of the way and try to keep yourselves safe. It's going to be okay."

He ran off again and Violet looked at the rest of them. "We better get our stuff just in case," she said. They all got their backpacks on and made sure their shoes were tied right. Nobody wanted to trip over a shoelace at the wrong time.

They stayed in the room as long as they could stand it, as the sounds of gunfire and people shouting—in anger, in fear, in pain—echoed through the Castle's halls and came in through its broken windows.

Then Saeed said, "I have to get a look outside."

He left the room and turned left down the hall, toward the big hall they used as a dining room. The rest of them looked at each other. They didn't want to be left behind. So they went, too. All of them clustered near a window that faced south toward the gate, but was far enough off to the side that it was mostly out of the way of the fighting.

What they saw scared them to death. Dozens of Sebastian's men were shooting from Independence Avenue and the buildings across from the line of abandoned cars. Some of the cars were on fire. Inside the garden area, they saw more people shooting at each other. A woman who had showed Violet how to run strings for beans to climb shot toward a soldier coming through the gate, then spun around and fell. She tried to crawl away but couldn't. Blood spread around her on the stones of the walkway between garden beds.

Some of the Castle defenders were down in the pavilion entrance to the Sackler Gallery, firing up at the invaders. The firefight went down into the underground levels of the museum. "That's kind of where we want to go, isn't it?" Amelia asked.

"Yeah," Saeed said. "But we come out way down in the basements under there. I doubt they'll go all the way down."

"If we have to use the plan," Noah said.

"Right," Saeed said. "If."

One of the invading soldiers stopped and threw a grenade down the stairs into the Sackler. A moment later, a gout of smoke bloomed on the pavilion, rising over the garden. The same soldier started to throw another grenade, but a sniper from the top of the Castle shot him. He fell, and three seconds later, the grenade went off at the edge of the garden. Violet knew it was dumb, but she was mad at the senseless destruction of the garden. They would have eaten those vegetables. Now they were all ruined.

They ran to the other side of the building to see what it looked like over there. Sebastian's soldiers were close to the Castle, trying to kick in the plywood covering the windows. One of them got a window open and then reeled back covered in blood. The kids could smell smoke, and see it curling up the main stairwell. Adults inside the Castle ran in every direction, trying to defend the entrances while bullets punched through the boarded-up windows.

It was time.

"Guys," Violet said. "Let's go." She was surprised how calm she sounded.

They went down the stairs, trying not to breathe in too much of the smoke. On the ground floor, the adults seemed calm. Violet heard one of them shout to Darryl, "We're holding. Long as we don't let them in here, we'll hold. They get in the garden, that's a shooting gallery."

Someone else was shouting orders about more enemies coming from the east.

The kids got down into the basement and found the steel door at the entrance to one of the tunnels. "We sure we don't want to take the long one and really get out of here?" Saeed asked.

"We don't know where it goes," Violet said.

"Yeah, but this one goes to the Sackler, which…" Saeed didn't have to finish the sentence. They'd all seen the explosion. But if their plan went right, they wouldn't get close to the fighting.

They ducked into the tunnel, Saeed and Violet in front, with Amelia and Ivan right behind, Shelby behind them, and Noah and Wiley at the rear. The tunnel was hot and dark, but they got to the other end with no problem and came out in the deepest level of the Sackler. There they paused to listen. There didn't seem to be any real fighting nearby right then.

Running up the stairs, they got to the ground level. There was a big glass entrance on the south side, but it was barricaded. The other ways out would lead them into the garden, where people were killing each other. So they went the other way, down halls between displays of beautiful artifacts of Asian art, and got to the outside windows on the west wall. There was a courtyard beyond, and then Twelfth Street. The windows were boarded up, but they pried off the plywood with a crowbar Saeed had taken from the Castle basement. Then they had to deal with the metal window frames. It took a few minutes, but eventually they broke one side free, and then they kicked out the rest.

Once they'd broken all the glass out of the frames, they could climb through. Shouting and gunfire came from the other side, inside the makeshift walls they had helped to build. "We have to get out of here. Tell the JTF," Saeed said.

"You said the JTF wasn't going to do anything," Amelia reminded him.

"Who else can we tell?" Saeed demanded. "The Division? You never know when they're going to be around."

Someone shouted from down at the corner of Independence. They looked that direction, and saw a group of Sebastian's men. One of them pointed, and four others started trotting toward the kids.

"Uh-oh," Ivan said. "We have to get out of here."

"To where?!" Shelby wailed. It was a good question. They couldn't outrun grown-ups. Not for long. And if they were caught, Violet was sure Sebastian's men would kill them. They had refused his offer. She might have been only eleven years old, but she knew that there were people in the world who would rather have you dead than telling them no.

Noah and Wiley were still getting through the window. Wiley winced as he climbed out. He was getting better, but his wound still hurt him when he had to exert himself. Violet kept her eyes on the approaching men. What could she say to them? What would they do?

One of them raised his gun. "Stay there!" he shouted.

They froze. Amelia said what they were all thinking. "We're kids! Help us!"

This didn't stop the men from coming closer, but at least the one who had pointed his rifle at them angled its barrel down. "Stay right there!" he ordered them. "Don't move."

Violet wanted to run. She knew with a bone-deep certainty that if they stayed, they would wish they hadn't. But she was too scared to move. Their plan had failed.

She saw movement out of the corner of her eye. When she glanced in that direction, she had a brief image of a red-haired woman with a Division backpack. The woman braced a rifle on the low wall separating the Sackler Gallery grounds from the sidewalk on Twelfth Street. She didn't say a word. She just opened fire.

Her first burst caught two of the approaching soldiers. The other two turned and she kept firing, hitting one of them and sending the other running for cover. She vaulted over the wall and ran to the children. "Come with me," she said. "Toward the Mall, across the street. Let's go."

They ran with her. She paused in the middle of Twelfth Street, all by herself, and sprayed a long burst back at more of Sebastian's soldiers, who were coming around the corner of the Sackler Gallery. "Keep going!" she shouted. Bullets ricocheted off the pavement near her. Violet saw a street sign twitch as a shot punched through it. She ran, with all the others around her. The woman staggered, but the kids kept running.

More of Sebastian's men came around the corner of the

museum, but now the Castle defenders on the upper floors had seen what was happening, and they started shooting. Sebastian's soldiers scrambled for cover or fell to the ground. The red-haired woman threw her rifle away and ran with the kids across Jefferson Avenue and the broad expanse of the Mall. They didn't stop until they got to the Washington Monument. By that time they were a little ahead of her, because she limped as she ran, but all of them clustered together at the base of the monument and waited for her to catch up.

She got there and leaned against the white marble wall of the monument, slowly sliding to the ground. There was blood on the left leg of her pants. She shrugged off her pack and winced as she tried to stand again.

Violet looked back toward the Castle. No one had followed them. The battle there was still going on, but they were out of it. With the rest of the kids, she drew closer to this woman.

"Are you a Division agent?" Saeed asked.

"No," she said. "I'm just here to help."

"You look like a Division agent," Ivan said.

She looked over at him and got slowly to her feet. "I'm not," she said. "But we're going to go find someone who is. Before we do, though…" She paused, breathing hard and resting against the wall. "Before we do, please tell me one of you is named Diaz."

CHAPTER 43

APRIL

"**A**ctually two of us are," one of the older girls in the group said. She pointed. "Amelia and Ivan."

Jackpot, April thought. The pain from the wound in her leg made it hard for her to think, but she knew she had to get these kids somewhere safe. She tested the leg. It didn't want to hold her weight. She felt the spot where the bullet had gone through, on the outside of her left thigh.

Everything I've been through since December, she thought, and this is the first time I've really been hurt.

Leaning against the wall of the Washington Monument, listening to the crackle of gunfire from the Smithsonian Castle... it all seemed unreal to her. But that was shock from the bullet wound talking. She still had one more thing to do. Well, two more things.

Amelia and Ivan Diaz stood together in the group of seven children. All of them looked to her for guidance about what to do next. April looked north, toward the White House. The main JTF base in DC was supposed to be there. There was a battle going on there, too. No help would be coming from that quarter.

She looked back east. Whoever was attacking the Castle seemed to be digging in. Groups of fighters were huddling together behind cover and the intensity of the fire was diminishing. She wasn't a trained soldier, but she could tell when an attack was starting to transform into a siege. That was what it looked like.

The battle around the White House was going a little better. The JTF seemed to be holding its own there. She felt exposed, and her leg was radiating waves of pain that made it hard to think. Seven children, she thought. Where do I take them?

The important thing was to take them somewhere. "We have to keep moving," she said. "Come on, we'll go around the other side of the White House and find help there."

"Wait," the girl who'd spoken before said. She was maybe ten or eleven years old, dark hair, serious face. "Someone shot Wiley over at the pond in Constitution Gardens."

"Where's that?" April asked. The girl pointed. "Okay," April said. "We'll go up toward the White House before we get that far."

She led the kids north across the Mall, angling toward the far side of the Ellipse south of the White House. The battle on the edge of the White House grounds seemed to be over for now. Glancing back south, she saw that the same was true down at the Smithsonian Castle. Smoke was pouring from one of the buildings near the Castle, but she couldn't tell what was happening inside the building. All that was on her mind at the moment was getting those kids someplace safe. And relaying a message.

When they had reached the far side of the White House grounds, just south of the Eisenhower Executive Building—she knew this from signs—she paused. "Okay," she said. "Which of you are the Diaz kids again?" She hadn't picked them out before when the other girl pointed them out in the group.

Two of them raised their hands. They sure looked like brother and sister, she thought. The girl, a few years older, looked more like Aurelio. "Your dad wanted me to tell you that he's okay," she said.

"You talked to him?" the boy said. Ivan.

April nodded. "We were on a mission. I guess that's what you'd call it. He's okay. He's planning to come back to DC soon."

Ivan broke down weeping. He sagged into his sister's arms, and April had a pang of sympathy for her. Amelia. She must have been feeling the same things he was, but she had to be the big sister. "Amelia," April said. The girl looked up from her brother. Tears stood in her eyes. "You've been brave. You took care of your brother. Your dad is all right. Hang in there and he'll be back." She didn't know this, but what else could she say?

Amelia nodded. Ivan still had his face buried in her chest. April turned to the other kids. "I'm sorry I don't have news about your parents," she said.

"We don't have parents," said the girl who had told her about Wiley getting shot.

"What's your name?"

"Violet," she said. "What's yours?"

"April." Looking around, April decided she had to try to get these kids to the JTF base. Whatever battle she'd walked into the middle of, it seemed to be over. "Let's go. We're going to talk to the JTF and see if they can help you find a place to stay."

"We tried to move over to Ford's Theatre," said one of the other boys. He seemed older than Ivan and the twins, one of whom was Wiley. "They wouldn't let us stay there."

"Okay," April said. "Tell me your name?"

"I'm Saeed," he said.

"Okay, Saeed," April said. "If Ford's Theatre isn't going to work out, we'll find something that does."

She led them to the JTF perimeter surrounding the South Lawn. "I've got kids here who need some help," she said to the guards. Looking down at her leg, she added, "I think I need some help myself." Blood had soaked her pants all the way down to her ankle.

The guard let them in and they rested for a minute inside the perimeter fence. April looked around. She'd never been to the White House. The last time she came to DC, her friend Mirabelle had tried to get her a tour, but they were booked up a long way in advance.

She saw a Division agent coming out of a command post between the White House basketball court and the fountain in the middle of the South Lawn. "Hey," she called.

The agent turned and saw April surrounded by a group of children. Then she saw April's pack and her expression changed. Here we go again, April thought. When the agent approached, she said, "I'm not in the Division. I just have the pack. It's a long story, and I have something else to tell you that's more important."

The Division agent looked skeptical. "More important than how you got an agent's gear?"

"Yes," April said. "But before I tell you, can you get these kids somewhere safe?"

"Stay here," the agent said.

"I've got a hole in my leg," April said. "I'm not going anywhere."

The agent led the children to a Quonset hut a little ways away, where an access road curved around the South Lawn. She went inside with them and came back out alone a few minutes later.

April was trying to stay on top of the pain in her leg, but it was hard. When the agent got close, she said, "I ran across those kids trying to get out of the Smithsonian Castle. I gave them a hand, but someone shot me."

"We'll get to that," the agent said. "First tell me more about how you got the gear."

April dug in the pocket of her pants and came up with Ike Ronson's watch. "Here's some more gear," she said.

"This watch belonged to an agent named Ike Ronson. He's a traitor. He sold me and a friend of mine out in Michigan. My friend was a Division agent named Aurelio Diaz."

She waited while the agent ran this information. "Okay," she said after a minute. "I know Aurelio Diaz, and there is an Ike Ronson in the SHD records. Is Ronson KIA?"

"I don't know," April said. "The last I saw him, Aurelio had tied him in a chair and we were running away from a helicopter attack on a lab at the University of Michigan. What's your name, anyway?"

"What's yours?" "April Kelleher."

"Alani Kelso," the agent said.

"Weird," April said. "We have the same initials. Can I tell you a story?"

"If it's quick," Kelso said.

"It may not be quick," April said. "But I promise you it's worth listening to."

By the time she finished, she was really feeling weak from the wound in her leg. A JTF medic had been by to bandage her up, but April was still feeling like she could fall asleep at any moment. At last the medic had shot her up with pain meds.

"Let me get this straight," Kelso said. "There's a treatment for the virus."

April nodded.

"Someone brought it here from Michigan."

April nodded again.

"But you don't know who has it now."

"That's right," April said.

Kelso thought this over. "Okay," she said. "You know I have to run this through some channels, right?"

"Yeah," April said. "Contact Aurelio if you don't believe me."

"I think I do believe you, as crazy as that sounds," Kelso said. "You came all the way from Michigan to tell me this?"

"Yeah," April said. "To tell someone, anyway. Where did the kids go?"

"They're safe for now," Kelso said. "The Castle's holding on for now. They held off the attack, with a little help from us. We won't send the kids back there, though, unless we can't find another place for them. It's not going to be safe for a while."

"Will you do me a favor? Two of them are Aurelio's kids. Can you get him a message that they're safe?" April was really feeling woozy now. It was hard to keep a thought in her head, but she was trying to stay focused on what was important.

"Sure," Agent Kelso said. "What's he doing in Connecticut?"

"I should let him explain that," April said. "But when you talk to him, could you tell him I checked in on his kids and they're okay?"

"I'll do that," Agent Kelso said. "I'm sure he'll be glad to hear it."

"And tell someone about the drug," April said. "It's here in DC."

Alani Kelso studied her for a long moment. "I have to be

honest with you," she said. "That's an insane story. But it's insane in exactly the right way to suggest that it's probably true. I'll see that this information gets where it needs to go."

"Thank you," April said. She sat there on the ground outside the JTF medical tent, thinking about all the things that had happened to her—no, all the things she had done—in the past five months. Nearly six. She realized she was drifting when Agent Kelso tapped her on the shoulder.

"Do you know anyone in DC?" Kelso asked.

"I used to," April said. "But I don't know if any of them are still alive." She was thinking of Mirabelle. She had lived not too far from here.

"Well, you can stay here for a few days," Agent Kelso said. "Then once you're back on your feet, we'll see what comes next."

April thought about that. What did come next? She'd spent every waking moment since the first week of December trying to piece together what had happened to Bill. Now she knew. Now she had passed on vital intelligence to the Division, about a treatment for the Dollar Bug. She was three hundred miles from New York, and never had to go back. She had a bullet wound in her left thigh. All of that came together into a strange sense of calm. She had the feeling that she had been given a mission, and not known it was a mission until she was already deep into it. Now she had completed it. She knew what Bill had been doing. She knew the battle for the future of the United States of America was not over, but she had done her part for now.

"I think I need to rest a little now," April said. "Makes sense to me," said Agent Kelso.

The world was going to be a better place, April thought. And she had played her part.

ACKNOWLEDGMENTS

A lot of people helped shape this book along the way. I'm grateful to each and every one of them, particularly Tom Colgan, Julian Gerighty, Jacob Kroon, John Björling, Richard Dansky, Eric Moutardier, Benoit Cohen, Caroline Lamache, Julien Fabre, Clémence Deleuze, Nicklas Cederstrom, and everyone else in the narrative and transmedia teams at Massive and Ubisoft. Thanks also to the players of *The Division* and readers of *New York Collapse*, for responding so warmly to April Kelleher and giving me the chance to take her story a little further.

ABOUT THE AUTHOR

ALEX IRVINE'S last foray into the world of *The Division* was the bestselling transmedia "meta-novel" *New York Collapse*. He is the author of both award-winning original fiction (*Buyout, The Narrows*) and licensed books in the worlds of Marvel, Transformers, *Pacific Rim, Supernatural, Halo*, and various other beloved franchises. He has also written a number of games, including *Marvel: Avengers Alliance* and *The Walking Dead: Road to Survival*, and done story development work for Blizzard and Amazon Game Studios, among others.

Connect online
www.alex-irvine.com

For more fantastic fiction, author events,
competitions, limited editions and more

Visit our website
titanbooks.com

Like us on Facebook
facebook.com/titanbooks

Follow us on Twitter
@TitanBooks

Email us
readerfeedback@titanemail.com